*Unholy Night in*

Deathlehem

Unholy Night in

Deathlehem

Edited by
Michael J. Evans
and
Harrison Graves

A
Grinning Skull Press
Publication

DEDICATION

As always, to all those who enjoy embrace
all things Christmas, light and dark.

TABLE OF CONTENTS

GRIM TIDINGS THIS HELLIDAY SEASON

When it comes to the holiday season, what's the first thing you think about? When I was a kid, it was the decorations and the presents. I didn't know diddly about Black Friday. For me, the first harbinger of the season was when they strung the Christmas lights along Fifth Avenue in Brooklyn. That's when we would start making out our Christmas lists and writing letters to Santa. It didn't matter that we didn't know his address; we were reassured by our parents that the letters would get there. And we trusted our parents.

As I got older, the decorative streetlights started to look a little ratty, and I guess that was the first sign that the holiday was starting to lose its magic. At least, for me. I was no longer up at the crack of dawn, chomping at the bit waiting for Mom and Dad to get up so we could go downstairs and open our presents. With each passing year, the magic died a little more, until I was no longer looking forward to the holidays. It became a necessary evil, if only for the kids. And on New Year's Eve 2004, the magic died altogether. That was the last year I truly

1

celebrated Christmas. In additional to the more personal reasons I touch on in the introduction to the very first Deathlehem anthology, the commercial way the holiday was treated... Well, it was a one-two punch that KO'd the holiday for a long time.

Now the first thing that comes to mind when I think about Christmas, besides Deathlehem, is Black Friday, the so-called "Official" start to the holiday season. I say so-called because as early as August you start to see Christmas displays going up right alongside the Halloween displays. It would be laughable if it wasn't so sad. The stores don't seem to realize that putting out the Christmas decorations so early ends up having the reverse effect. People become so sick of it that by the time Black Friday rolls around, they no longer want to think about Christmas. They just want it to be over with.

But when I hear Black Friday mentioned, the first image that comes to mind is the mindless hordes descending upon the stores, hungry for whatever bargains they can find. Sometimes they don't even need a particular item but want it simply because somebody else wants it. And God forbid it's the last of that item. The fights that break out over who gets it are frightening. Yeah, I know the media paints it more viciously than it actually is, but I've seen some of the fights first hand.

Yeah, I made the mistake of going out on Black Friday once. I was standing outside FAO Schwartz, a high-end toy store in New York City, for three hours in the freezing rain because my mother wanted to make certain she got whatever collectible Barbie was out that year. They had this Barbie Boutique that stocked every kind of Barbie you can imagine. Once I got through the doors, it was another hour before I was allowed to actually enter that particular part of the store. They had guards in attendance at the entrance and exit. As one person left, the radio would squawk, and somebody else would be allowed entry. It was a nightmare, and I swore I would never do it again. And yeah, I saw a number of fights break out. Not as bad as the ones you see broadcasted in the news and social media, but they did get pretty nasty. Thinking about it now, it conjures up images of a horde of zombies in a feeding frenzy, with that flat screen TV the hapless victim and the crazed shoppers the walking dead, which is why I find it appropriate to open the year's collection with Todd Keisling's "Black Friday."

I'm glad to see your survived that harrowing trip to the mall. You might wish you hadn't because now you need to deal with the other joys of the holidays. You know the ones I mean. Making sure you have enough batteries for all those electronic toys you bought the wee ones, trying to find the perfect tree, the decorating, the lights. All seems safe enough, right? Guess again. You might be better off keeping an exorcist on speed dial, especially after reading "Manufacturer's Defect" by B.L. Daniels, "Family Heirloom" by Karen Thrower, or "X Marks Xmas" by Debra Robinson. And you may want to forego the decorating this year if your decorations are anything like those in DJ Tyrer's "Baubles" or S.E. Casey's "Traditions and Rotten Delicacies."

You've done a nice job with the decorating. I have to admit, I had my doubts. I think Santa will be quite pleased. Then again, Santa isn't quite the jolly ol' elf we've come to know and love. Just check out Christopher Stanley's "Sack of Souls" or Terry Miller's "Santa Slay" if you don't believe me. You might fare better against Wiebo Grobler's Grýla or Patrick Winters' "Mrs. Krampen."

As you can see, nothing much has changed around here. Christmas is just as deadly now as it has always been. There's murder and mayhem, and you may encounter a ghost or two. And what's Christmas without a couple of ugly Christmas sweaters. They're to die for.

This year, though, is not all doom and gloom. Surprising, right? We do have cause for celebration. See that coal shed out back? Yeah, that one. A child was born there this night. A child who just might grow up to be famous. Or should that be infamous. Well, that remains to be seen.

So without further ado, turn the page, if you dare, and I bid you welcome to Deathlehem...again.

Michael J. Evans
and the staff at
Grinning Skull Press,
Best Wishes for a Happy Helliday
and a frightful New Year!

B*LACK F*RIDAY

Todd Keisling

In case anyone finds this—

I can hear them outside the door, scratching to get inside. Their moans are almost sad, like they're mourning the loss of their shopping holiday, and maybe that's not too far off the mark. A million shoppers ravenous for a deal. Maybe this is what humanity's death rattle sounds like. Maybe we've been hearing it for a while and just didn't notice.

Look, if I'm wrong about things, if this plague isn't the end of us, then I pray you'll take these final words to heart. Learn something from this and do better than we did. We deserved better, even if we deserved this.

My name is Doug. I have one bullet left, and I'm going to use it, but first I need to get this down.

This is what happened:

* * *

I awoke around three that morning and fought the urge to call in. You could call in all you wanted and not get repri-

5

manded for it (except maybe on your paycheck), but God couldn't help you from Lyle's wrath if you called in sick on one of the major "shopping holidays." The day after Thanksgiving was no exception.

Instead, I called Jenna to make sure she was awake.

"Hello?"

Hearing her voice made me wish we'd spent the night together. Even now I wish that, and my heart hurts just thinking about it.

"Morning. Ready for another grand day working for The Man?"

She yawned. "That's giving Lyle too much credit, don't you think? Missed you last night."

"You'll see me soon."

"I know. At least we'll get out of there at the same time for a change. What do you say about dinner with Mom and Dad tonight?"

"Sounds good. Go on and get ready. I'll see you at five."

"Love you," she said.

"Love you, too."

An hour later I sat at my tiny kitchen table looking over our store's sales flyer while sucking down a cup of coffee. Our manager wanted us all to be familiar with the so-called "super saver" ads. After working there for three years and being promoted to the vague status of "Specialist," I'd grown accustomed to the standard bait-and-switch bullshit the geniuses at Corporate decided to send our way. Our Black Friday ad was the same bag of tricks with a different year on it.

I'd worked my share of Black Fridays over the years, and every single one of them had devolved into some form of chaotic consumerism. At the last store meeting, the weird guy in our store, Thomas, quipped that we should get holiday pay for working on Black Friday. Lord knows he was right. Everyone found his comment amusing except for the manager, Lyle.

That morning, I was determined not to let Lyle's demand for rigid corporatism ruin my mood. I had a girl, I had an apartment, and I had a job. Things were good, and if you were to walk up to me and say, "Hey, how's it going, Doug?," I would've grinned and said, "Pretty damn good, man. No complaints here."

Someone long ago used to say that I was the kind of guy who'd take lemons and make lemonade, or something like that. He was my science teacher from high school, Mr. Martin, and the last I heard, he'd retired early due to an ongoing battle with cancer.

I saw him today, shuffling about with the rest of the crowd, a bag of merchandise hanging limply from one hand, his eyes vacant and mouth agape. The poor bastard's shirt was stained black with dried blood, and when I saw him, I couldn't help but laugh. Mr. Martin used to be a neat freak.

But I guess none of that matters anymore because he's dead now.

❅ ❅ ❅

Lyle's car wasn't the only one in the parking lot that morning. I counted at least ten others on our side of the lot, and that was at a quarter after four. A short line had already formed outside the store, and when I trudged toward the building, some of the early morning wise guys asked for a head start on the goods.

I politely told them they'd get their chance at six and was careful to close the sliding doors behind me. Lyle was in my face as soon as I stepped inside.

"Get the registers up and running." He shoved a cash till into my hands and beat a speedy retreat to the manager's office.

"My Thanksgiving was great, Lyle. Thanks for asking."

He spun on his heels and grinned. "You're welcome."

I swallowed back a snarky reply and turned my attention to the line of people outside the window. The queue had grown by at least six people. If so-called consumer reports and internal projections were to be believed, this would be the biggest Black Friday sale in the company's short history, so there was a huge push to "go for the sale." I tried to imagine the number of people who were, at that very moment, lining up at other stores across the country, and the sheer enormity of that number boggled my mind.

All those people out in the open, unprotected, ill-prepared, with pointless products in their eyes and money burning holes in their wallets.

The weight of those thoughts was too heavy to bear at such an early hour. I turned away from the line outside and went about prepping for the store's opening.

※ ※ ※

I stood in the doorway of the employee lounge while Jenna brushed her hair.

"Morning," she said. "What are the odds we'll get out of here early today?"

"I wouldn't bet on it."

Jenna smirked and went back to her hair.

"Where's dinner tonight?"

She caught my eye in the mirror. "Don't know yet. I'm going to call Mom at lunch and figure that out. Oh! I almost forgot!" She reached into her purse and pulled out a sales flyer for the jewelry store on the other side of the shopping center. "There's a necklace on sale today. I'm going to try and sneak over on my break and snag it for Mom. What do you think?"

I flipped through the ad and happened upon a sale for diamond engagement rings. She pointed to the opposite page at the necklace.

"Wow, that's really nice."

I stared at the ring for a moment longer, but not long enough for her to notice. At least, I don't think she did. I guess I'll never know. In that instant, my brain managed to wake up and do some rough calculations. Combined with what was in my wallet and the discount promised by the vendor, I might be able to grab one of those rings.

Proposing to Jenna had been on my mind a lot lately. We'd been together almost two years, and we'd talked about it a couple of times. She didn't want to pressure me even though I knew it's what she wanted, and the more I thought about it, the more I realized it's what I wanted, too.

"Do you think she'll like it?"

Jenna's smile snapped me from my reverie. "Yeah," I said, thinking of placing that ring on her finger. "I think she'll love it."

* * *

Crazy Carl wandered in a few minutes before five to give the store a once-over. He'd been the custodian for longer than I'd worked there, and during all that time, I'd maybe spoken to him only a handful of times. He wasn't much of a talker, and for good reason.

I stood outside of the store once while Mike and Jack took a smoke break, just shooting the shit about whatever you please, when Carl arrived to do his cleaning duties. After he entered the store, Mike nudged me and said, "Ever talk to him?"

"Me? No. Guy's not much for words, really."

"No shit." Jack took a drag from his cigarette and exhaled a thick plume of smoke. "He's practically a mute."

"Yeah." Mike pocketed his pack of smokes. "I talked to old Crazy Carl once."

"Seriously?"

He had our attention now. I tried to avoid store gossip as a rule, but this was too good to pass up.

"Yeah, man. I was standing out here once, no lie, and Carl just waddled up beside me and asked for a ciggy."

Jack finished off his own cigarette and stamped it out on the sidewalk. "No shit? I didn't know he smoked."

"Neither did I. Anyway, he comes up to me, bums a cigarette, and he just starts talking like we'd been friends for years. And get this—he says the reason he doesn't talk much is because he hears voices. He doesn't respond to people because he doesn't know if what he's hearing is real or imaginary."

"Voices? Like schizophrenia?"

"Yeah. He said he spent most of his childhood in one of them psychiatric wards or some shit."

"You mean like shock treatments?" Jack asked. "Lobotomies?"

"Who knows," Mike went on, "but that sure threw me for a loop. I've worked at this place going on seven years, and until that day I'd never heard Carl so much as squeak out a single fucking word, man. But yeah, he opened up to me that day. And it gets better, too."

Jack pulled another cigarette from the pack with his teeth. It was, as he'd said on so many occasions, a two-cigarette break.

We spoke in unison: "Go on."

Mike leaned in and spoke low, the corners of his mouth turned up into a twitchy grin. "The guy packs heat every time he comes to work."

Jack dropped his cigarette. "Bullshit."

"I'm serious! He showed me the piece, too."

I looked through the large storefront window. Carl walked by, pushing one of those giant mechanized floor cleaners. "You mean he's carrying a gun right now?"

Mike nodded. "I think it's a Glock. He said the only time he can really tune out the voices is when he's down at the range, popping cap after cap." He pantomimed firing a gun with his thumb and index finger.

"Jesus," Jack whispered, "what if that guy snaps?"

"I doubt that." Mike crossed his arms. He seemed satisfied by his sudden authority on all things Carl. "They've got him on some serious meds."

I admit the prospect of saying the wrong thing to Carl at the wrong time made me feel uneasy. Just this morning I passed him on the way to the restroom. I gave him a friendly nod and noted the faraway look in his brown eyes. Looking back, I'm not sure if I was chilled more by the thought that he heard voices or by the fact that he always felt more at ease by carrying a hand cannon.

Now that I think about it, the fact that Carl was a bit crazy and found solace in carrying a gun probably saved my life.

❅ ❅ ❅

Around a quarter after five, Lyle sent me and Jack outside to hand out product vouchers to the crowd. This was typical practice. We only had fifty of this item, ten of another, and the first few folks got dibs. Jack was in the process of handing out vouchers for the morning's laptop offer when I glanced across the parking lot and saw a handful of people standing in front of the jewelry store.

"Hey, Jack."

"Yeah, boss?"

I pointed to the jewelry store and reached for my wallet.

"Did you finish up your area?"

"Yeah, man. Right before Lyle sent us out here to the wolves."

"Good," I said. "Listen, I've got a favor to ask."

He looked at my wallet and smiled. "Buyin' something for the missus?"

My cheeks flushed with heat as I pointed across the parking lot. "They've got a sale on engagement rings. Just a diamond solitaire, silver band if you can manage it, but I'll take gold if that's all they've got left. Size seven. This should be enough."

I gave him the cash.

"Won't Lyle pitch a fit?"

"Let me worry about that."

✻ ✻ ✻

Lyle didn't notice Jack's absence. He didn't even go outside when the time came to open the store. At ten minutes to six, there were at least two hundred people lined up outside, and from the look of things, over two thousand in our shopping complex. All across the country, thousands of others were doing the same thing.

Maybe that's too modest a number. Maybe it was more. I couldn't say, and now I guess it's something I'll never know.

The morning shift had all arrived on time. Thomas waited in the Print Center, checking his watch every few minutes. His backup, Alice, wasn't scheduled to arrive for three more hours.

Jenna, Lois, and Matt were all at their registers. Lyle and I could man two more registers should the lines become too long. There were floaters, too—employees who didn't belong to any one department but wandered around the store offering assistance when needed. Their names were Nick, Alicia, and

Bill. They were some of the first to die.

"Are you excited?"

Jenna tugged at my sleeve, grinning. I should've kissed her, but I didn't. I've regretted that decision. I never had another chance to do it.

I rolled my eyes. "Oh yes. I can't wait to help a conglomerate make more money."

We laughed together, turning our attention back to the crowd lined up outside the doors. Jenna said, "What happened to Jack? I haven't seen him for almost an hour."

"Last-minute shopping decision," I said. "His area's in order, so I let him go. He should be back soon."

"Aren't you worried Lyle will lose his shit?"

I shrugged. "I doubt he's even noticed. What time is it?"

She checked her phone. "Five minutes to six. Time for the speech. Go get 'em, tiger."

The speech was something we'd adopted over the years. Every Black Friday morning, a few minutes before opening, we'd go over some simple rules about voucher redemption, product quantities, and safety concerns. In recent years, there were cases of overcrowding at other stores, resulting in several injuries. The company didn't want that kind of liability and preempted such things by making us walk out to give a little speech before opening.

As I was going over basic safety precautions, I spotted a man dressed as Santa Claus staggering across the parking lot. He tripped over his own feet in front of an oncoming car. The squeal of brakes was enough to tear the crowd's attention from me. Most of them turned and murmured to one another as the car's driver slammed on the horn.

Someone in the crowd said, "Is he drunk?"

The guy in the Santa suit climbed to his feet and staggered away. The car swerved around him just as he bent over and vomited. Everyone groaned in disgust.

One guy was on his phone, trying to call the cops, but he frowned and hung up after only a few seconds. "Line's busy," he said. Someone else pocketed their phone and said the same thing.

A lady turned to them. "Since when is 9-1-1 busy?"

"Beats the hell out of me," he said, shrugging.

That's when I stopped talking and started paying more attention. That's when things started slowing down and happening too fast all at once. It's when I saw Jack walking back across the parking lot with that dumb grin on his face and a plastic bag in his hand.

It's when Santa Claus stumbled after him.

Something about the way Santa moved did not seem right to me. He walked with a kind of fidgeting gait, and as he moved closer to us, the details became clearer in the hazy morning light. A dark blotch spread down the front of his red suit coat, staining it black, like he'd been splashed with oil. I didn't want to consider what that stain might be. All I wanted was for Jack to walk just a little faster.

Then Jack dropped the bag, and everything played out in slow motion.

Jack paused and bent over to pick up the bag.

Jack looked up and saw I was staring at him. He smiled at me.

Jack straightened and was about to resume his stride.

Santa Claus stumbled forward and put a fidgeting hand on Jack's shoulder.

I heard Jack say something that sounded like, "Hey, what's up, Santa?"

Santa gurgled and groaned, spraying black oil from his mouth, and Jack recoiled in horror. He wiped the dark sludge from his cheek.

"What the fuck, man? Jesus, you sick fuck, what the shit—"

Santa Claus reached for him, but Jack swatted him away and kept on walking.

"Christ," one of the shoppers muttered, "did you see that?"

"That guy's gotta be drunk out of his mind," someone else said.

"Must've had one hell of a Thanksgiving," said another, prompting a few nervous laughs. The clumsy man in the Santa suit reached out once more for Jack, grabbed his arm, and yanked him back.

"Goddammit, dude, what the fuck is your prob—"

But then Jack was screaming. God, he was screaming like a baby as that crazy bastard took a bite out of his hand. When he jerked his hand free of Santa's teeth, he left two fingers behind in the crazy guy's mouth. Jack's bloody stumps spurt gore into Santa's face, staining the fake beard a sickening crimson, and suddenly I realized what that big black stain was down the front of his suit.

Blood. The guy was vomiting blood.

Jack's screams dwindled into weakened sobs as he stumbled back toward the crowd. He almost made it, too, before collapsing at the curb. I pushed my way through the line of shoppers and fell to my knees beside him.

"Jack, oh shit, oh shit—"

"Keep pressure on your hand—"

"He bit off my fucking fingers, man, the crazy fuck, he—"

Some of the shoppers circled around us. One of them said, "Hey, it's after six, man. Unlock the damn doors." I almost whipped around to tell the little shit to call an ambulance, but then someone else said, "That dude's coming over here."

I looked up. Jolly Saint Nick shook and jerked with some kind of diseased palsy as he staggered toward us. He snarled and chewed absently on Jack's missing fingers.

"Get on your feet," I whispered. Jack's eyes were vacant, his pupils dilated, and the last thing I needed was for him to faint. Blood gushed from the stumps of his fingers. "Come on, Jack, stay with me. We'll get you to the hospital, but you gotta stay with me."

"I got your ring," he mumbled, and tried to hand me the plastic bag. I pushed it away, but he insisted, and I stuffed it into my pocket. Then he clenched his teeth and growled. "Fuck, this really hurts, man. Really hurts—"

Somehow, I got him to his feet. Adrenaline, maybe. I don't remember. All I can recall is that the crazy Santa Claus attacked another customer, which prompted most of the crowd to make a mad dash for the doors. By this point, someone inside had switched them on, and they slid open as the first few people approached. A couple others remained to fend off the attacker, and I heard someone scream, "He bit me! *The crazy shit bit me!*"

I remember seeing footage of the LA riots when I was a kid. I remember the way the camera was always at a safe distance with all the rioters looking like ants on the screen. That image hung in my head during the first few minutes of the attack. I could watch something from a distance, but being there, being *right there* with the blood in my face was a whole other matter.

After getting Jack to the service desk, and after Lois ran to the office for the first-aid kit, I couldn't help but stand in shock as the horde of shoppers shoved their way into the store like cattle. Shock and fear are what kept me rooted in place beside the doors. When Mike shouted for me to flip the switch and lock the doors, I just froze up. The little black switch that shut off the automatic doors was on the other side of that human river, and they were all starting to scream in panic.

"Doug!"

Mike stood on top of the service desk, looking over the throng of terrified faces and down at me. He held up his hands.

"What the hell is going on?"

I opened my mouth to speak but found I couldn't muster the words. Instead, I pointed toward the window. Mike turned just as Santa Claus tore a chunk out of a customer's neck. A dark geyser of blood splattered the storefront window, covering the glass like a thick curtain.

Jenna's scream woke me from my terrified trance. I pushed my way through the crowd and back to the sidewalk, grimacing as the cold air stung my cheeks.

Santa was off to the side, making short work of his victim's neck. I nearly vomited when I saw the darkened ring of gore around his mouth and chin. And his eyes. My God, his eyes were so vacant and cloudy. He groaned and gurgled as a fresh mess of dark blood oozed from his mouth and dribbled down his chin.

This creature sized me up with those empty eyes before returning to its meal. There was a soft crunch; a moment later the victim's head slipped back an inch, suspended by the cords of exposed tendons.

It's going to chew his fucking head off, I thought, and that's when I screamed, *"EVERYBODY INSIDE RIGHT NOW!"*

I spun on my heels and was about to make my way inside when I saw Carl standing in the doorway with his handgun, his finger on the trigger, a twitchy frown on his face.

"Please move, Doug."

He spoke calmly, almost nonchalantly, as if he'd practiced this a million times before. I followed the last few customers inside and asked Carl to step back so I could close the door, but he ignored me. He trained the gun on Santa.

The creature in the Santa suit rose to its feet, twitching and vomiting a slow stream of blood down its chin, and dragged its feet toward us. Everyone screamed for me to close the door.

"Carl—" I began, but then my ears were ringing, and I couldn't hear anyone. I saw mouths moving, shrieking words I couldn't understand, and when I turned back, I saw Santa staggering backward. A large black hole had burst open in its chest.

I put my hand on Carl's shoulder. "Come on." My words were muffled, and my ears were ringing so loudly that I could only feel the vibrating hum of my vocal cords. "God-dammit, I need to close the door."

Thomas approached us and tapped Carl on the shoulder. "Shoot it in the head, Carl."

I looked at my coworker, and I remember being stunned because of how smug he looked. Smiling and nodding, like he expected this. Or that he knew what was happening. And he did, too.

Thomas said, "Headshots are the only shots that count, Carl."

Carl centered his aim, steadied himself, and fired again. The bullet struck Santa square between the eyes; a moment later the creature collapsed in a heap and did not get back up.

I grabbed the back of Carl's shirt and yanked him inside the store. Just before pulling the doors closed, I thought I heard sirens and gunfire through the ringing in my head. I flipped the switch and locked the doors in place.

We pushed our way back through the murmuring crowd and to the service desk. Jenna hung up the phone and shook her head. "Line's busy," she whispered, her eyes wrapped in tears.

Thomas pushed forward through the crowd. "You guys okay?"

"How'd you know to do that back there?"

He shrugged. "Zombies, man. Works every time."

* * *

Thomas was a weird guy and relatively new to the company. Lyle put him back in the Print Center to replace someone who'd got so fed up with the job that they just stopped showing up one day. Couldn't blame them, either. When they hired Thomas, I didn't think he'd last very long.

The Print Center required a certain type of person, and I'm saying that from experience. Lyle stuck me over there once to cover for someone who was out sick. A service-oriented department like the Print Center commanded a higher profit margin for the company, which meant higher expectations from the district manager. The department printed money, if you'll pardon the pun, and working there was synonymous with pressure.

No, I didn't think Thomas would last. Not at first. Not based on the way he kept to himself and seemed to internalize everything. I once told Jenna, "If anyone goes apeshit and walks into the store with a semi-automatic, it'll be Thomas." This was before I knew about Carl packing heat every day. Even then, I still clung to my prediction.

I think his silence was what unnerved most of us. He was just so quiet, you know? I once overheard a conversation Jenna was having with Lois and Matt, two of the dedicated cashiers. Lois said, "There's something not right about that boy. He looks like he's got plenty to say, but he just won't talk."

She was right. Thomas had plenty to say, but the key was

getting into his comfort zone. On one of Jenna's days off, I offered to take Thomas out to lunch. My treat, of course, as a sort of olive branch. To my surprise, he didn't turn me down.

"I know some people don't like me," he said between bites of his burger. "I hear them talking about me. It doesn't piss me off or anything. I just find it annoying."

I cleared my throat. "They just don't like that you're so quiet."

"Got nothing to say."

"Is that so?"

He smirked. "No, it's a lie. I'm just doing my time, okay? I'm not here to get chummy with people. I'm here for a paycheck. I told that pencil-neck, Lyle, the same thing. Four years of college, a degree, a hundred grand in debt, and here I am making copies for illiterate shits who are too proud to wipe their own asses."

"Too proud?"

I admit I enjoyed watching him realize the irony of what he'd said.

"Fair enough. Four years ago, I didn't expect to find myself doing this, you know? I think that's how most of the folks who end up working retail must feel. Like they're caught in a net somehow and can't find a way out."

He had a point. I certainly didn't want to make retail my career. I saw what it did to people. Work retail long enough and you turn into Lyle. "But someone has to do it," I offered, "and hey, some people are even good at it. Dare I say they even enjoy it."

Thomas finished off his meal. "You're probably right. I'm just not a very talkative guy."

I leaned back in my seat and smiled. "Could've fooled me."

"Yeah, I'm lying again. I just have this thing about futility.

Ever heard of Sisyphus?"

"That's the guy with the rock?"

Thomas nodded. "Damned by the gods to roll a rock up a hill every day for all eternity. No matter how much or how little he struggled with that rock, it would always roll back down to where he started. That was his punishment for being such a tricky bastard."

I clapped slowly, applauding his dissertation. "Well done, Professor."

"Sorry," he said. "I majored in classical studies."

We fell silent for a few minutes, watching customers come and go. I realized then, watching him, that he was silent because he spent most of his time thinking. He wasn't anti-social, just introspective, and once I grasped that about him, I found him easier to understand.

As we walked back to the store, hands shoved in our pockets, he continued his soliloquy about the existential myth of Sisyphus. He motioned to all the cars in the parking lot around our shopping complex. I never thought I'd make a connection between Greek myth, existential philosophy, and the modern shopper, but Thomas made a believer out of me that day, and all in the time it took us to walk back to our store.

"The real tragedy," he said, "is that all those people out there, the ones we're on our way to serve, are locked in this endless cycle. Work and spend. Produce and consume. There's no end to that cycle. Cut off all conscious thought and I'll bet you a million dollars they'll still continue that cycle."

We both laughed at that.

"Alright," I told him, "you're on, Professor."

❋ ❋ ❋

Jack changed about an hour after the Santa attack. Lois

took charge of his care and was sitting with him when he lost consciousness. She thought he was sleeping.

Jenna was still on the phone trying to get through to 9-1-1, but the line was still busy. We'd all tried our phones over the course of the morning, but the result was the same: our calls couldn't be completed as dialed.

Lyle emerged from his office to find out just what the hell was going on, why we weren't at our posts, why the customers weren't shopping, and so on. He screamed in both mine and Mike's faces for about five minutes before Thomas stepped between us.

"Lyle, shut the fuck up."

"What did you say?" Lyle's face blossomed in red splotches, spreading from his cheeks to his forehead.

"I told you to shut the fuck up, Lyle." Thomas brushed the hair from his eyes and shrugged. "In case you hadn't noticed, we've got a situation here."

"The only situation we have here is insubordination," Lyle snapped. I still can't believe he said "insubordination."

Thomas pointed to Jack, who lay motionless on the floor behind the service desk. "We need to get these people out of here, Lyle."

"No, no, no, just stop, Tom. That's it. You're gone, okay? You're fired. Done. Get out of m—"

And then something amazing happened. Something that I never thought I'd see, though I'd wanted to do it myself for quite some time. Thomas grinned, reared back, and slugged Lyle in the face. Blood from his nose splattered my shirt as he fell to the floor.

"Holy shit," Mike gasped. He looked at Thomas. "I can't believe you just did that. Did you see that? Did he really just do that?"

I was in too much shock to respond. Lyle scrambled to

his feet. "Fine," he stammered, "if that's how it's gonna be, I'm calling the cops and pressing charges."

Jenna slammed the phone down in its cradle. I heard her whisper "fuck" under her breath. Thomas shook his head. "Good luck with that, Lyle."

Our fearless manager stumbled back against the service desk. "Insubordination," he muttered. He was halfway to the manager's office when Lois got our attention.

"There's something wrong with Jack."

Lyle stopped. His cheeks were wet with tears, and a thin line of blood trickled from his left nostril. "What do you mean? What's wrong with him?"

"I tried to tell you," Thomas sighed.

Lyle grimaced. "That's enough out of you. You're through, mister, you hear me?"

He doubled back to the service desk, knelt beside Jack, and began to shake him. Jack's head rolled to one side, and Lyle pressed two fingers against his neck. All that redness in Lyle's face drained away slowly. "He's dead."

A lump rose in my throat. Jenna walked over to me and began to cry. I held her as she buried her face in my chest. "We need an ambulance," I whispered.

Jenna sniffed and shook her head. "The line's still busy."

There were murmurs from the crowd of shoppers. Sounds of crying erupted somewhere in the back, and no sooner had we discovered Jack's untimely demise, a few people ran up the aisle toward us. A young blonde woman nearly collapsed at our feet, her words nearly incomprehensible through long sobs.

"Jeff's dead," she cried. "My husband's dead."

"My wife just fainted," another man screamed. "Honey, wake up! *Wake up!*"

By the time we figured out who'd been bitten or scratched,

it was already too late. We didn't have time to figure how when or how. We were just a gang of retail workers earning barely more than minimum wage. What the hell did we know about pathogens or quarantine procedures? Most of us didn't even know how to give proper first aid or count back correct change.

Lyle rose to his feet and opened his mouth to try and gain some kind of control over the situation, but his words were overpowered by frantic screaming and a heavy *thud-thud-thudding* against the front window.

We turned and saw a young man standing outside with his hands on the glass. He wore a green smock, gloves, and a gold name tag. Half his left cheek was missing, and I could see the faint traces of teeth through the ripped maw of his face. His gloves left bloody smudges all over the glass.

I tightened my grip on Jenna and forced myself to look away. The guy at the window. I knew him. His name was Sean, and he worked at the grocery store next door. My stomach churned.

Someone in the back of the store screamed, and we turned in time to see the crowd of shoppers rushing back toward us.

"Hold on," Lyle began, "everyone just keep calm—"

A low growl split the air, interrupting all of us into silence. A middle-aged man with a bloody stain down the front of his sweater stumbled down the aisle between the printers and tablets. He had a bloody bite mark on his arm, and blackish bile spewed out of his mouth.

Jenna screamed. I thought she was screaming at this impossible thing working its way down the aisle toward us, but I was wrong. She was screaming at Lyle, imploring him to look out, but she was too late. Our manager spun around just as Jack rose to his feet, only he wasn't Jack anymore. His eyes were clouded over, stained the color of sour milk. More of that thickened black mess oozed from the corner of his mouth.

Lyle stumbled back and shrieked. "What is this?"

Jack groaned as he reached for Lyle. His pale fingers gripped our manager's collar and yanked him close. He sank his teeth into Lyle's left eye. That was the moment the giant Fate Monkey hurled a collective mound of shit into the fan called Life.

And to think I used to be such a positive guy.

* * *

At some point in the ensuing chaos, someone scrambled toward the front doors and flipped the switch. This was after those things in the store started waking up, and after Lyle retreated to his office minus one eye courtesy of Jack's sudden appetite. Opening those doors was a move motivated solely by panic—I mean, think about it. You're trapped inside a store with an undead monster. Do you remain inside or remove yourself from the premises? You do the math.

The problem was, whoever flipped that switch forgot about Sean, the grocery clerk from next door.

There were others, of course. All those shoppers who'd ventured out on Black Friday had all been bitten or half-consumed by the living dead, only to die and reanimate less than an hour later. Now I understood why the emergency lines were busy. This was happening everywhere, with everyone out in the open, unprotected, and trying to do their Christmas shopping. This year Santa had brought a plague, and we were all on the naughty list.

Once those doors opened and some of the first people made their exit, I realized just how fucked we were. Those who went outside met the same fate, as there were hundreds of others who'd died and come back. I saw people I'd worked with for years being eaten alive.

After Jack finished choking down Lyle's eyeball, he turned his milky gaze toward Mike, who was too busy trying to hold back the rush of customers to notice the danger he was in. Jack fell upon him, and Mike screamed as he tried to push away his attacker, but the current of people swarming the service desk was too strong. Jack bared his teeth and sank them into Mike's cheek.

I don't remember how long our panic held us captive, but we went from standing to sprinting down the aisles of the store to outrun those who had changed. I gripped Jenna's hand and pulled her along. My mind was on autopilot. *Get to the back of the store*, I thought. *Get to the storage room, the loading dock, the fire exit in the employee lounge—somewhere with an alternate exit.*

Carl rounded the corner, spun on his heels, and fired another round into the horde. Blood poured from a bloody gash on his chin, staining the front of his work shirt.

"Oh Christ, Carl."

He stumbled and fell to his knees. "Get away," he croaked. "Too many. Always too many. And they won't shut up."

I put my hand on Jenna's shoulder and gently pulled her toward me. Carl looked up and caught my eye. The paranoid, dodgy gaze was gone from him; in its place was a hardened stare of absolute clarity.

"*Unnnnngh.*"

One of the undead staggered from around the corner and caught its leg on an end-cap. An assortment of pencils and pens clattered to the floor. Carl raised his weapon and fired. The round pierced the dead man's eye and exploded from the back of his head in a dark floral pattern across the wall. The impact sent him tumbling backward against a row of three-ring binders.

"Go," Carl gasped. We did.

We raced through the maze of aisles and overturned displays, circling the inner perimeter, leading the diseased masses through the store. When we happened upon Carl again, he was serving himself up as a feast for three of the undead. His gun was gone. Jenna was crying, babbling something about her mom, but I couldn't bring myself to smack her. I wanted to cry and babble, too.

"Guys, up here!"

Thomas looked down on us from the top of a steel shelving unit. He stood among boxes of overstock merchandise and waved his arms to get our attention. The rolling staircase we used to access the higher shelves was just a few feet away, and a small group of those dead things was trying to navigate the steps.

"Can we get up there?" she asked.

I squeezed Jenna's hand. The shuffling feet and ravenous moans behind us didn't leave us time to think it over. We ran.

✻ ✻ ✻

Thomas had Carl's gun. He'd swiped it from the dead custodian's hand while the undead feasted upon poor Carl's corpse. Carl was a big guy, after all, and he'd become a buffet.

"I'll see if I can pick them off."

His voice carried over the moans, grunts, and screams, and the crack of gunfire punctuated the store's grim ambiance. By the time we'd circled back to the rolling staircase, Thomas had managed to clear most of the zombies from the steps. We were halfway up when the wheels started to turn. My heart leaped into my throat, and I wanted to scream, *It's not locked down!*

But no words came. Jenna screamed for me, and the world as I knew it stopped turning.

The stairs rolled forward, throwing off her center of gravity, and she began to fall back. Her arms pinwheeled like a cartoon, and I reached out for her, took hold of her wrist.

But the momentum, you see. If Thomas had let her, she would've pulled me down with her. I can still hear myself screaming, *"Thomas, I can't hold her, I'm losing her—FUCK, SHE'S SLIPPING, I CAN'T—"*

Jenna screamed once more, a shrill sound of mortality and fear. That sound still haunts me. And the look in her eyes, the look of terror, the cold *knowing* that she was about to die—

I can't get that look out of my head.

Jenna's hand went limp as she slipped from my grasp, as Thomas pulled me back from following her.

She watched me as she fell, and I closed my eyes. The coward that I am, I fucking closed my eyes.

Thomas left me on the edge of the shelf while he kicked away the staircase. Several of the undead were pinned beneath that rickety web of iron.

I couldn't get her eyes out of my mind. I sat there, sobbing like a baby, telling myself that this couldn't be happening, shit like this didn't happen anywhere but in the movies, and it all came to a single point in my head, sharpened and driven home by the pulse of blood rushing through my brain: *this was my fault.*

Overhead, the speaker system pumped out holiday music, mostly mediocre covers of classic Christmas songs. The moment when she fell, when the horde claimed her, Wham!'s "Last Christmas" started to play. And then that song was etched forever in my head, destined to play back in an awful flash reel.

"Doug."

I rocked back and forth on the edge, tears streaming down my face. I squeezed the ring box in my hand.

"Doug," Thomas said again, and I heard him clearly, but my lips wouldn't work. Finally, Thomas sighed and sat back against a boxed fire-proof safe. I crawled away from the edge of the shelf, stretched out on the cold metal surface, and closed my eyes to the world.

❊ ❊ ❊

An hour later, Thomas put his hand on my shoulder and shook me. I couldn't take my eyes off the dead, kept thinking that if I just slipped, or God help me, happened to roll over while asleep or something, it would all be over. Sure, I'd scream and bleed while they ripped me to pieces, but soon the light in my brain would flicker out and I'd be up again in no time, coming after those who were left.

"Doug." He shook me again. "You can't keep doing this to yourself. You need to pull yourself together so we can work on getting the fuck out of here, man."

Their hands reached up for us. They were down there, *right there*, a six- or seven-foot drop, and if I just stretched far enough, I might be able to brush their dead fingertips. One of them touched me during the surge. It was one of the freshly dead, maybe only an hour or two, and its skin was still clammy, cold.

Mindless drones, every one of them. Clamoring over one another, arms held out, bile and blood spewing from their mouths. I couldn't tell the difference between them and what

they were like when they were still alive. Alive, dead, undead —
did it matter anymore? They're still marching up and down
the aisles, their hollow moans filling the store to its rafters.
They're still searching for their desired prize.

I started to cry, but my tears didn't last long. Thomas back-
handed me, and the jolt of pain yanked me back to reality.

"If you want to die, Doug, just say the word." He put the
barrel of Carl's handgun to my forehead. "At least this way
you'll go out as a human being and not as one of those things."
He put his finger on the trigger. "Your choice, friend. I can
make it very quick, which is more than you'll get from them."

I stared at him through the tears, wondering if he'd lost
his mind, wondering if maybe he'd snap and shoot me, but
then I realized the only one who'd lost his mind was me. I
shook my head and grimaced. He lowered the gun.

"Are we cool now?"

"Yeah," I said, averting my eyes from the horde below.
"We're cool."

❄ ❄ ❄

Thomas and I pushed flat-packed boxes of unassembled
furniture off the top shelf and down onto the growing crowd
below. The boxes landed with *thuds* and *cracks*, and the sound
made my stomach twist into knots, but I kept telling myself
that they weren't people anymore. Easier said than done.

He stood on one end of a long box containing the pieces
of a desk. I stood on the other side. At the count of three, we
both lifted, carefully stepping to the edge where we let go.
The box landed on Mike, cracking open his skull and splatter-
ing his neighbors with reddish-black goo.

"You owe me a million dollars."

"Wait, what?"

"A million bucks," Thomas said. "Don't you remember?"

I thought for a moment, and then it hit me. "Shit, now how was I supposed to know this would happen?"

"That doesn't matter. You still owe me a million dollars. You're not going to back out of our deal, are you?"

I dusted off my hands and readied myself for another box. "Tell you what, Professor. If we get out of this alive, I'll roll the rock as long as I have to so I can earn that million bucks for you."

Thomas considered this for a moment before frowning and shaking his head. I thought he was still kidding around, but when he spoke again, I realized he wasn't.

"No," he said, gripping the edge of the next box of cubicle parts. "I doubt either of us will live that long."

I looked down at the rest of the store. Standing on top of the storage shelves, we were maybe eight feet from touching the ceiling. This high up, you were practically in the rafters and could see the entire store. Every aisle, every department, was filled with those bloody things, their mouths open, eyes cloudy and unblinking, all clamoring over each other looking for the next "it" thing.

Thomas and I were the only ones left.

We stood at the edge and exchanged glances for one grim moment.

"You could've just lied to me," I muttered. We let go of the box. *Crack.*

* * *

We sat with our backs against a couple of boxes containing desktop computers. I washed down my dinner of jelly beans and potato chips with a can of warm soda. Just the sort of thing that one could pick up for an office party while also buying the necessities like paper, binders, and envelopes. "Up-sell opportunities," Lyle used to call them before he lost the ability to speak in comprehensible words.

Building a makeshift bridge between the shelving units with a long box of furniture was my idea. It had taken us most of the day to sift through them and find one just long enough, and when we did, the box barely covered the distance.

Watching Thomas tip-toe across while things below reached up for him was both comical and terrifying. When he made it to the other side, he began sorting through the boxes of goods, tossing them across that writhing, moaning canyon between us. I almost lost my balance a couple of times while catching the supplies. When Thomas was finished, he raced back across the bridge with not a moment to spare. The box shook and tumbled down onto the mob below just as he stepped away.

Our feast of junk food was hard-won, and we ate like kings.

"I'm serious," Thomas said, munching on a chocolate bar, "that's how I knew."

I finished off my chips and crumpled the bag in my hands. "You mean to tell me that because you've seen every zombie film ever made, that that's how you knew to shoot them in the head? It never once occurred to you that maybe there was some other explanation?"

He smirked. "Are you complaining?"

"No, I'm not. But the rest of us didn't even consider that option. You, however, knew right away. You suspended disbelief right away. Tell me, Professor, why do you think that is?"

Thomas thought for a moment, and then said, "Too many movies and video games, maybe." He popped open another can of soda.

"Too many movies and games," I said. "Cheers."

We tapped our cans together.

Fifty years from now, if civilization somehow manages to survive this undead plague, historians will rule that pop culture saved us after all.

* * *

"FUCK!"

Thomas fired a round into the forehead of the dead man who bit him. The dead man who used to be Jack. The back of his head flew off like a bloody toupee.

He'd almost made it. He was climbing up the shelves with a shopping bag full of batteries and a radio, and that's when Jack rounded the corner. Our dead coworker reached out, clutched Thomas's ankle, and took a bite.

I pulled my friend to safety. He grimaced and cursed through clenched teeth.

"Here," he growled, tossing the bag. The packages of batteries spilled out. The radio was still in its box—on sale in Aisle 9—and going for it had seemed like a good idea at the time. If I stood at one edge of the top shelf and made as much noise as possible, I could lure them away while he climbed down for the goods.

Now he was dead. Not yet, but soon. I sat him down against the boxed safe and looked at the wound. The bite was minor, barely even a nick, but we both knew the damage was done. The look on his face confirmed as much.

"Had a good run," he said. He gave me Carl's handgun. "You know what to do."

"I can't—"

Thomas laughed. The plague was already working its terrible magic. His whole body trembled, his forehead dotted with fevered sweat, and black veins sprouted from his wound.

"You'll have to," he said. "It's either that or you'll have

one more of those things to deal with up here."

"I don't think this is very funny," I said.

"Of course it is!" He turned and spat black fluid from his mouth. "This is how it's supposed to happen. You buy the ticket, you watch the movie, and it always comes down to one person. No offense, man, but I figured I'd be the last. Didn't think you'd make it after Jenna fell."

Tears welled up in my eyes, and I fought to hold them back. I'd done enough crying. "This isn't a fucking movie."

"No, you're right. It's not. But that doesn't mean it's not happening. Say, what do you think is a good price for a giant rock in Hell?"

"You're not funny, Professor."

But I wanted to laugh. I wanted to laugh and cry and vomit.

Thomas tapped the barrel of the gun. "Three shots left. One for me, you, and Jenna, if you can find her."

The lump returned to my throat, and my stomach burned. The thought of her wandering around down there among them, seeking living flesh to consume, made my skin crawl.

And then the gravity of our situation fell upon me, crushing the last of my spirit. I wouldn't survive this. The whole reason for getting the radio was because we'd neither heard nor seen any sort of enforcing presence that might clean up this mess. For all we knew, we were the only ones left in town.

That thought quieted my mind. For the first time since her death, I realized what was going through Jenna's head in her final moments. The knowledge of your own demise, the grim acceptance of it, was enough to bring calm to anyone in their ending.

No, I wouldn't survive this. None of us would. That fact alone empowered me, and finally, I understood the point of Thomas's rock analogy.

"Do you think we all deserved this?"

The sound of his voice startled me. "What do you mean?"

"All this." He gestured in the air around us. "The height of civilization and decadence, and now it's all gone. We were celebrating a shopping day, for fuck's sake."

"It's a bit late to get philosophical, don't you think?"

He chuckled and fell silent again. Of course, Thomas was right. Even I had fallen prey to that mentality. Produce and consume, spend and please, and this is where we ended up regardless of the outcome: dead, or close to it.

"Yeah," I said finally. "I guess we do."

When he didn't respond, I pulled back the slide and chambered one of the three rounds left. One for my friend. One for Jenna. One for me.

We sat there for a long time, Thomas breathing slower and slower, me getting used to the weight of the gun in my hand.

His eyes widened. He pointed to the undead mob below and cracked a smile. The light in his eyes was already starting to fade.

"You still owe me a million dollars."

And with that, Thomas closed his eyes for the last time. I checked his pulse just to be sure. I told him goodbye, took a breath, and put the gun to his temple.

❊ ❊ ❊

He was all over my shirt and face. After I pulled the trigger, I cried and dry-heaved and clawed at my face to get the blood off me. I could taste it on my tongue. The stench of blood and gun oil wouldn't leave my nose. I left his body up there where they couldn't get to him. He deserved better than that.

An explosion from somewhere outside drew them away from the shelving unit long enough for me to make my escape.

I climbed down and retreated to the back of the store. She was waiting for me there.

There wasn't much left of my love. Those monsters had torn away half her scalp, and her nose was chewed off. She grinned at me through a blackened hole in her cheek. The badge on her vest confirmed my worst fears. Until then, I think maybe I still had some slim hope that she'd managed to survive, that it was all just a nightmare from which I'd yet to awaken.

Reality is a bitch, though. It doesn't take prisoners. All it leaves is a body count.

Grimacing, fighting back the urge to puke, I lured Jenna to the back of the store, through the receiving area, and toward the back office.

I pushed open the door and peeked inside. The old cash office was empty, isolated, and windowless. There was only one way out of this. I knew that. But I couldn't go through with my plan while knowing Jenna was still out there, wandering for all eternity, her body slowly rotting away. I couldn't let that happen.

She staggered down the hallway, convulsing while black bile oozed from the gaping hole in her face.

I wiped tears from my eyes, raised the gun, and aimed down the sight. The gravity pressing down on my heart took care of the rest.

"I bought something for you, honey."

I have one bullet left. One ticket out of this mess, and I aim to take it.

I don't know why I wrote this down. Maybe this was my rock, and I've been rolling it ceaselessly these last few hours.

Maybe I wrote it all down in case someone finds it. In case there's someone left to find it.

These words are my final testament, written upon sheets of our store's stationery. This was the best I could do. There wasn't much else in here besides rolls of receipt paper and stale coffee.

Maybe this is just the old me trying to make lemons from lemonade. Maybe if people survive this plague, Black Friday will become a day remembered for all the right reasons—a day when humanity's excess came tumbling down around its ears.

Or maybe nothing will change at all.

But I won't know.

That uncertain future may be for sale, but I'm not buying.

Manufacturer's Defect

B.L. Daniels

"Thanks for calling Create-A-Bear workshop. This is Tim."

"You have to help me! This bear is trying to kill my family! How do I stop it?"

Tim's face twisted. He looked at the handset, then put it back to his ear. "Uh, sir, this is a toy store, not the police, I think you need to call 9-1-1."

"No, please, don't hang up! Tom—"

"Tim."

"Tim, sorry. Tim, my name is Alan Watts, and I already tried calling the cops. They just laughed at me. They thought I was high or pulling a prank or something. They hung up on me, twice…"

* * *

Alan heard the scratching again and watched Catherine hug the children tighter as they huddled in the corner of the room.

"Sir, are you there? Hello?" Tim's voice buzzed from the

smartphone.

"Yeah, sorry. I'm still here."

"So there's a problem with your kid's Create-A-Bear?"

"We always let them open a present the night before, and when she unwrapped the box, it seemed okay, but then something happened. It started glowing, and the thing went nuts and attacked her."

"Wait, the bear attacked your daughter?"

"Yes! I managed to pull it off, and then it went after our Pomeranian."

"I'm sorry about your plant—"

"Not a Geranium, a *Pomeranian*. The thing killed our goddamned dog."

"Mommy, what happened to Mister Jingles?" Jenny asked, tears welling up in her eyes. A low growl vibrated through the door. Alan felt electric terror jolt through his fingers, and his hair stood on end as the guttural noise stretched and twisted into a high-pitched shriek. Catherine and the children screamed and covered their ears.

"Whoa, what's that noise?" Tim said.

"It's that thing." Alan winced and clasped his free hand over his other ear. "Now do you believe me?"

There was a momentary silence on the line. "Uh...yeah, I'm gonna go get my manager. Can you hang on a second? Joanne!"

Tim's voice disappeared, replaced by the sound of dogs barking "Jingle Bells."

"Alan, what's happening? Are they calling the cops?" Catherine said.

"Uh, no. They put me on hold."

"What?" Catherine's eyes grew as wide as dinner plates.

"They're getting a manager." He shrugged. "I'm sure she'll help."

The door rattled on its hinges as the creature slammed into it. The children yelped and buried their faces into their mother.

"Dad? Is it going to kill us?" Jeremiah peered up from the safety of his mom's ugly red sweater.

"JJ, don't say that," Catherine snapped.

"Hey, calm down. Everyone just calm down." Alan shushed them with a hand motion. "No, buddy, we'll be fine. It's just a teddy bear. It can't get through the door, and the people on the phone are going to help."

"Hello?" a deadpan voice interrupted the caroling hounds. "Create-A-Bear Workshop, this is Joanne."

"Oh, thank God, Joanne, this is Alan Wa—"

"Yes, sir, Tim already told me. What's the issue with your Holiday Harvey?"

"Holiday Harvey?"

"Yes, the bear. Holiday Harvey."

"The bear attacked my family when my daughter unwrapped it. It bit my little girl, and now we're trapped upstairs, barricaded in my son's room, and the thing is trying to claw through the door."

The silence on the other end of the line was punctuated by the doorknob shaking and jiggling, the creature probing for a way in.

"It's unlikely there's a problem, Mister Watts," Joanne said.

"Excuse me?" Alan stared at his phone in disbelief.

"Holiday Harvey doesn't have teeth or claws. The only Cuddle Friend with fangs or claws is Barry Bat, and he's gone after Halloween. Plus, they're made of felt, so even if there was a manufacturer's defect, it shouldn't be a danger to you."

Alan's chest grew tight, and his heart pounded into his throat. "Okay, listen to me, Joanne. The bear is trying to kill us. I don't know why, and I don't care. Just tell me how to turn it off. Please."

Joanne's voice faded into a muffled echo. "Tim, go get me the Holiday Harvey manufacturer's guide. What? I dunno where. I think it was in that box of weird-looking batteries with the squiggly writing on it. Yeah, it's probably in the trash, and tell Vicki to cover the register, the line is getting huge. Yes, ma'am… I know it's late. Someone will be right here to help you."

A chorus of dogs barking "Up on the Housetop" sounded through the phone.

"For Christ's sake…" Alan said, rubbing his forehead.

"Mister Watts, you still there?" Joanne returned. "Okay. So I think I have a solution to your problem."

"Thank God! What is it?" Alan said.

"Well, Tim and I are trying to read the book, but it's real weird. There's pictures of Cuddle Friends I haven't seen— Yeah, Tim, I know the book smells bad. No, I don't know why the cover is all wrinkly."

The door made a loud snap as something hit it from the outside.

"I can't figure this gobbledygook writing out," Joanne said. "I think it's Indonesian or something? Tim, get Vicki, maybe she can read it. Wait, Vicki's Filipino? Hey, I am NOT racist—"

"Jesus Christ!" Alan shouted as the children's sobs erupted into full-blown wails. "Tell me what to do. It's getting in!"

"Let me just look at the diagrams," Joanne said. "So there's a picture of a child laying down, and…uh…a circle of other people…and the Cuddle Friend seems to be holding a heart up. Tim, does that look like a heart to you?"

It hammered against the door again, hard, and the knob rattled loose, bouncing off the floor with a *thud* as wood buckled and fractured.

"Hurry," Alan said.

"All right, we figured it out," Joanne breathed a sigh of relief. "Mister Watts, you and your family need to go and lay in a circle, with your daughter in the middle. Then Holiday Harvey will hug her until he eventually falls in love with her. If that doesn't work, then maybe try unbuttoning his sweater vest and removing his battery pack?"

"What...the...FUCK?" Alan screamed into the phone, his face burning with rage. "I'm not sacrificing my daughter to that fucking thing out there!"

"Oh my God!" Catherine clasped her hand over her mouth, "Oh my god, that's what they said?"

Alan looked out the window and watched snowflakes melt into tiny droplets as they touched the warm glass. It was at least a twenty-foot drop straight to the frozen ground, and he imagined JJ and Jenny living their lives in braces or a wheelchair if they survived.

"Mister Watts, I don't like your attitude," Joanne's corpse of a voice crawled through the tiny speaker, snapping Alan's attention back to the phone. "It's Christmas Eve, and I'm sorry you're having problems with your kid's toy, but I've been here going on almost thirteen hours now, and I don't appreciate being cussed at. So I suggest if you don't like my advice, you come back here Tuesday when you've cooled off a bit, and if you bring Harvey's box and your receipt, we'll see about getting you a gift car—"

Splinters showered the room as the ax split the door open.

Alan's ears rang with his family's screams as Harvey tore its way in, chewing and clawing at chunks of the door panel to make an opening.

Goddamned fool, Alan cursed himself for leaving the ax laying out after he built the fire. The bear was determined and learned to improvise.

"Run!" Alan dove at the door and flung it open, pulling

Harvey with it, and smashed the bear's face into the wall. Its arms and legs flailed, bloody, silver claws recklessly swiping at anyone within reach. Harvey fought against the door, and a cold, purple light bathed the hallway, radiating from under its sweater vest.

Catherine and the children flew from the room, their feet pounding the staircase like a herd of spooked deer. Alan snatched the ax off the floor and headed for the stairs. He heard Jenny's scream halfway down.

"Mister Jingles!" Jenny shrieked. Alan rounded the corner and saw his wife's mouth agape as she gagged and covered their daughter's eyes. JJ trembled in a muted panic.

On the far wall, above the fireplace, a message was scrawled in crimson and matted clumps of orange fur. Strange symbols—geometric patterns inked in blood—surrounded a single word, "YULE," painted from Mr. Jingle's insides. A plastic angel gently cradled the dog's head atop the tree, its swollen, purple tongue dangling to one side. Blood trickled down, pinstriping the twinkling silver ornaments below.

"Dad! Look out!" JJ shouted.

Alan felt the hot pain of teeth sinking in as Harvey bit his shoulder. "Aaaaaaaagh!" Alan screamed and pulled at the bear. Its jaws clamped tighter; teeth like knives sliced his flesh as it dug claws into his back. "Run! RUN!" he screamed as he successfully dislodged Harvey. He flung the bear and a chunk of his shoulder at the fireplace. Harvey recovered and jumped onto the back of the couch. The toy unleashed an ear-piercing shriek, and the room was bathed in purple light pouring from its back. Alan grabbed the ax with his working hand and limped forward, the blade scraping hardwood as he dragged it across the floor.

"Catherine, get out of here. Get to the Thompsons and call the cops." Alan said, his eyes locked on Harvey. "Come on, you fuzzy sonofabitch! Come and get me!"

Harvey lunged. It flew across the room, tackling Alan and knocking the ax across the floor.

Alan's hand spasmed as Harvey bit into the meat of it; dark blood flowed between the bear's teeth as it severed his thumb and index finger. He smashed its head with all the strength he had left, but his fist only sank into soft plushness of the toy animal as the bear continued gnawing through bones and tendons. Christmas lights dissolved into shimmering blurs as Alan's eyes watered, and numbness crept up his mangled arm.

"Die, you fucking monster!" Catherine screamed as she swung the ax.

The steel head smashed into Harvey's back, tearing open the sweater vest to expose a cracked purple crystal. Harvey cried out, releasing Alan's dangling fingers, as a fountain of purple sparks erupted from its back. The sparks grew into thin fibers of lightning, arcing from the burning stone. A bolt cracked into Catherine's hand, and she yelped as it scorched her flesh.

Harvey stumbled backward. It wailed and shuddered as the energy swelled into lavender flames that engulfed his body. Button eyes melted, and fabric burned. Alan watched as the things face warped and twisted, a demonic visage emerging within the cloud of purple fire. "YUUUUUUULE," it croaked as the blaze consumed the last of its body before it finally collapsed to the floor, a charred lump.

"C'mon, we need help," Catherine said, picking up Alan and wrapping a throw blanket over his arm. Sirens howled in the distance, "Thank God. Alan, you're going to be all right. Missus Thompson must have heard us and called 9-1-1."

"We need to get outside," Alan said, shivering as shock settled in. "We need to go. Where are the kids?" He limped forward with help from his wife, and the cold air stung his face as she swung open the front door.

Alan saw flames lick from the windows of Mrs. Thompson's house as Catherine's shouts faded into a high-pitched whine. The old woman lay face down in the yard outside her front step; a tiny unicorn was plunging a kitchen knife into her back. The blade struck her again and again, and black blood spattered across the fresh snow.

Alan staggered, and through the smoky haze, he watched Dr. Feldman, confined to a wheelchair, roll into the street as a teddy bear strangled him. The fire engine's brakes squealed as it barreled around the corner, and Mrs. Feldman howled into the night air as the truck shattered her husband across the cold asphalt.

The Cuddle Friends had awoken from their cardboard prisons and brought the gift of an ancient chaos.

Alan's last thought before the darkness claimed his vision was of Harvey, and how if there was a next Christmas, his daughter was getting a bike.

X❄ Marks X❄mas

Debra Robinson

Jake trudged through ankle-deep snow on Christmas Eve, dragging the ax, weaving in and out between the rows of pines, looking for the perfect Christmas tree.

A-Plus, Number One Dad.

His personal mantra ran through his head.

His kids followed close behind, in his tracks mostly, Michelle complaining a bit, but Evan was as gung-ho as he was.

"Dad, what about this one," Michelle whined. "It looks great." She obviously wanted to go home.

"No, Honey, it's too sparse. We want a full one."

She pointed to another tree. "That one?"

"Not quite tall enough, Michelle. We want it to go to the ceiling, almost!"

"Look at this one, Dad! It's kind of weird, but in a good way," Evan called from a row over.

Jake diverted from his lane of trees and walked into the next row. A tall evergreen jutted from the ground, leaning aggressively toward the tree beside it. Two ancient, hand-hewn stones, stacked on each other, stood behind it, part of an old foundation, it looked like. The tree's branches were strange—the last four inches of each end turned upward, almost at right angles, like fingers bent backward.

"Wow, that's kind of interesting looking, isn't it?" Jake mused.

"It's nice and tall, and really full, too. What do you think, Dad? I kind of like it. It's different!"

Jake liked it, too. "Different is good, Evan! What do you think, Michelle? Shall we take it?"

Michelle shifted from foot to foot, staring at the strange tree. She made a face. "I don't know. I guess."

Jake ignored his daughter in favor of his son's endorsement. He knew this was a problem but couldn't stop himself. It had been this way since Evan had been born. He craved his son's approval in a way he knew led to a dysfunctional family dynamic. He tried to overcome it in various ways to make it up to Michelle. But this was not one of those times.

A-Plus, Number One Dad.

Jake swung the ax, congratulating himself for thinking of this cut-your-own-tree nursery as another way to bond with his kids, to be a better parent than his parents were to him. To have the perfect Christmas Eve.

Jake loaded the tree onto the sled provided by the nursery and pulled it back to the small building at the front of the property.

The old man in charge took one look at the odd tree and laughed.

"You got the Demon Tree."

"How so?" asked Jake as he turned in the borrowed ax and rolled the tree off the sled.

"Oh, that's just what we call it around here. There's not another one like it on the entire acreage, and things just somehow seem to 'happen' when we get near it. The tractor overturning on a rut. Jeremy, our teenage helper, breaking his leg. That sort of thing."

The kids stood google-eyed, but Jake just laughed. "Well, now. That's interesting. But different is *good* in this family." He gave the old man a dazzling devil-may-care grin, but with a hard glint in his eyes that dared him to say more.

The old man blanched slightly. "No offense meant, of course. We're not superstitious around here." He hesitated a moment, then added, "That tree grew right on the spot where the Deacon cabin sat." The old man stared hard at him, as though that should mean something.

Jake paid him. "We're from the next county over, so not real familiar with your local history here." He didn't smile this time, which worked. The old man didn't offer any other explanations.

As he dragged the evergreen back to the SUV, Evan hugged him around the waist, giddy with excitement. His heart soared.

A-Plus, Number One Dad.

Jake thought back to his own childhood, as he often did. Those experiences had informed his opinion that some people should not have children. It was a near-miracle he'd overcome his initial reluctance to have them. And he'd been rewarded with Evan.

Jake's childhood had been a living hell.

His parents were religious, fundamentalist extremists. No TV or movies were allowed in their house. Each morning, his dad would carefully ration the milk on young Jake's daily breakfast cereal; only enough to wet it was the rule. Accumulated hours spent on his knees, praying for forgiveness, was the prevalent memory of Jake's younger days. He supposed if you added them all up, those hours would actually amount to years.

With the clarity provided by time, Jake came to believe it

was a control issue behind his parents' obsessions all along. Sure, it was couched in the Holy Roller, hive-mind, group-think indoctrination stuff, but when it came right down to it, the struggle for control of Jake's words, thoughts, and deeds seemed to be what was at stake.

He remembered being allowed to play with only one young classmate because his parents approved of *that* kid's parents. This friend would get angry when Jake insisted the dirtiest parts of Forest Gump be played over and over on their DVD. Jake's sexual obsessions only escalated from there: sexual addiction, alcoholism, control issues; he'd dealt with them all.

One day, at age fifteen, he'd snapped and killed them all; his parents, brother, and sister. On Christmas Eve. He'd stayed in a facility until the age of twenty-one when he'd been deemed to no longer be a threat to anyone, his abusive family considered the catalyst for the tragedy.

Later on, beginning his second life, his past a total secret from his *new* family, Jake began to understand *his* need for control was a result of having zero control in his youth.

He didn't quite understand why *Evan* had become like the dad figure in his head and he'd become the kid trying to please him. Not to mention poor Michelle, and her total neglect.

He didn't allow himself to dwell on this for long. It was too painful, too effed up.

Jake started singing Christmas carols, egging on the kids to join in, and they sang them all the way home. But watching Michelle in the rearview mirror, he could tell she was pissed.

Wait until she sees the stuff I bought her. That will fix things.

His wife was nowhere to be found when he got home. The kids ran to their respective rooms and their electronic devices, Evan yelling he was going to look up the Deacon cabin.

Jake untied the tree from the top of the SUV and pulled

it inside. He found the tree stand in the garage, the ornaments in the attic, and planned to call the kids to decorate it as soon as he got it set up.

His tree stand was an old one, inherited from his parents. You had to screw three L-shaped rods into the trunk to hold it in place. Jake balanced the tree upright with one hand as he tried to do this. Then he realized he needed to lay it down and set it up after the stand was attached.

As he eased the evergreen onto its side, he moved to let go of the trunk to start on the stand.

His hand was stuck.

His fingers were wrapped around the trunk as though glued there. Puzzled, he reached in with his other hand.

That's some serious pine tar. Better than super glue.

Jake pulled at his fingers, trying to pry them away from the bark. The turned-up ends of branches scratched his face, his throat, jammed into his chest.

Suddenly, one of those odd, turned-up branches folded completely back on itself in front of his eyes and slid slowly toward his mouth. Jake squeezed his lips shut, but the pointed branch and needles forced them apart and pushed its way inside.

The tangy, pungent smell of evergreen overwhelmed his senses, and pain flared as two more branches folded back upon themselves, these ones aiming for his nostrils. He jerked his head from side to side, making it harder for them to find their target.

The branch in his mouth pushed deep into his throat while the others forced themselves into each nostril, breaching his gullet and joining the first one. Jake gagged and choked for air. More branches pried their way into his mouth, and Jake, in horror, agony, and disbelief, began to suffocate.

He felt the branches ripping open the seat of his pants,

seeking another orifice. He heard Evan run into the room, yelling something about the Deacon cabin, about the witch burnt there, the curse she left behind as she died.

And then Evan was beside him, pulling him, but the Demon Tree had other plans. Evan's high-pitched squeals were snuffed out as branches crammed their way into his mouth and down *his* throat. Michelle's cries came next as she tried to save her big brother.

As Jake blacked out, the last thought in his head was relief that they would all die together on Christmas Eve, as a good family should.

A-Plus, Number One Dad.

THE TREE-LIGHTING CEREMONY

Mark L. Eshbaugh

"So what's it going to be this year, Johnny?" slurred Eric, leaning heavily on his friend's shoulder for fear of falling off his bar stool. "Last year was pretty epic. That ice castle took up nearly the entire town common. I thought it was something extraordinary. And the knights you designed to repel the frost giants crashing the front gate were so fun to make."

Eric Ducharme was the town drunk and John's high school buddy. Both men, townies to the core, had lived their entire lives in the same neighborhood. Taking very different paths, they each eventually found work in the school system. Eric was the high school maintenance man. Throughout his entire life, Eric was often the butt end of jokes and the victim of cruel pranks among the townsfolk. Some may have been deserved, but most of them were not. Despite his dependence on alcohol, Eric was a good man. The students had nicknamed him "Flex" based on an entirely false rumor from his high school days that refused to die. In short, an unnamed classmate of Eric's had supposedly walked in on him in the school bathroom; supposedly, he had been standing in front of the mirror and masturbating with one hand while flexing the muscles of his free arm.

"Thank you, Eric. That was a fun display to design," John replied. "But I just dream them up. You're the one who gives them life," he said with a grin.

For the past several years, they—with an army of seasoned volunteers—worked as a team building large-scale ice and snow sculptures. Each year, they decorated not only their own yards but also the school grounds and the town common. Eric's undiagnosed dyslexia as a child had made him a terrible student and an unpopular one. But to his credit, despite his difficulties reading, the heightened visual and spatial ability his dyslexia also provided made him an exceptional sculptor, in addition to making him invaluable at his job able to fix anything. He could envision and build anything three-dimensionally.

Eric was John's right-hand man since the beginning of freshman year in high school. Both had a love of live music and had formed a short-lived high school punk band, with Eric on drums, John on vocals, and a mutual friend, Jason Luminello, on guitar. In addition to never deciding on a name, they had no bassist—and figured that was just fine because, first of all, who knew what a bassist was, and second, no one can hear them anyway, right? Besides, wasn't it "punk" to not have a full-lineup? Their fourteen-year-old selves certainly thought so.

Academically, they were on opposite ends of the spectrum. John excelled in school and took several AP courses that included calculus, physics, and art. He long dreamed of being a famous artist but was enough of a realist—and his parents were insistent enough—that he stuck to the STEM programs throughout high school, college, and later his graduate studies.

It was, however, his background in art that allowed him to design the plans for the ice and snow sculptures that Eric would then make a reality each year.

John was first hired at the high school as a math teacher. He loved planning and guiding the curriculum, while his colleagues and subordinates preferred teaching to the tests and copying directly from the teacher's editions. Though he enjoyed his time in the classroom, John decided that he was more suited to administration, so after seven years in the trenches, he became one of three Deans at the school. As the Dean of Emerson House, he knew every student in his house by name and called home when they were out sick, not to see if they were playing hooky, but out of legitimate concern for their well-being. After three fast years as Dean and earning a Doctorate in Education during his nights and weekends, John worked his way out of that job and into a private corner office with a plaque on the door that read: John Galante, Principal.

"Hey, man. Why don't I drive you home after this round?"

John's tone told Eric everything he needed to hear: he had hit his limit. "Okay, buddy. I know you got to get home to the family," he replied.

After finishing their drinks, John paid the tab for both of them and guided his friend out to the parking lot. Snow was gently falling as they made their way to John's Prius. Eric leaned heavily on the side of the car as John began fishing for his keys when a loud voice from across the street called out, "Hey Flex! Drunk again? You useless prick!"

Both men looked toward the sound of the voice. A seventeen-year-old boy stood in an open bay of Connolly's Auto Body. "Trevor Connolly, why don't you head back inside and help your old man," John called back. "And I trust I'll see you at your usual detention after school tomorrow?"

Without another word, the boy turned and disappeared into the garage. A moment later the door slid down behind him. Trevor was the only son of Rob Connolly, who had also been a maladjusted bully in his day. Rob Connolly had been in the same graduating class as them. Rob and Eric were classmates for most of their schedules, as they faced many of the same academic struggles, and each pined after the same girl in those classes, Shannon Miller. John always suspected Rob of creating the "Flex" narrative out of jealous rivalry. Eric managed to date her first, but it didn't last more than a few months. Within days after the "Flex" narrative began circulating, she had dropped Eric and started dating Rob. When Rob tried to gloat, Eric simply replied that he'd had her first, and she was a "Shantastic" lay. The ensuing fist fight left Eric with six weeks of detention and Rob spending an equal amount of time eating through a straw; Eric had fractured Rob's jaw in three places. And it had been wired shut in order to heal. From that day on, Connolly and his best friend, Frankie Faulds, did everything they could to make Eric's life a living hell.

Shannon went on to marry Rob when, shortly after graduation, she discovered she was pregnant with their son. Shannon couldn't afford college and a child, so after the baby was born, she began working as a stripper at Sanctuary. Over the years, Shannon, unbeknownst to her husband, had had regular affairs with a few select, high-paying customers. She also made it a point to arrange to spend a weekend around the holidays with Eric every year, which she referred to as her "Christmas bonus." This was in addition to the several times they met up during the year.

Trevor was Rob and Shannon's son, and he too, with Kevin Faulds by his side tried his best to keep the legacy of abusing Eric going. Like their fathers before them, Kevin was Trevor's best friend, that is until Kevin and his father were found dead

in their home three years ago. The two Faulds were found mur-
dered in their bedrooms, victims of blunt force trauma. The
only clues the police had to work with was a shattered bay
window and large pools of water throughout the home, which
could have just been the result of snow blowing in through
the broken glass.

"You giving Shan her 'Christmas bonus' again this year?"
asked John as he unlocked the car doors. "Just put the books
in the backseat, would you?"

"You know it. I don't know why Shan stays with that jerk.
It's getting harder to keep it a secret now that they keep trying to schedule her for the day shifts. It's harder to come up
with reasons she'd be out all day and night. Manager says she's
getting too old for the job. I guess she's looking for other
options, maybe drive a school bus, or the grocery store, or
something..." Eric grabbed the pile of books on the front seat
and sat down heavily, setting the books in his lap. He began
flipping through the books as John went around the car and
settled himself in the driver's seat. Snapping the topmost book
closed, he stared at the title on the nondescript cover.

"John, am I that drunk? Or is this book not in English? Sefer
Yetzirah?"

"You're definitely that drunk, man," John replied. "But, no...
That one is in Hebrew. I read that one around the holidays
every year. In fact, I had to borrow that copy from Shannon.
I lost my copy."

"Oh. Okay, some Chanukah thing then. The snow is really
starting to come down. Glad you're driving."

"Yeah, me, too," John said. "You shouldn't be driving anytime soon. So we've got two and a half weeks to the holiday
tree-lighting ceremony to design and build our sculptures.
I'll sketch up some ideas tonight and over the weekend so
you can start planning."

"At least we'll have some fresh snow to work with. Not like two years ago when we had to rent that snow-maker from the ski place."

"Yeah, that cost a fortune, and the town only paid a tenth of the bill. The rest was out of my own pocket." John pulled the car into Eric's driveway. "Alright, here you go. Time to go sleep it off."

Eric nodded sleepily to his friend and got out of the car. As he made his way slowly to his front door, a large, black dog came racing up from the yard next door. Eric noticed a little too late as the dog clamped down on his calf, knocking him to the ground. Eric began kicking the dog as it bit down harder on his leg. John, noticing what was happening, laid on the car horn despite the late hour, trying to spook the dog into letting go. Whether it was the horn, another well-placed kick from Eric, or the neighbor calling the dog to come, it finally released Eric and retreated back to its yard.

"Goddamn it, Ed! Keep that son-of-bitch on a leash. That's twice this week! If he comes after me again, it will be the last time!"

John watched as Eric slowly got up and made his way into the house. He looked toward the neighbor and glared at him as the man retreated with the dog in tow. As Ed went back to his house, he returned John's glare and flipped his middle finger in John's direction. Shaking his head, John pulled out into the street and headed for home.

The following morning, Eric woke up to a raging hangover and an insistent knocking on his front door. After a few false starts and muttering curses under his breath, he made his way to the front door and pulled it open.

"Here are the plans for this year's display," John said, handing his friend a large hazelnut dark roast and a sketchbook. Eric gratefully took the coffee and swallowed a large gulp, which burned the roof of his mouth. With a grimace, he turned his attention to the sketchbook Eric eagerly shoved in his face. "How's the leg?"

"That goddamned dog. I swear, if Ed lets it get out again, I'm going to punt it over the fence. So what are we making this year?" Eric flipped open the sketchbook and began thumbing through the images John had produced.

"It's probably a bit off the rails, but I was thinking about holiday classics. And then I thought classics in general. So we have the whole of the town common and the front of the school to fill…"

"Don't forget our front lawns," interjected Eric, still looking through the sketchbook.

"Right, it's all in there. So the town common will have the holiday classics by the tree-lighting stage: all the reindeer, Santa, Frosty, Yukon Cornelius, Bumble the Abominable Snowman, et cetera. The kids and parents will love it. But leading in from the municipal parking lot toward the stage, we will have a section of Hollywood movie classics on one side: Frankenstein's Monster, Dracula, Godzilla, the works. Then on the other side, we'll have cartoon and comic book classics: Bugs, Daffy, Woody Woodpecker, Snoopy, Spider-man, Batman, and such."

"I get you. What do you want in your yard?" asked Eric as he continued looking through the display sketches.

"I was thinking Star Wars characters," said John, stabbing his finger on a page of the sketchbook. "We can put them all in Christmas scenes and hats. They did a holiday special we can draw from. I know it's not totally original this year, but we're short on time, and it's fun."

"Yeah, it works...as long we don't get sued for copyright infringement. What are we putting in my lawn then, John?"

"I would hope corporate America has better things to do than sue people over their lawn ornaments. What do you want? Because I was thinking..."

"Horror movie classics," they said in unison.

"Yeah. Freddy, Jason, Myers," Eric said, flipping through the sketchbook and turning toward the kitchen.

"Perfect. Let's get to work," John said, sitting down at the kitchen table. Eric sat beside him, and the two went through the sketches and refined their display ideas.

❄ ❄ ❄

The next two weeks were busy ones. Between the kids at school entering their holiday craze and getting the displays together, Eric and John were working non-stop. It took ten days to complete the town common display alone. They prioritized the common as it had the largest display and was the most important to finish in time for the lighting ceremony. Eric did the precision sculpting while John and a team of volunteers did the heavy lifting, moving the ice blocks into place and carving the rough forms ahead of him. They then repeated the process for the front of the school, which took an additional four days. Eric and John's lawns took a day each to detail.

"You truly are a wonder creating these sculptures," John said, taking a step back from the completed scene on Eric's lawn.

"You just got to feel the flow within the ice, then picture the sculptures in your mind and start your hands working. Before you know it, that synergy is pouring through the cosmos."

"You just make that B.S. up on the spot, or have you

been rehearsing that?" asked John.

"Rehearsed. Dude, I just carve the ice and fill a few gaps with snow. It's not that hard."

"Well, you make it look easy, anyway," John said.

The sun struck the scene, making the crystal clear ice shine brightly as they stood admiring their work. Translucent versions of Hannibal Lecter, Angela from Sleepaway Camp, and Chucky shined in the center of the mock nativity display portraying Joseph, Mary, and Jesus, respectively. Just behind them stood the three wise men—Freddy Krueger, Jason Voorhees, and Michael Myers. Off the left side stood Leatherface and Pennywise the Clown portraying angels. On the right, portraying shepherds were Jigsaw, Candyman, and Ghostface. In the foreground of the display, in place of donkeys and sheep, there was a collection of Alien xenomorphs, Bruce the shark, and tying it all together were Gremlins running around and between the entire display.

"Well, we did it. Tomorrow night is the lighting ceremony. I'll come by and pick you up about four. We can eat something, then get there early to hear all the wonderful praise headed our way," John said as the neighbor's dog began barking wildly behind them.

"You expect praise for that blasphemous crap! I should let him off his leash!" yelled Ed from the street.

"Piss off, Ed! You let that dog off his leash anywhere near me, and it's the last time you'll ever see him!" Eric responded as he watched his neighbor drag the dog past and into his yard and into the house. "God, I hate that guy and his stupid mutt."

"Don't let him get to you. I'll see you tomorrow."

Eric went inside and opened a beer, which led to several more. Inspired by the display, he cultivated a stack of Blu-ray discs from his collection and started playing a horror movie marathon. He passed out drunk a few hours later just as Jack Nicholson called out, "Here's Johnny!"

* * *

Ed didn't wake up when the glass window that adorned the side of his front door shattered. Even his dog didn't stir when a cold gust of wind blew through the opening, followed by a crystalline arm reaching through and unlocking the door. It wasn't until a razor-sharp stiletto of ice pierced its stomach that the dog yelped and began barking. Ed finally awoke to the cries of his dog and cautiously got out of bed. He opened his bedroom door as his dog let out an agonizing whimper. Then silence fell over the house.

Ed crept slowly down the hallway. As fear gripped at his insides, he wished he had something to use as a weapon, but there was nothing. He turned toward his living room, where his dog made it a habit of sleeping by the heating vent. It took Ed a moment to process the scene before him. His dog's head and hind legs were completely severed and lay several feet from its torso, which had been flayed open. Viscera trailed out in several odd angles. A scream rose in his throat, but before it could escape his lips, he felt a sharp, cold sting across his neck. Ed had just enough time to process the pain before his own severed head rolled off his shoulders and hit the floor with a thud.

* * *

John pulled up to Eric's house at five minutes past four the following afternoon. He hated running late, even by five minutes, but his wife kept asking him to do a variety of tasks. She and the kids were to meet him later at the lighting cere-mony, and he impolitely reminded her he needed to pick up

Eric and get there himself, then rushed out the door. He knew he would pay for it later, but he would face that music when the time came. He parked in the driveway and honked the horn to alert Eric to his arrival.

As Eric rushed out the front door and jumped in the passenger seat, John glanced over at the ice sculptures in the front yard. "Don't you think the blood stains are a bit much? What'd you use? Food coloring or something?" he asked, turning to look at Eric.

"What are you talking about?"

"The display, dude. They all have blood stains, and I would swear some of them have moved slightly," John said.

"Wasn't me, man. Maybe some kids were having a laugh, used paint or food coloring or something. It was warm today, the first day above freezing all month, so they could have shifted some from slight melting."

John shrugged. "I guess," he said as he pulled out of the driveway and turned toward town.

The two men ate a quick dinner at the tavern and then walked to the town common. The official lighting wasn't for another hour, but a healthy crowd was already forming. They wandered through the people as the townsfolk admired the displays. Several of them took pictures with the sculptures, and he overheard a large number commenting on how this year's display was more family-friendly than past years. John's previous displays having been original creations often depicted large-scale, unified, thematic scenes like last year's ice castle and medieval knights versus frost giants battle display. He never really considered those exhibits as not being family-friendly, but he could understand the appeal of recognizable cartoons and such as a parent.

At the designated time, Eric and John made their way to the stage for the lighting. By then, nearly the entire town had congregated in the common and turned their attention to the Town Manager as he began the ceremony. He went through the written program and thanked Eric and John by name. To acknowledge his hard work, he asked Eric to step forward and do the honor of flipping the switch for the lights. Eric smiled, took a deep breath, and threw the toggle switch. The entire common shined. The substantial Christmas tree behind the stage washed them all in multi-colored lights. The large Menorah that stood beside it was illuminated by a deep blue flood light. The other trees and shrubs throughout the common were lit with a series of red and white lights that reflected off the ice sculptures in a dizzying display of illumination. Eric was smiling at the display when the snowball hit him square in the face.

"Flex, you suck!" he heard someone yell as another snowball hit his temple. A barrage immediately followed the second snowball. Eric ducked away as best he could, but the onslaught was unavoidable. His anger rose within him. He looked toward the source of the attack and saw Trevor and his father, Rob Connolly, still throwing snowballs in his direction and laughing with delight. Beside them was a small group of lackeys they had enlisted. Eric recognized one as an employee of Rob's at the Auto Body shop. The group broadened their attack to include John. The townspeople murmured their disapproval but did nothing to stop the small group as they humiliated Eric on the stage. Nor did they move when the ice sculpture of Yukon Cornelius stepped forward to protect Eric, flipping his ice-made ice pick in the air, catching it and licking the tip, then hurling it toward the attackers. The pick buried itself deep in Trevor's chest.

Trevor staggered backward, bewildered as the ice entered his chest. He looked toward his father with shock on his face. Rob Connolly reached toward his son as a set of crystalline antlers burst through his own chest from behind. He looked down at the antlers as he coughed up blood and fell forward as the antlers slid from his body. The ice golem reindeer lifted its head, blood dripping from his horns to fall on its nose, staining it crimson. In the bright white and red holiday lights, you could've even said it glowed.

The crowd panicked. The townspeople screamed and ran in every direction, but nowhere was safe. The ice sculptures all began to move among the frightened crowd. The entire exhibition of ice became a violent, murderous rampage. Godzilla cleared swaths of the crowd with his tail. Woody Woodpecker impaled several people with his beak. Batman fought through the crowd, snapping necks as he went.

John rushed to Eric's side. "Are you okay?" he asked.

"Yes, but we should get out of here," Eric replied.

The two men began to run from the carnage. Bodies were everywhere. Children cried and clutched at fallen parents. The snow all across the common melted into pink pools and ruby rivulets from the warm, fresh blood. Eric slipped and fell on the slick ground; he looked to his left to see John about to be impaled from behind by an ice reindeer. He was about to call out as the reindeer skidded to a stop inches from hitting John and turned abruptly and charged off to skewer another fleeing member of the crowd. John rushed to Eric's side and helped him up. "We have to do something! Find a way to stop this!"

"There's nothing we can do, Eric! We just have to get to safety," replied John, pulling his friend to his feet. The two men looked one another in the eye. Eric nodded, and the two began to run again. The ice golems seemed to clear a path for them as they ran. The sculptures cut down anyone who got in their way as they slipped on the ice, blood, and snow and jumped over bodies. They were nearly to the street when

Godzilla's tail swatted Eric full-on in the chest. The breath was knocked from his lungs as the blow hit him. He lost consciousness as his head bounced off the frozen ground.

John slid to a stop when he saw Eric go down. "No!" he yelled, turning to aid his friend and tripping over a severed arm in the process. Spinning away as he fell, his hand struck Eric's leg a glancing blow as he went down. John landed hard on the ground and found himself face-to-face with a severed head. Recognition came slowly as the expression of terror distorted the once-beautiful face of his wife. He let out a sob as he realized his wife was gone. He struggled to his knees and looked around. The bodies of his children were broken and bleeding out beside him. The pain of despair seized him but only for a second; ice-cold hands grabbed his head and jerked it violently, snapping his neck with a sharp crack.

Eric awoke to the sound of a television and someone holding his right hand. He moaned and gave a gentle squeeze to the hand.

"Welcome back. I was getting worried," a soft voice said. "I didn't mean to lose John. I'm so sorry. They were just supposed to protect us. At first, they did. I saw them turn away from you both, and then... Ever since the Faulds incident when I... John usually does the rites, but I insisted this year, and he trusted me... I just... I just wanted to right some wrongs, and for the two of us to be alone...to be together just you and me. That's what did it. My instructions, now I see... I just wasn't specific enough." The voice took a sobbing breath. "They only act if we're threatened, so when Rob and Trevor attacked with the snowballs... I'm sorry."

Eric lay silent, taking it all in. After a moment of silence, he squeezed the hand once more. The familiar voice continued weakly, "You woke just in time to hear my interview." The television volume rose slightly.

"Now reporting is Terry Winestrom..."

"Thank you, Jim. I'm standing here at the scene of last night's massacre. The area is still cordoned off as the investigation continues into what transpired, but I can confirm two-hundred-and-four dead, with several more wounded. I'm here with one lucky survivor, who miraculously came out unharmed. Shannon Connolly, please tell us what you experienced..."

A Victorian Christmas

R.A. Goli

ictoria grabbed the baluster with one hand, grasping it with a knuckle-whitening grip, as her father began to speak. The feast had been devoured, the parlor games played, and she had been sent to bed so the adults could drink claret and tell haunting tales as the rain pelted the window panes. This was her favorite part of the night. Her heart began to thud with such force she thought the grown-ups would hear it downstairs. Their laughter and chatter abated her fears for now, but she knew she would receive a lashing from her father's belt should he find her on the stairs instead of in her bed.

Over the next hour she was enthralled by the stories as each person tried to best the previous guest's tale. The one where a murderer dressed as Santa Claus snuck into houses to steal children from their beds sent icy chills down her spine. The story where the guests all played hide-and-seek while drunk on egg nog and discovered there was an extra ghostly player had Victoria looking over her shoulder. But it was the last one, which her mother told, that caused a needle of terror to worm its way through her body and settle in her gut like a lump of coal. In the story, a disobedient child was punished, and when she unwrapped her Christmas present, she discovered the severed head of her pet dog. Victoria's eyes welled with tears as she thought of her cat, Merlin, asleep on her bed, as she was supposed to be.

The oohs and mock gasps from downstairs ceased suddenly, and she sucked in a breath. *Did they hear me?* She stood slowly and tip-toed up the stairs to her room, her breath quick and heavy, then climbed into bed.

Merlin was no longer napping at the end. Victoria scanned the room and thought she saw a fleeting whisper of white near the door. Now, she lay restless and worried as she listened to the party downstairs wind down as each guest took their leave. She tried to focus on the hiss of the pouring rain against her window as her parents readied themselves for bed, though the knot in her belly felt heavier with each passing moment. She'd had the cat since she was six, and he always slept in her room. Perhaps the noise of the party had upset him and he went to hide elsewhere.

Did they know I was on the stairs? Was it a warning? The vein in her temple throbbed and bulged as her heart raced. She began to worry that her parents were fed up with her sneaking out of her room and not always being obedient. She took a deep, calming breath. *I'm being silly. They would never do that.* She knew she wouldn't be able to sleep so she waited for over an hour before quietly removing herself from the warmth of her blankets and went in search of the elusive cat. She grabbed the oil lamp from the dresser and crept into the hall.

She walked silently past her parent's room, swinging the lamp carefully to illuminate every corner of the hall, not daring to call the cat's name. Her search upstairs proved fruitless so she headed for the staircase. Her heartbeat quickened with each step she took until she was at the bottom landing. The dark was so stygian it swallowed the light of her small lamp. She turned the dial, releasing a bit more wick, and the flame flickered bright and comforting. She continued her quest, checking each room and under furniture, but there was no sign of Merlin.

A cough from upstairs sent a spark of fear through her, and she froze. If her father found her sneaking around, she would be in serious trouble, but there was one room to go.

She turned the corner and stood at the sitting-room entrance. The candle light cast eerie shadows against the walls, and her scalp tingled and tightened. *It's just shadows from the tree.*

The fir stood tall, decorated with home-made baubles, popcorn garlands, painted pine cones, and wrapped sweets. She stepped toward the hearth, the blackened embers with their red-streaked glow made her think of a demon's eyes, and she shivered and turned her gaze to the stockings. She felt the outside, comforted by their shape. She knew what treasures they held even without looking. There would be a new penny in the toe, a handful of chocolates and nuts, and she knew the round ball-like shape was an orange by the sweet scent that invaded her nostrils when she squeezed the stocking.

With no sign of the cat, but the presents so temptingly close, she squatted beneath the tree, placing the lamp beside her. She would feel the gifts to settle her curious mind and perhaps even take a peek at the treasures that awaited her in the morning.

She carefully rummaged through the pile. The hiss of rain had faded, and outside was silent. A shadow darted out from the bottom of the stairs, and an icy fear gripped her. Too big to be a cat. Her chest heaved as she stared into the darkness of the other room. *Was it Father? Or the hide-and-seek ghost from the tales?* It was neither, and after a moment, her heartbeat slowed and her breath steadied.

When she found a gift with her name on it, hard and rectangular, she knew it was a book and relaxed further. A second present, soft and malleable, she was unsure of, so she carefully opened the tiniest corner of the wrapping. Disappointment squirmed its way into her chest when she saw it was a pair of gloves. *I'll have to try hard to pretend I'm excited about these tomorrow.* She was about to stand when she noticed the box in the back, and once again her heart raced. She reached for it, her fingertips awkwardly gripping the corners, and dragged it closer. It was the perfect size for the head of a cat, and Victoria choked back a sob as she undid the top layer of paper.

The unadorned wooden box gave no clues as to what was inside, so when she lifted the lid and the papier-mâché doll dressed in blue shirt with ruffled white collar sprung up at her, she flinched and dropped the box.

It happened quickly then. Victoria barely registered what the *whoomp* sound was until she saw the fir blazing and felt the heat of flames climb her arm. Lamp oil coated her skin, and the fire sluiced along her body like melting snow from a slanted roof. Her screams pierced the night as her skin crackled and burned.

Victoria flailed and dropped to the floor in an attempt to douse the flames, but her hair was alight, and the fire quickly consumed the skin from her scalp and face. Her screams stopped, but her limbs jerked wildly as the fire ate her white linen nightgown and her skin, causing it to blister and burst, red and weeping. Still the fire ate greedily until Victoria's flesh was gone and her arms and legs stopped moving.

By the time her parents raced down the stairs to discover

the inferno, she was dead. They threw wet towels and buckets of water over her, but Victoria was barely more than a skeleton. A hideously twisted and unrecognizable pile of charred bones and cinders.

Merlin emerged from his hiding place in the laundry and peeked around the doorframe, not understanding what he saw. He darted upstairs to the safety of Victoria's arms, only to find the bed empty.

Her father continued to extinguish the tree while her mother wept by Victoria's corpse. When the flames were out, her father joined the lamentation. Neither of them would ever know Victoria had crept down to search for the cat, her imagination running wild after hearing the spooky story. Or that the gift they'd carefully picked for her, the most expensive of all the gifts they'd purchased that year, a reward for her good behavior, had been the catalyst of her death.

B*AUBLE

DJ Tyrer

ane was practically bouncing with excitement as they exited the tube station for the chill evening. Andrew had never invited her to his home before. They'd been dating for nearly a year, having met at Dana's New Year party, but had always gone out or back to her flat, never his place.

Clinging to his arm, she leaned in against his shoulder and gazed up at him.

Andrew smiled down at her.

Jane grinned back. "I'm so excited."

He raised his free hand to smooth back his hair and said, "It's only a flat." But she was certain she could hear a hint of excitement in his voice: he was looking forward to this Christmas as much as she was.

Reaching out toward the road, he waved for a taxi, and one pulled over to pick them up.

She let go of his arm so he could open the door for her, and she slipped inside.

Andrew slid in after her, saying, "Jewel Street, please."

The cab driver nodded. "Right you are."

As the taxi pulled back into traffic, Jane turned to Andrew and said, "I'm really looking forward to seeing what your place is like."

"I think you'll like it."

The bright lights of a city decorated for Christmas washed over them, refracted through raindrop-speckled windows.

They passed the end of Oxford Street, and Jane pressed her face against the window, the glass frosting at her breath, and stared out at the display of lights.

"It's beautiful."

He looked past her. "Like a fantastic fairyland."

Jane laughed. "That's so sweet."

"I can recite poetry, too," he said with a chuckle.

Progress was slow through the crowded London streets, but the journey was short: despite never having seen the place before, Jane thought it conveniently sited. Andrew had always been vague about his work, something "in the City," but he had to be doing exceptionally well to live here.

She looked away, a little embarrassed to have even thought such a thing.

"Jewel Street," said the driver over his shoulder. "Where abouts?"

"Ah, just over here, thanks."

Andrew handed him the fare and a decent tip, then they climbed out.

"It's this one over here," he told Jane, guiding her toward a shopfront with a sign that said *Jewel Street Novelties* and which was decorated for Christmas with a huge tree, hung with a multitude of baubles in a variety of colors and sizes, and holly and mistletoe fringing the scene.

There was a door marked 12A beside the shop, set back a little way from the street, with a lion-head knocker. Andrew stepped up to it, slipped out a large iron key, slid it into the lock, and opened it.

"Wow." Jane shook her head in delight. "It's like something out of Dickens, Scrooge, I mean." She laughed. "And, the number—it's perfect. I mean, twelve—very Christmassy."

He stepped through the door. There was a flight of stairs going up above the shop.

"Follow me."

She entered after him and closed the door behind her as Andrew flicked a light switch and started up the stairs.

The Dickensian feel continued as they reached his flat, which was decorated with the sort of dark, heavy wallpaper Jane associated with the Victorian era. Each room was a different color, with embossed patterns upon the paper in a darker shade of the same color: one room was decorated with green paper patterned with holly leaves, another was red with birds like robins, the lounge was a dark gold in color with a pattern of circles upon it.

"Please, sit," said Andrew genially, gesturing toward a large mustard-colored settee that was sagging a little in the middle. "Can I get you a drink?"

Jane sat. "Please."

Andrew disappeared into a kitchen that, she saw through the open doorway, was tiled in blue and white.

As she waited for him, she took in the large lounge. There were several chairs in the same mustard yellow and a bookcase along one wall; looking at the titles, she laughed and clapped in delight to see *A Christmas Carol* and a number of other Dickens titles.

There was no sign of a TV, and she assumed it must be tastefully hidden when not in use, but there was a large Christmas tree in one corner of the room hung with numerous baubles that shimmered as they reflected the light: each, she realized, was a globe of glass. She hadn't seen any like them before, save amongst those decorating the tree in the window of the shop below.

"I love your tree," she called out.

"Thanks." He re-entered the room, a glass in each hand. He handed one to her. "Here."

She sipped the warming liquid; sherry, she realized.

"Hmm, lovely." She nodded toward the bookcase. "I see you collect Dickens. They look old."

Andrew gave a vague shrug. "First editions."

"Really? Wow!"

"Yes. Gifts, actually. Dickens gave them to...my, er, great grandfather."

"Amazing," she murmured, shaking her head.

She drank down the rest of the sherry, enjoying the warming glow that filled first her stomach, then the rest of her body.

"I'll be back in a minute." Andrew patted her on the head, took her glass, and headed back to the kitchen.

Jane furrowed her brow, blinked, and shook her head. She felt fuzzy, as if her head was wrapped in cotton-wool and her eyes smeared with Vaseline.

She groaned—this was not the time for her to develop a cold—and tried rubbing her temples, but it didn't help.

The room seemed to be swaying, just a little, and through the odd, muffled sensation in her ears, she thought she could hear a soft hum, like the distant murmur of a conversation, and a faint tinkling of glass.

"Odd..." She looked about, confused. Maybe it was the sound of a radio or TV in the neighboring flat?

Then she realized the sound seemed to be coming from the direction of the tree.

"Odder..." She pushed herself up from the settee with some difficulty and stood on shaky legs. Her body seemed to be far away and, somehow, both heavy and light, as if she were floating just above the floor, but her limbs were transformed to lead.

She stumbled toward the tree, the room stretching out before her as if it were made of rubber.

Her head felt hot, the warm glow of the sherry becoming a raging furnace as it reached her brow.

"Feverish..." she murmured, despite a churning feeling in her guts that told it was nothing such.

She tried calling Andrew's name, but he didn't respond, and she began to feel a welling panic in her chest.

Jane leaned toward the tree and looked at the nearest bauble: there was something in it. An imperfection in the otherwise perfect glass? She looked more closely. Yes, there was something in the bauble... *inside it*. Something moving.

Pressing her face close to the glass globe, she realized it was a tiny, miniature figure—a woman in a ballgown, who was hammering her fists against the glass and mouthing inaudible words.

With a shriek, Jane stumbled backward to fall back onto the settee. "Andrew!"

There was a sound behind her, movement, and she sensed her boyfriend's presence, but he didn't speak.

"Andrew?" She was finding it hard to form the sounds of his name.

He didn't answer, but his arm appeared on the edge of her vision and placed a little parcel, neatly wrapped, on her lap. She looked down at it, stupidly, mind too foggy to think.

Andrew's arms reached around her and undid the bow, slipped it free, then removed the wrapping and opened the wooden box it revealed. Inside, protected by crimson felt padding, was a clear globe of glass with a length of golden twine through a loop at its top: a bauble like those upon the tree; only, this one was empty.

Jane stared at it, and it seemed to grow larger and larger…

She screamed Andrew's name and looked wildly about in confusion. No longer befuddled, she was certain she must be mad, for she was surrounded by crimson walls.

With a sudden lurch, the room began to rise, the walls grew clear, and she realized they were made of curved glass.

Hammering upon the glass, she called Andrew's name, again, then screamed as his face loomed horrifically huge before her. She shrieked and leaped back.

Andrew leered at her and tapped the glass, which shuddered at his touch. Then he carried her to the tree and hung her bauble upon it, amongst the many others.

A chill of terror flowed through her as she realized each glass globe must contain a woman, like her, one a year…for how many years?

No, no, it couldn't be true…

She closed her eyes, but the nightmare remained when she opened them again and refused to evaporate as, for twelve days, Andrew sat staring at the tree and those imprisoned upon it. Nor did it end when he packed each one away in darkness.

Then, twelve months later, he took her out and hung her, once more, upon the tree, and she beat her hands upon the glass in impotent rage, knowing exactly what was soon to occur…

Another Christmas, another woman, another bauble.

A CHRISTMAS PILGRIM
Neil Davies

The old man grumbled to himself as he shuffled through the slush on the pavement, worn shoes squelching as ice-cold water seeped in with each step. He pointedly ignored the carolers singing "Jingle Bells" outside a brightly lit shop doorway, was equally disdainful of the glittering window displays and the hurrying late-night shoppers, all wrapped in coats and gloves and warm hats.

He felt every icy breeze through the thin, torn jacket and old t-shirt hanging loosely on his emaciated frame.

It wasn't that he hated Christmas, but it was an inconvenience, a trouble. The rest of the year he could lie low, hide from most people, live his own solitary existence. True, he would be hungry most of the time, but he preferred it that way. The hunger kept him focused. When he was well fed, he changed, became a different person. Even his personality changed, and he didn't like what he became.

"Sorry."

He looked up at the woman he had walked into and smiled, almost laughed at the automatic politeness that led her to apologize, even as she stared at him in disgust and horror.

"Fuck off, lady!"

He didn't watch, but he knew she would be pushing fast away from him, turning to look back. She probably felt nauseous, and that did make him laugh.

He hadn't looked in a mirror since last Christmas, but he didn't need to. Every time he touched his face, he felt the sagging skin, dripping like melted plastic off his bones. Not even the beard he allowed to grow could hide the horror of his ill-fitting flesh. Once he had tried to shave, but chunks of flesh had come away with the hair, and it had taken months to heal. He had never tried since.

His stomach growled, reminding him of his hunger. This was the one time of year he looked for food.

No, not looked. *Hunted.*

He shuffled further through the crowds, finding a certain grim amusement in the way they parted in front of him, afraid to touch him.

So much for the Christmas spirit.

Still, if they knew what he fed on, what he hunted, they would be on the other side of the street.

That thought made him laugh so hard he fell into a coughing fit, stopping, bending forward, spitting phlegm into the dirty-white slush at his feet.

He lifted the black plastic sack he carried in his right fist, shifted it to his left to balance the agony that shot through his bent, claw-like fingers, and turned into the alleyway that opened on his right.

He knew it well. This was a good hunting ground.

As the bright, Christmas sounds of the main shopping street faded behind him, he heard the less joyful, but more welcoming, sounds of hushed voices up ahead.

He did not hesitate in his shuffling gait, did not care if he was heard or seen. Why would they bother about a crumbling old man like him? They were young. They were strong. They would be so high by this time that, even if they did notice him, they'd find him a joke. Certainly not a threat.

The stench of dog shit and overflowing restaurant bins drifted around him, and he found it comforting. So like home. Home, except at this time of year.

He never looked forward to the hunt, the kill. It was not a pleasure. It was a compulsion.

The five teenagers, sharing a bottle of vodka and a poorly rolled joint, barely noticed the old man until it was too late to do anything but scream.

He fell on them, not with relish or satisfaction, but with an almost bored resignation. This was what he did, not who he was.

Except at Christmas.

He tore at their throats with sharp, ragged fingernails, ripped windpipes with stained teeth, pulled still-pumping arteries out with arthritic fingers and drank the hot blood that spurted, then dripped, then pooled on the alley floor. Handfuls of flesh and organs were pushed into his mouth, his chin dripping with lumps of bloody tissue. He lapped at the spilled blood like an animal.

And as he fed, his body began to fill out.

The sagging skin of his face grew taut as his cheeks expanded, so tight the wrinkles smoothed out and the eyes no longer hid in deep sockets. His t-shirt grew taut across his growing belly, and he had to loosen his trousers before they burst.

Still, he ate and drank, a glutton sitting among the raw, steaming mess that was his food. He sucked the last flesh from a finger, gnawed at a soft, well-fed arm, teasing out strings of muscle from between his teeth, too tough to digest. He amused himself for a while in a spitting contest, seeing which traveled further, fingernails or toenails. He judged the toenails won, but only because one was deformed, thicker, and therefore heavier, than the others.

He did not hurry his food, not wanting to suffer indigestion later.

At the end of the alley, shoppers hurried past, laden with parcels and bags. None looked down the alleyway, and he was able to savor every last morsel of flesh, of organs, every last drop of blood.

Fully sated, he allowed the next part of his compulsion to take control.

He stripped naked, pulling off his now tight clothes over rolls of fat, and washed himself in the pools of ice-cold water gathered in the hollows of the alley floor and the still-fresh drifts of snow against the alley walls. Opening the black sack at his feet, he drew out his new clothes, his once-a-year, special occasion clothes.

As he dressed in the red trousers, the black boots, the red coat, he could no longer remember why he thought he hated Christmas so much. Christmas was the *best* time of year, a time of giving and caring. This was the time he waited for all through the annoyingly bright spring, the unbearably hot summer, the depressingly long autumn. This was *his* time of year.

Stepping from the alleyway, back into the packed throng of shoppers, he smiled and stretched smooth, straight fingers over the bulge of his stomach. Once more the people parted before him, but this time with a cheery "Merry Christmas" or a laugh and a wave. He no longer sneered at the window displays but marveled at the ingenious animatronic animals and sparkling fairy lights. In a moment of spontaneity, he stopped and sang a couple of verses of "The Holly and the

Ivy" with the carolers, shaking hands with their leader before moving on his way once more.

Laughing, smiling, and full of the joys of the season, Santa Claus made his way along the decorated city streets on the start of his annual pilgrimage North.

Mrs. Krampen

Patrick Winters

've got something great lined up, man. You won't freaking believe it!

Carter kept wondering about that cryptic text that Brandon had sent him just this morning. And now, waiting in Daisy's Diner, he was wondering what was taking his friend and partner in crime so damn long to show. He was a good ten minutes late, and the suspense of waiting on his buddy's little mystery was making Carter fidgety.

He was about to get up and drain the lizard—more to relieve his nerves than his bladder—when he saw Brandon's old Honda Accord pull into the lot just outside. He watched as his friend bolted out of the car, through the snow and up to the diner's entrance, and came right in at a rush toward Carter's corner booth. Brandon had that glint in his eye, the one that came with a breeze of a job. Maybe he *was* on to something.

"'Bout damn time, man," Carter said, giving a cautionary look-over of the nearest booths. The closest customers were clear across the room, focused on their pancake platters, and the lone waitress was hunched over at her counter, but he kept up his whisper anyways. Best to be quiet when they were talking "business."

"Yeah, yeah," Brandon said, flipping him off. "Now shut up, listen, and be glad I'm letting you in on this."

He hunched forward and let loose a shit-eating grin that would have shamed the craftiest car salesman. "I'm gonna get us laid."

Carter just looked at him. "Say wha'?"

"Get this," Brandon started, keeping up the smile. "I was casing a house up on Barber the night before last, looking for a place for us to hit. Mailbox said Krampen on it, or some shit like that. Place looked like a safe bet—dark, quiet, and probably shit security. Also figured that anyone in there was asleep, that time of night. Shit, was I wrong! I was in back, looking through the windows, and I saw..."

Brandon started laughing and tried holding it in. Carter urged him on, wanting him to get to the point.

"I saw this total MILF inside, half-naked in some BDSM strap-outfit and a big, red Missus Claus-lookin' coat, whippin' a dude in his underwear while he knelt on the hardwood floor in front of her. And she was recordin' it! Probably for some fuckin' porn site or somethin'."

Carter started laughing himself. It sounded rather unbelievable, but it seemed to him that Brandon wasn't pulling a fast one.

"So, what'd you do?"

"I took out my phone and did some recordin' myself. And I made sure to get her good side, which, my man, is just about all of her. Big and beautiful. Ass that won't quit and tits that'd knock out an NFL center. And then I had me an idea. The next day, I knocked on her door and showed her the video."

Carter blinked, amazed at his friend. Even for thieves and home-invaders, that took some balls to do.

"I told her that if she didn't show you and me some equally freaky attention, I'd make her a *real* star and show the entire town my little movie. And you know what, man? She's down. Shit, I think I could've just asked her to do us without the blackmail and she'd have still said yes. This babe's up for anything, I tell you."

Carter asked to see the video. He wanted to see this supposed Holy Grail of hotness.

"Nah, man, I want you to be surprised. You'll get to see her for yourself...*tonight*. It's all set up. So, you down, man?"

It didn't take Carter long to answer. "Fuck yeah, man."

"Good." Brandon gave a thumbs up and called the waitress over to get their orders. "Now that I'm helping you get your dick wet, the least you can do is buy me breakfast."

❄ ❄ ❄

The mailbox in front of the old, dark home did read Krampen, just as Brandon had thought. The Christmas lights blinking next door to the bare household illuminated the faded moniker in quick, colorful flashes. A strange name, for sure, but what did Carter care? As long as the woman looked better than her name sounded.

He and Brandon were bundled up against the cold; they climbed the porch and to get out from the evening wind. They looked forward to being warmed up once they got inside.

"So how's this gonna work, exactly?" Carter asked. "Do we take turns with her, or spit-roast her chestnuts by an open fire?"

"If we take turns, I call dibs on the first go-round." Brandon leaned toward the door and gave the ornate bell a long push. He leaned back and looked to Carter, making his eyebrows dance in anticipation.

They heard floorboards creaking behind the door a moment later, along with the sound of a lock sliding away. The door opened slowly, a surprising amount of heat from within escaping out into the night and hitting their faces. Carter saw a red-tinged shadow stepping out of the dark hall; it took the shape of a woman as it came into the blinking light.

And what a shape it was. A five-foot-four bombshell stood before them, her body covered in a fuzzy scarlet robe, of sorts, which hung down to her feet, its trimming white and fluffy. Though it hid away the exact angles of her curves, there was no doubt that a luscious and fairly plump frame waited beneath the clothing; more than a hint of a buxom bosom begged the attention of the eye. To Carter's, it looked like she possessed the fabled G cup.

The woman gave them a lusty smile with her full, pink lips, her blue eyes narrowing in a show of allure and mascara. Short, golden locks hung around her pleasantly round face. She gave them a playful shake as she spoke.

"Hello, boys," her velvety tones said. "You've kept me waiting. Come on in; let's get right to it." Her smile widened, the tip of her tongue playing puckishly across her lips. She beckoned them in with a turn of her head.

Carter gave Brandon a *Dude, nice job!* look, as they stepped on in, their libidos revving. They kicked off their boots on the mat (because even in blackmail, there had to be some courtesy) and followed the swish of the well-built woman's full backside through the dim, warm household. It was so dark that they could hardly see a thing on the walls or in the rooms they passed. They came to a stop beside a black stairwell that led upwards, and before a back room closed off by a sliding partition. The woman opened it, revealing the bare, hardwood-floored room that Brandon had mentioned in his account. It was lit by a roaring fire blazing in the fireplace across the room, shadows and light dancing and swaying together like lovers' bodies.

The boys stepped on in, regarding the empty room as the woman followed them in.

"I've gotta say," Brandon put in, "the whole naughty Missus Claus deal you've got going is really doing it for me."

The boys turned back to face the woman—right as she pulled her robe off and let it fall to the floor. Her nearly naked body—covered only by scant, overlapping strips of leather—was on arousing display, her enormous breasts hanging and with nipples that silver dollars would envy. Between her thick thighs, her shaved womanhood waited, teasing the boys, whose hearts were now thoroughly racing and whose pants were straining at the crotch.

"Missus Claus hasn't got shit on this," the woman said with attitude. "Now, it's your turn. Strip."

The boys didn't have to be told twice. They pulled off their clothes in a frenzy until they were naked before her. She looked over their erections with a teasing half-smile. "I didn't think it was *that* cold out."

Brandon returned her jab with one of his own. "Yeah, well...isn't this floor gonna hurt your knees, bitch?"

The woman inched closer to them slowly, her breasts bouncing a tad and her hips rolling. "Even the littlest pain can bring the greatest pleasure, honey. And yours will bring me a *lot* of pleasure."

Then her eyes flashed with silver, and the sounds of snapping chains cracked to life. The boys looked up only to see a barrage of rusted steel chains coming from the dark, alive and snaking toward them. The chains bound up their arms and legs and lifted them up into the air as they screamed out their fears and amazement. No sooner had they done this, though, then more chains wrapped about them, this time around and through their mouths, cutting off their cries.

"Well, what'd you expect, boys?" the woman said, bearing a look of mock pity as she watched the strange scene. "Trouble always comes from wanting to fool around with a married woman."

She bent over and pulled Brandon's phone from his pants. She flicked it into the fireplace, destroying the video he'd taken of her. As if by magic, something materialized in her hand the moment she held it up to them. It was a bundle of white birch sticks, long in length and strapped together.

"People somehow got it into their heads that *my husband's* the one who likes to whip and punish bad boys and girls, when really, that's my thing. He just likes to watch."

She stepped closer to them, tickling Carter's crotch with the tip of the sticks.

"He's normally so busy this time of year. That's why I record my occasional…sessions…for him to have. But it just so happens he has tonight off. And he'll get a front row seat for *our* little bit of punishment."

At that, the ceiling above them creaked. The woman looked up, positively beaming. "Here he comes now."

The creaks across the ceiling continued until they moved out into the hall and down the dark staircase. A huge, lumbering figure dressed in a tattered red cloak was coming down the stairs, horns sprouting from the top of its colossal head and a bushy white beard hanging out from within the dark hood, the thing's faced concealed.

As it stepped into the room, stopping beside its wife, Carter's bladder let loose out of fear.

Mrs. Krampen looked at him with an excited smile. "Ooh,

another reason to whip these bad boys..."

While the towering monstrosity behind her gave a pleased grumble, she stepped up to Carter and brought the sticks across his chest.

He hollered in agony, Brandon groaned in terror, and Mrs. Krampen moaned in ecstasy at all of the pleasurable pain that would follow into the night.

Merciful Goremas

Kurt Newton

It was the night before Goremas, and the Down Under was
still,
all the murks were a-snorkeling in their dreams
of the kill.

All the axes and adzes (it was quite a selection),
all the sickles and scythes were all honed to perfection,
as visions of those to be skinned alive
danced in the fire pit coals of their minds.

But for centuries the murks had been kept out of sight,
by do-gooders and goodie-two-shoers doing what's right.
Forever they longed for the good ol' dark days
when blood flowed like wine beneath a smoldering haze.

And just when it appeared this year would be as

ho-hum as before,
there came a loud crash through their hot
chamber door.

The murks awoke startled, their pillows soaked
in dark drool,
and there stood an angry Santa with more elfin
minions than Azul.
"I'm sick of those humans," he said with snarling aggression,
"they appreciate nothing, it's time we taught them a lesson!"

And so it was on that grim, sulfurous-smelling early morn
that the thing that came to be called "Goremas" was born.

At midnight, the grates of the Down Under were ungrated,
and up into the world crawled the murks unabated.
With Santa's list trailing like a long paper tongue,
they snuck into each address and addressed each
wish one by one.

If a kitten was requested along with a juice mixer, you see,
they would put both gifts together to make fresh kitty puree.
Fruitcakes were decorated with intestinal mold,
while stuffed animals and dollies were rigged to explode.

Train sets and game boards were demonically cursed
to blind or to amputate fingers or worse.
Each specially-warped gift under Santa's prescription,
was designed to provide maximum pain infliction.

The murks didn't mind all this attention to gore,
but what they really wanted was something more.
Something involving their blades and their teeth,

not simply a long string of hamsters made into a wreath.

"But Santa, wouldn't it be better," the Murk Master said,
"if we just slaughtered them all as they slept in their beds?"
But Santa was much wiser than any lower depths lord,
"If we kill them then how will their faith be restored?"

It was then Santa pulled his red pointed cap from his ears,
and to each murk's amazement, a halo appeared.
"I've appreciated your help in this most worthy cause,
but it's now time I show you who's really the boss."

And with a point of his finger, his chin gave a jerk,
the ground opened up and swallowed each murk.
It was then Santa—or whatever name he goes by—
ascended with all of his helpers into the sky.

And as the sun rose across the frozen valleys and streams,
you could hear the first in a series of blood-curdling
screams.
Goremas was here, and it would not long be forgotten,
remembered with fear as the day Christmas turned rotten.

But if truth be told, a golden age had returned,
an appreciation of all things small and great had
been learned,
handed down from fingerless grandfathers to grandsons,
told by blind-eyed grandmothers to granddaughters
one by one.

And though times were hard, it somehow felt right.
So have a merciful Goremas, and to all a good night!

GRÝLA'S SWEET YULE TREATS
Wiebo Grobler

Hymir drove past the row of houses brightly decorated with blinking Christmas lights. Blow-up snowmen and plastic reindeers adorned snow-covered lawns. He was dazzled by the oncoming lights of a snowplow, and for a few seconds, the night was a flurry of white before darkness returned to match the mood inside his car.

On the radio, Nat King Cole was midway through "The Christmas Song." The houses were getting further and further apart until they disappeared altogether and there was only a hypnotic monochrome of darkness and snow.

He nearly missed the hidden left turn; it had been several years since he'd last visited Amma Frida's cottage.

After his parents died when he was eight, she took him in. They argued and rubbed each other the wrong way, but she loved him, and he loved her. When he finished his degree, he was offered a position in New York he couldn't turn down. He would come back to visit, often at first, but five years have passed since he'd last seen Amma, and now she was dead.

The Volvo bounced over the uneven road, the snow chains

biting into the frozen earth. The road was narrow and surrounded by old pines. The cottage was remote, Amma liked—
used to like—her privacy. The radio began to spit static; the
reception was bad this close to the lava fields.

He drove around a bend in the road, and the cottage appeared, sitting squat at the top of a slight rise. It looked exactly
the same as he remembered.

He parked the car and killed the engine. Taking a deep
breath of the heated air inside the car, he exhaled loudly and
opened his door. It was below zero, and his breath misted in
the frosty air. It was always so dark, especially in December,
dark yet beautiful without all the light pollution from the cities.
You never saw the stars in New York.

He pulled the key for the cabin from his pocket; he'd picked
it up earlier from the lawyer who was dealing with Amma's
estate. He was here to sort through her belongings and box it
up. The cabin was to be sold, as he no longer considered it
home.

He unlocked the front door and slowly pushed it open. The
familiar smells brought back a flood of memories—pepper
cookies, the faint aroma of wood smoke and pine needles and
Amma's violet perfume. He turned on the light. Stale pepper
cookies in the shape of stars and wrapped with red ribbons
hung from the wood rafters along with bunches of dried holly
and berries. The Christmas tree in the corner had dropped most
of its needles; there were no presents beneath its drooping
branches.

He closed the door, stamped his feet, and rubbed his arms.
It was freezing. He went over to the wood burner and opened
the hatch. It was clean. He took kindling, bunched up the trash
mail Amma saved for the fire, and lit the stove. There were
only a couple of logs in the basket next to the burner. Amma
had gone to get more from the rear of the house, slipped, and

broken her hip. That's where the delivery driver found her. She'd died of exposure.

It didn't take long for the cabin to warm up. Hymir walked to his old room and switched on the lights. It still looked the same, even the old patchwork quilt at the foot of the bed. He could still see her, sitting on the side of his bed and whispering to him, her breath carrying the aroma of warm milk, honey, and nutmeg they shared before bedtime. Her silver hair hung in two long plaits that would brush his face as she told him tales of Grýla, the giantess troll who lived with her husband, Leppalúði, in a cave deep inside Lofthellir mountain. Grýla had a ferocious appetite for children who misbehaved, especially during the Christmas season.

The lava fields of Dimmuborgir were dotted with collapsed magma tubes that twisted deep into the earth. Amongst the thickets and birch trees, dark basalt chimneys rose from the bedrock, long-silent exhausts that used to vent the fires from Hell. Keyhole rocks stared like empty eye sockets over the vast landscape named the Black Fortress.

Amma Frida had told him the tunnels connected the earth with the underworld. When Lucifer was cast from the heavens, Dimmuborgir was where he landed, and he created the tunnels, caverns, and caves, which led down to Hell.

On more than one occasion he would wake petrified, his pajama bottoms and bed soaked. Outside, an elemental monster howled around the corners of Amma's cabin, tapping at the windows with wet, icy fingers and flaying the roof tiles with biting winds.

He'd had terrifying nightmares of Grýla coming down from her cave and crossing the lava plains on her hooves to Amma's house. She would break through his window and, with her long arms and bony hands, pull him from his bed. Dangling him in the air like a sardine, she'd slurp him down legs first like a noodle.

Amma would scold him for wetting the bed, scrubbing him with a cold flannel, while he peered over her shoulders, shivering and staring at the window. Flurries of snow created monsters outside, which the howling winds would blow apart. But that was a long time ago.

He put on his headphones and began to sort through his grandmothers belongs. He had three separate boxes. One for charity, one for rubbish, and another for sentimental bits that he might take back to New York.

He threw the dead tree outside and swept up the fallen needles. In Amma's room, he paused for a second before opening her closet. He gently placed her clothes and old furs into the charity box. At the bottom of the wardrobe, he found five wrapped parcels.

Hymir bent down and pulled them out. They were Christmas gifts from Amma, one for each year he'd been away since his last visit. There wouldn't be one for him this year. He already knew what they were, but opened one anyway. It was a new shirt. Legend said the Yule Cat, Grýla's pet, ate children who didn't receive new clothes on Christmas. Amma had always given him something new to wear for as long as he could remember.

Hymir sighed. He was drained; the day had taken its toll. He would finish packing tomorrow.

His night was restless; it was too quiet, and he woke several times. He turned over and froze. Something big was walking outside, slow, calculated steps that would stop often. They were accompanied by a loud snuffling; something was testing the air. Hymir slowly pushed himself upright, his left hand searching for his rucksack next to the bed. He carried mace inside.

A large object crashed through the window, showering

him in glass, and landed at the foot of the bed. It was the Christmas tree.

Hymir slowly looked up. A giant head slowly pushed through the window. Large nostrils flared, sniffing the air inside the room. Green eyes the size of dinner plates stared straight at him.

He screamed and tried to scramble out of bed. This was his childhood nightmare come to life. Grýla had finally found him.

A large hand clamped over his left calf, and she dragged him toward the window. He twisted around, trying to kick at her arm.

She grinned, large, yellow teeth like chunks of Cheddar hovered over his legs. Her arms were thin but corded with muscle. In the light of the moon, her skin was dirty white with mossy green patches. Filthy black hair spread like a fan behind her. He struggled, but her other hand came through the window and grabbed his right foot, then guide them toward that gaping maw.

His feet were inside her hot cavernous mouth. Her fetid breath made him retch. She made a sucking sound, and his legs slid deeper down her throat. Hymir wailed and felt his bladder go.

Amma was going to be so angry with him.

Red Reconnaissance
Vicky MacDonald Harris

For hundreds of years, people had a theory about a hollow earth: that the world on which we lived had hollow spaces below the verdant surface, layer upon layer, like an inhabited onion. They did not know of the true, long-forgotten story that I can now tell.

The North Pole did indeed have holes. Holes to a place that no human would ever want to be and definitely wouldn't want to go. It happened a long time ago, and consequently, what we know about Santa Claus now, because of his yearly sacrifice, cannot go untold.

Before recorded time, creatures who called themselves The Uisuil, whose essence was electrical, rode solar winds into cracks in the magnetosphere to the North Pole. They breached deep cracks in the earth, water, and ice, dug down and lived in rock layers below, siphoning heat from the earth as food. Time was different for them, so they did not perceive it passing as people did. During what we know as the Ice Ages, thick glacial ice trapped them below.

These beings had changed some over the years while inhabiting the layers. They used the rock around them to take form. They became a strange mix of electrical power and rock, a merged hybrid that was strong and flexible. Their sealed skin formed from rock kept their electrical properties contained.

The peopling of Earth continued. No humans living then knew the danger beneath them. They went on with their tough lives, expanding around the world, the edge of the ice leading their way.

When The Uisuil decided to rise, the heat they generated was later termed the Younger Dryas. The flood waters eased their way out. Some of the world chilled once more. The Uisuil spread south in all directions, their pace varying depending on what and who they encountered.

History recorded in the tree rings and ice cores now began to be recorded in song. Evidence began to build for those who would find the rings, the cores, and the stories one day.

The Uisuil began to kill many people and thus erased whole groups from history. They had an impact on cultures all around the world. Soon, stories and songs told of wars with giants, wars with winged creatures. All were The Uisuil. The electrical power the creatures wielded sometimes melted rock into glass during their battles, causing speculation in future times about comets and various other astronomical theories for the glass.

Until one day a man who recently learned the knowledge of smelting metal from rock said, "Enough."

San Clas was wild, muscled, and thoughtful, the leader of a village near a great river. He and his people had encountered The Uisuil enough times to know to stay out of their way. Seeing surrounding villages decimated and burned to the ground enraged him. His partner, Hel, was brilliant and had vast war experience, a titan in the slaughter of her enemies. Together they soared into history.

San and Hel recruited the local warriors, men and women for whom battle was a belief, who felt time inconsequential, and saving people their God-given right to express. He called them all to the top of the hill overlooking their village and told them to prepare for battle. Swords were struck. They brought their Yule goats, animals that were both their beast of burden and their partners in war. San brought wagonloads of lodestone rock because he noticed years ago that lightning often struck where that rock was mined. He had his men carve sharp tips out of the rock and attach them to arrows. Hel had them fill barrels of water, hoping that, because water and lighting don't mix, the strategy might help against The Uisuil. Other people in the town donated other needed provisions. Healers joined as well. Others fanned out and found even more lodestone. When they were ready, his group marched north in their village colors of red and white.

After several days, they began to see the remnants of battle: burned trees, scorched earth, and the dead, electrocuted where they stood. San shook his head, turned to his soldiers, and said, "This is why we do what we do."

Hel added, "We have the means necessary to overcome these creatures. We will prevail."

The group began to cheer as they marched past the dead village, their flags waving like a potent ocean wave moving toward shore.

The sky began to darken and crackle. Electricity, like lightning from the ground up, began to show itself in the distance. Hel looked at San and took his hand. They kissed, and then they drew their swords. The archers took their place, and the water pumpers stood at the ready by the barrels.

The Uisuil climbed toward the hill. They were like a rolling ball of rock and electricity. The archers released their arrows. The goats, laden with lodestone, ran toward the enemy.

San and Hel watched carefully to see the reaction, if the lodestone tips would have an effect and break through The Uisuil's tough skin. They heard many sounds: howls below from the goats, scratching noises, and stone on metal clashing. The pumpers sent water in a cold, arcing spray down the hills. The screams grew louder as a few of The Uisuil got closer. The archers reloaded and released. Their arrows didn't need to go far, and they appeared to be effective. The pumpers continued, all soaked to the bone, freezing in the cold. Three Uisuil creatures made their way toward San. He held his sword high. They made contact. His sword and the electricity conducted, sending him flying. He rolled several times, the snow dusting him over.

The archers finished off the last of the creatures; the water from the pumpers dampened any resistance their enemy might have tried to gather.

San stood up, dusted ice off his pants, and returned for his sword. The Uisuil were beaten. He raised his sword and yelled, "Compatriots, we are victorious. Well done! Our job now is to go to every village we know, every town and every city in the path of the other Uisuil, and teach the people what we have learned today. We will go north and beat back every creature we see. We will infiltrate their homes and destroy them. We will make it so that no person is ever hurt by these creatures again."

For the next several years, San and Hel made their way from village to village, both the large and small, in concentric circles, angling toward the direction from which The Uisuil came. People of all cultures joined the growing army and banded together to help. Success was at hand.

When they reached the North Pole, the area, despite all the snow and ice, was black. The remains of rock and the scorched electricity had defaced the once-pristine land.

Hel took a reconnaissance party forward to survey The Uisuil's home. They could see nothing. They then realized that The Uisuil came out of a hole in the ice. The battle would have to be above the ice, not below.

They made their way back to relay the information to the others. They saw The Uisuil in the distance, heading out in all directions. It seemed as if there was a never-ending number of them.

When she got back to San, Hel said, "We need to stop them and cap the hole from which they come. The hole is not large, so it can be done. Find the largest tree."

San nodded and sat down to formulate a strategy. Hel said, "We might not be able to stop all those that are out in the world, but we can stop others from getting out."

He was quiet for a moment and then speculated, "Since all the Yule goats are gone, a noble sacrifice indeed, we need to find a creature that we can make fly over the hole. We need more reconnaissance. The magnetism in the rock we have might be able to help."

Hel said, "We can get nearby reindeer to fly, though not high, by using the lodestone strapped to their chests, and then they can jump and be pulled by the other stones on the other side of the hole. One of us can ride it and see below. Perhaps that can work?"

"It never hurts to try," said San. "Let's round up some reindeer."

They sent several warriors out to gather the deer. They found eight nearby. The animals, too, were fearful of The Uisuil, so they were willing to do anything the kind and gentle humans taught them. It didn't take long, as San fed them a treat of arctic char and greens.

Strapping the rock to them was more difficult. They didn't understand the weighted bags put on their backs and fastened tight. As they began to run away, the magnets did their job, and the reindeer flew. Not far, and not high, but far enough and high enough to work. Hel got up on one reindeer and did a test flight, and it worked! From above, the hole was as black as she had ever seen, with a deep electrical shimmer. The hole had to be closed permanently. The reindeer received berries when they landed. Soon they were jumping all on their own.

San and a few others went to a nearby forest and cut down the tallest pine tree. He scraped off all the bark while others trimmed the branches. They would use the pole to fill the hole and trap The Uisuil forever. He studded it with chips of lodestone they had from making the many arrow tips.

All the soldiers, the archers, the water pumpers, the reindeer, and the people carrying the pole gathered. They were a remarkable sight, proud and strong. San and Hel stood before them, raised their swords, and San said, "People will not know what we do tonight. If we are successful, it will be buried under the ice, forgotten forever. We do this for all the people of the world. We do this for peace."

They marched toward the black hole, their wagons pulled by reindeer, wheels bumping over the ice road, the clinking stone chimed their way forward.

They repeated the strategy that had worked before. First, the archers, then the water pumpers. When the stream of creatures started coming out of the hole, Hel yelled, "Water! We need more water toward the hole!"

A barrage of arrows and water flew toward the hole, and they started to hear sizzling.

When the creatures stopped, San yelled, "Now the stone, all the stone we have, around the hole."

Everyone began to throw stones. Several reindeer flew over, releasing their stones as they descended. The stone formed a flat cairn around the hole." Then San yelled, "Now the pole."

All the soldiers lifted the wood pole into position, and then they continued to raise the one end until it was vertical. Gravity did the rest and helped them place it tightly into the ice.

Then Hel yelled, "More stone."

They brought more toward the pole, locking it into position forever. They added more snow and ice scraped from nearby areas to ensure the hole was capped and filled securely so that nothing ever could get out. They cheered for the peoples' victory.

After a night's rest, Hel said the next morning, "San and I will build a home here, at the top of the world. We will live here forever, guarding this space. We will go around the world once every year to destroy any Uisuil that live. We will watch over the Earth. You soldiers can stay and join us, or you can go back to your homes. Your work here, if you choose, is done or just beginning. The world is grateful to you."

The reindeer were happy to stay, as were many of the people.

After a time, San and Hel noticed that electricity flowed from the hole. They learned to use it to warm their home and, in a few short years, to build the toys they would deliver around the world one night every year on their reconnaissance runs.

The Uisuil were never heard from again.

Santa Claus and Helga, as they were now known, did have cause for concern for what might still lurk beneath, now more than ever because of the melting global ice, an even for which they were currently preparing.

Ugly Sweater

Evan Baughfman

It was hideous. The sweater's arms weren't even the same length, and its fabric was the wrong color green. Not the color of a Christmas tree, but instead a neon, snotty hue, like the inside of a kiwi.

On its front, a misshapen snowman expressed heartbreak with a frown made of coal. The snowman had no nose, carrot or otherwise, and the poor bastard slouched forward as if he were slowly melting beneath a hot sun. His eyes were crimson, and one seemed to be sliding down the snowman's right cheek, no longer content with being paired with the other. Frail twigs jutted awkwardly from the snowman's side like the useless limbs of a tyrannosaurus.

Wow, Gramma, thought Liam. *Shitty gift.*

Before he'd torn away the black wrapping paper, Liam wasn't sure what to expect. After all, Gramma didn't really know him that well anymore. It had been fifteen years since the last time he walked down the block to spend a weekend with her while Mom did Vegas with friends.

Fifteen years since he'd stumbled across Gramma in her

attic reading a crumbling book by candlelight and speaking in otherworldly tongues.

Fifteen years since Mom had listened to his story with wide-eyed terror and discovered pentagrams scrawled in blood, hidden in shadows around Gramma's house.

Fifteen years since Liam and Mom had both fled across the country, clumsily attempting to jumpstart new lives for themselves far away from the dangerous old woman.

Gramma had been able to find them a few times, however, no matter where they'd fled—north, south, east, or west. She'd always spoken through the mouth of an animal. A cat, a raven, a bat. Even a goat, once.

It wasn't until Mom had changed both of their names and relented to finding an ancient book of her own that Gramma's little familiars finally stopped coming around.

After realizing that her mother's interests had evolved past cribbage and episodes of *Jeopardy!*, Mom had vowed to protect Liam. Unfortunately, she broke that vow last month when she died.

Apparently, Gramma was still alive because she'd found Liam, even though that hadn't been his name when he knew her last. She'd left on his welcome mat an unwelcome Christmas present with a candy cane-shaped tag affixed to it.

It read simply, "Love, Gramma."

Liam wasn't convinced that Gramma loved him. After all, it had been his big mouth that had led to the implosion of their family unit.

At first, Liam wasn't even going to open the gift. Who knew what kind of horror was contained within? But here it was, two days before Christmas, and he hadn't received any other presents, which was to be expected since Mom was no longer around to check things off his wish list. Plus, all the moving around had never made it easy for him to make close friends.

Ultimately, Liam's curiosity won out, just as it had when he'd ignored Gramma's warnings to stay out of the attic all those years ago. So he sat on his couch and unveiled the ugly sweater. He was glad to see that Gramma's hobbies now included knitting. Though, by the sad state of the snowman and the sleeves, she was still learning the ropes.

She hasn't seen me in a while, but this thing's made for someone twice my size. Made it on the bigger side, just in case I was addicted to donuts and allergic to exercise.

No way in hell was Liam going to climb inside that probably-cursed itch factory. He threw it into a heap on the coffee table even though the temperature in his living room felt like it had suddenly dropped thirty degrees.

Then he saw the note at the bottom of the box. It read, "I'm sorry, please, call me," and was followed by a phone number that bore the same area code as his own.

Awesome. Gramma's already settled in nearby.

The next three numbers were "666". Of course, they were.

Liam doubted her apology would be very sincere.

Well, maybe I can get outta here before she notices I'm gone.

Liam spent the next thirteen minutes stuffing items into a duffel bag, a travel suitcase, and an empty tank that once housed several species of goldfish. Mom was never too crazy about pets but had allowed goldfish, her thoughts being that even if goldfish could somehow communicate, it would be difficult to hear them underwater.

Before long, Liam began to yawn. His eyelids grew heavy, like they were weighed down with tiny cement blocks.

Even though it was mid-day and Gramma was closing in, he couldn't shake the sudden compulsion to sleep.

Oh, God, no. Don't do that!

At the bathroom sink, he splashed water onto his face.

He yawned wider. He slapped himself across both cheeks, but the jolts of pain faded quickly. He yawned more. More.

Why was he so damn tired?

Gramma. Somehow she's doing this, trying to make me vulnerable.

She sprinkled something in through the vents. Or she enchanted the wrapping paper.

Liam went back to his bedroom to pack, to focus on anything other than the encroaching shadow of slumber. But the need to sleep persisted.

With each blink of his eyes, it became more difficult for Liam to lift his lids. Finally, he blinked too hard, for too long.

Nineteen hours later, on Christmas Eve, Liam woke up in bed somehow wearing the snowman sweater.

The hell?!

He leaped to his feet, not believing his eyes.

The sweater fit him snugly, as if it had shrunk overnight. Its sleeves were of equal length, too. However, they weren't long enough to cover his wrists.

Liam tugged at the fabric, but as he did so, the sweater seemed to hug him tighter. To constrict him like a python. Pain flared up in his chest and shoulders as the sweater attempted to vacuum-seal around his frame.

He screamed when it felt like one of his ribs cracked.

The sweater stopped.

Liam stumbled from bed and went to the full-length mirror secured to the back of the door. Indeed, he wore the sweater like a second skin. His ribcage was visible behind the snowman.

Goddamn it, Gramma! What is this?!

And then the itching began. The annoying sensation first crawled up along his spine like a marching squad of ants. Soon, it spread across his whole back, around to his chest and stomach, and down the length of his arms. An entire fucking ant army!

Liam scratched and scratched and scratched, but there was no relief to be had.

Jesus Christ, enough already!

He had to get the godforsaken garment off. He couldn't remove it like he would a normal sweater. It probably wouldn't let him, anyway.

Scissors! Fucking scissors!

Liam ran to the junk drawer in the kitchen and found a pair.

When he brought the scissors toward the sweater, it squeezed him some more. Liam moaned but still managed to slide a blade under the quickly closing cuff of the left sleeve. He sliced into the sweater and howled as blood gushed from his arm.

It was too late. The sweater had already grafted to his skin. He'd also carved into his own flesh.

Oh, God, oh, God, oh, God!

He'd hit a vein. Blood spurted from him like water from a fountain.

Woozy from the sudden blood loss, Liam tossed the scissors onto the counter, then slowly lowered himself to the tiled floor. He leaned back against the cabinet and reached for the dishtowel hanging below the sink. He grimaced as he held the dirty rag against his open wound.

Under the towel, the sleeve shifted. The pain slowly faded. The bleeding stopped.

The sweater had stitched itself—and Liam's arm—back together with kiwi-colored thread.

He threw the dripping dishcloth aside, where it wetly slapped against the refrigerator door. Liam stood on shaky legs, momentarily slipping in a puddle of his own gore.

That's when he noticed the terrible taste on his tongue. Liam gagged and spat a nasty, chalky glob onto the stove-top.

He reached up to inspect his teeth. When he pulled back his fingers, their tips were dark, covered with soot.

Liam thrust his face close to the microwave's glassy front. His reflection showed a pitch-black grimace.

THE FUCK?!

He touched an incisor. It broke free of his gums.

He held a small piece of coal in his palm.

What...?

Whatwhatwhatwhat?

Liam's heart jackhammered against bruised ribs. For a moment, he worried that it would leap out of him like an alien and scuttle off to wherever Gramma was residing. She wanted him so scared that he'd have to come to her, no matter what happened in the past.

Fuck, it's hot.

Hot, hot, HOT!

Sweat dripped down his face and pooled in the tight spaces that somehow still remained between sweater and skin.

He looked back into the makeshift microwave mirror and saw that his right eye drooped down his cheek and the flesh on his face sagged. He was melting like a fucking ice cream cone.

No, like...like...

Like a snowman.

The meat was falling off his fingers in thick, viscous chunks. The exposed phalanges resembled gnarled twigs. He felt himself liquefying inside the sweater, forcing it to loosen the hold it had on him. He felt himself turning to slush inside his pants.

Liam lurched to the fridge on softening feet. He gritted coal teeth as he used all his strength to open the refrigerator and freezer doors with skeletal hands. The blast of frigid air gave him fleeting relief. Even if it were able to make Liam solid again, he'd congeal in all the wrong places. He'd be an unsightly sculpture, forever stuck in the kitchen.

He knew of only one person who could possibly make things right again.

Goddamn it, Gramma. Just like you wanted.

He staggered to the living room, where he'd last left his phone. Parts of him were left behind on the carpet, like a snail trailing slime.

It was a struggle, but Liam was finally able to dial Gramma's number.

Obviously expecting him, she picked up after the first ring. "Hello, honey," she said. "How do you like your gift?"

He had a lot he wanted to say, but his lips had fallen onto the floor. His thoughts, too, were beginning to dissolve inside his brain.

"Gramma..." He choked. "Help..."

"That's all I've ever wanted, honey. To help you. But your mother, she didn't like what I had planned for your future."

"Gramma..."

"Now that the wall she's built between us has finally been torn down, I wanted to extend a greeting to you. You're a big boy. Free to make your own decisions. Sorry, I had to go about things the way I have, but I wanted you to feel the need to extend yourself to me. You understand, don't you, honey?"

"Yes...come...please..."

"That's wonderful to hear. No one should be alone for the holidays. I'll be right over. I've got a few more surprises for my grandson."

"No..."

But Gramma had already hung up.

Liam slowly melted into the couch cushions and waited.

Granddad's Candles

Steven Van Patten

Gabe knew his grandfather loved him, but it was hard not to feel intimidated.

"Did you drink all the damn orange juice again?" the old man asked.

"No, sir!" Gabe answered.

"And keep your ass out of my room! I'll let you know when you can have the candles!"

The barrel-chested patriarch wasn't making any sense. "What candles, Granddad?"

"The ones you were messing with when you went in my room!"

Gabe's eyes widened with fright. One glare from the deep-voiced, smoky-haired, chocolate-brown man had always been enough to set his stomach quivering to the point of nausea.

"No, sir, I didn't do that!" Panic began to set in. While his grandfather had never laid a hand on him before, Gabe had also never before been accused of breaking the one cardinal rule of the house. There was no way to know what the repercussions might be.

"You will inherit the candles soon enough, Gabe!" His grandfather's voice seemed to echo throughout the house. "After I'm gone!"

"I didn't touch any candles, Granddad! Please! You have to believe me!"

"Gabe!" a woman's voice called.

Hearing the words "after I'm gone" brought back the memory of his grandfather in a coffin.

"Gabe Marks! Wake up!"

Gabe's eyes opened. The vision of his grandfather and the kitchen peeled away. Taking the place of the dream was the harsh reality of Mrs. Morgenthau scowling at him from behind her desk while his thirty classmates turned in their seats to look at him.

He hesitated before answering. "I'm sorry, Missus Morgenthau!"

"Come out in the hallway, Gabe. Now!" Mrs. Morgenthau rose from her chair. "The rest of you, turn to page eight in the workbook. I expect all of you to be finished in ten minutes."

"Sleepy punk ass!" problem child Kenny Nesbit called out.

"Quiet, Kenneth!" Morgenthau shouted.

Kenny pouted, slammed his workbook on his desk, and pretended to do the assignment.

Once they were in the hallway, her face softened. "Gabe, you've always exhibited a great deal of maturity for a ten-year-old, so I'm going to be straight with you." Morgenthau dropped to a knee so they could be face to face. "As you know, we have a couple of bad apples in our class. I mean, I can barely control Kenny Nesbit..."

"I know, Missus Morgenthau."

"So, if I let you fall asleep in class, it makes me look bad. Now, did you sleep last night?"

"Not really." He looked down at his shoes. "I keep thinking about my granddad."

Mrs. Morgenthau knew about the grandfather's passing. "It's horrible, losing a close family member, especially around the holidays. Do you want to go home, Gabe? Maybe we brought you back to school too soon."

"I can't go home," Gabe told his pretty Asian teacher. "My mom has to work." Suddenly, the weight of feeling like a burden to his mother struck him. He started to cry.

Tears welled in Mrs. Morgenthau's eyes as she hugged Gabe. "It'll be okay, Gabe."

"I'm making you miss class," he said between sniffles.

"It's all right. They can wait."

❋ ❋ ❋

"Yo! Wassup, playa!" Freddy's overly cheerful voice said over the cell phone.

"Don't 'wassup, playa' me! Where's my money? Don't make me have to beat yo' ass at Christmastime!" If there was one thing that brought out the beast in Roscoe, it was someone trying to be cute with his cash.

"Why you stressing me, anyway?" Freddy was Roscoe's former weed-dealing partner, whose newest vice was a gambling addiction. "I mean, you should be in a good mood, what with good fortune just falling out of the sky like that."

"Nigga, what are you talking about?"

"My condolences, by the way!"

Roscoe's eyes widened with anger. "I'm gonna ask you again! What are you talking about?"

Freddy coughed deeply, a telltale sign he was smoking something. "Your fucking father-in-law! I mean, I know you didn't like the old bastard, but I still gotta offer condolences.

114

'Cause, you know, I'm a polite motherfucker!"

"Time out! Are you saying that bougie ass Augustus is dead?"

"Dead as Biggie, Tupac, Prince, Michael Jackson, take your fuckin' pick!" Freddy laughed. "Wait, you mean your wife ain't tell you her father's dead?"

"Shit, I haven't seen her in two weeks! Bitch was always running back and forth between our place and her daddy's. Always talking about how I'm childish and unfaithful and shit! Anyway, I'm hanging with this new one. The stripper I met at that spot on Gun Hill Road."

"Well, you do fuck a lotta broads! You're like Captain Kirk and shit!"

"Yo! I was always like this, son!" Roscoe's yelling prompted people in the street to turn and look at him. "Bitches be trying to change you!"

"Exactly! That's what I tell my sisters! Don't be out here tryna change a nobody! Deal with it or be out!"

"Anyway, forget that shit, man! When am I going to see my loot?"

"Look, man, I got you! I'm not trying to cheat you outta your inheritance like your wife, my dude! Anyway, I just gotta hit this poker game tonight!"

"Poker game? Isn't there a blizzard tonight?"

"We ain't playing poker outside, nigga!"

Roscoe's short supply of patience with the one man in New York more trifling than he was had finally been exhausted. "Whatever, man! Snow or no snow, you better have my money!"

Roscoe ended the call before Freddy said something reckless to add further fuel to the raging fire inside of him. "This bitch got the house! And has the nerve to try to hide that shit from me! I'll be damned."

There weren't many bars open in this section of The Bronx, especially on Christmas Eve, but EVO's Lounge would be a good spot to stop and drink some Hennessy.

Yeah, I'm gonna get fucked up, then head down to Harlem and start whipping some ass. I'm gonna fuck this broad up for not telling me we inherited a house. I'm gonna fuck Gabe up just on general principle. Shit, if she got a new man up in the crib, he can get some, too. I'm tired of these motherfuckers tryin' to play me! It's time I start lettin' these lame ass motherfuckers know I'm Gun Hill Roscoe! And these motherfuckers are worried about snow? Shit! I'm gonna give them something to worry about.

"Yo! Give me a Henny!" Roscoe yelled as he entered EVO. "In fact, I'm gonna get some bottle service up in here! I'm celebrating! I just got equity and whatnot!!"

✳ ✳ ✳

Working a shift at the strip club on Christmas Eve may have been the most soul-draining thing Alisa ever had to do. She hated leaving Gabe on his own, but Christmas presents don't materialize from outer space; a mother had to do what a mother had to do. As with any other night, the actual bartending was simple enough. Most patrons stuck to tequila shots and beers, a departure from the service model she'd learned in her mixology class, where she'd been taught a litany of drink recipes and how a friendly demeanor garnered more tips. Unfortunately, to be tipped in a place where customers could, contrary to what Chris Rock believed, have sex in the champagne room, a bartender had to be friendly. That's a problem when friendliness gets interpreted as a willingness to be fondled, or worse.

Her ass had already been grabbed several times during trips to the cellar or the ladies' room. The manager had long ago assured her customers weren't allowed to do such things, but the bouncers were always looking in the wrong direction whenever someone got too grabby. She had been asked repeatedly why she wasn't on stage or available for lap dances. A tragically obese man adorned in a mink coat and holding two hundred dollars in singles introduced her to a very attractive, light-skinned video vixen-type he claimed to be "representing," before suggesting they all have a threesome when her shift ended. For someone who simply wanted to make drinks and go home, it was all very tiresome.

Alisa recalled her father's reaction when she told him she'd started waitressing at a strip club, aptly named *Titifield* for its proximity to *Citifield,* the baseball stadium the New York Mets called home.

"Did I kill a school bus full of kids in a past life? Seriously, what did I do to deserve this?" It was the first time she'd seen the normally feisty and energetic man look defeated.

"I'm not stripping, and I'm not turning tricks," she protested. "The money is good. I just have to serve drinks and avoid the drama until I find something better."

"I raised you to set higher goals."

"Look, I'm sorry! I didn't get the good grades you wanted. I didn't get accepted into a fancy college, and I got knocked up by a loser! I've disappointed you over and over again! I know it!"

"Come home. Forget the loser. I'll take care of everything. I'll help you with Gabe!"

"No, daddy!" She stomped her left foot, one of the few times she'd ever said no to him. Her stomach trembled as the words left her lips. "I'm a grown woman, and I have to figure it out. You're done raising a child. You should enjoy your retirement."

"If I didn't already hate that damn useless husband of yours, I'd surely hate him now. And it's not like me to hate anyone! But I hate him. Deeply and fully, I hate him for what he did to my child."

There were only a few superficial conversations with her father after that. By the time she'd left the apartment she had shared with Roscoe a week later, her father looked worn down. He died quietly in his sleep two nights after she'd come home. Finding him, she realized she'd spent so much time arguing with him that she never acknowledged she knew the old curmudgeon always meant well. She was inconsolable for days. To get through the wake and funeral, she focused on being strong for Gabe or she might have had a nervous breakdown.

As she hustled more drinks, she feared she might have one now. *Should have listened to you, dad! I fucked up...but I'm gonna make it right.*

"Ladies, I need singles!!" she shouted over the music. After a moment, a topless, chocolate-toned girl in a pink thong, burgundy pumps, and a Santa hat made her way to the bar. Alisa knew her real name was Samantha, but in the bar, she was known as "Rocket."

"Hey, girl! Here you go!" Rocket pulled a five one dollar bills out the lower half of her thong, added it to the stack of money folded into her garter belt, and held it out to Alisa.

Alisa took the singles, counted to forty, and gave Rocket two twenty dollar bills. *I gotta remember to buy hand sanitizer.* "Thank you, Rocket!"

"Hey, you're leaving soon, right?" Rocket leaned in to ask.

"Yes! In two hours! Ginger is coming to relieve me. We split the shift so we could both at least do some time with our kids."

"How are you getting home? There's like a foot of snow on the ground in Long Island. The mayor is talking about shutting down the trains."

"What?!" She couldn't believe it. Half of her night's take would be going to a cab driver now. "If it's that bad, why are all these people still here? Why did we even open tonight?"

"People probably didn't take the news seriously. Last time there was supposed to be a blizzard, only upstate and Jersey got hit. These fools are so busy trying to get their little dicks wet they won't know anything until the weather advisory hits their cell phones!"

Rocket's words proved prophetic. A high-pitched electronic squeal emitted from multiple smartphones at once. Eyes widened. Mouths gulped drinks. Hands grabbed coats. Lap dances ended.

As the club emptied, Petrov, the manager, emerged from his office. Petrov dressed like a man who had a great sex life in the seventies and refused to progress as a human being afterward. His cologne cloud presented itself five seconds before he did.

"You don't think you're leaving without cleaning the bar first, do you?" Petrov's cologne stung Alisa's eyes. "I take you home if there is problem, but bar has to be clean."

"Don't worry, I'll figure it out!" she answered without even looking at him.

Get in a car with you? I don't think so, Russian Bill Cosby! I'm not waking up in some hotel room with a pierogi in my ass!

She turned from Petrov to clean up when she noticed her cell phone blinking, most likely with the weather alert. She spent the minutes that followed as a living blur of multitasking, taking last-minute orders, packing away the garnish containers, and sealing and storing liquor bottles.

Meanwhile, strippers who had cars ran out; the ones who didn't negotiated rides with lingering customers even as the two gigantic bouncers encouraged everyone to leave. She thought about asking the DJ for a lift, but he'd packed up his equipment and was gone before she could catch him. Rocket had slipped by her as well.

She was working up the nerve to ask the bouncers if either of them were going to Manhattan when she finally checked her blinking phone and saw a message from Roscoe:

"YO! Merry Christmas, bitch! I'm coming for my house! That's right! MY house! I'll see that ass tonight!"

Roscoe's message had come in over forty minutes ago, so the digital stamp read. Then the phone screen went black. In her haste to get settled into work, she forgot to charge her phone.

Panic set in. She repressed a scream and turned toward her boss. She would spend the next few minutes explaining the situation to Petrov and hope that somewhere, underneath the Russian's grimy exterior, there was a decent human being who wouldn't take advantage of the fact that she needed his help to rescue her child.

❋ ❋ ❋

"Try to have a happy Christmas, Gabe. I hope you and your mother can do something festive to keep your mind off things." Mrs. Morgenthau pulled her Buick Skylark up to Augustus Marks's house.

"I don't know if being trapped alone with mom during a blizzard will be all that festive," Gabe said with a sigh, "but it beats being in a classroom with Kenny Nesbit. I'll give it a shot. Thanks for driving me home, Missus Morgenthau."

"You're very welcome, Gabe."

He climbed out of her car, ran up the stone steps, and let himself inside the dusty four-story brownstone.

Inside, he made a beeline for the kitchen and cooked up

some burgers on the George Foreman grill, just like his grandfather had taught him. He planned to study and play video games once he'd eaten but ended up thwarted by a food coma. Unaware of his mother's worries or his father's impending arrival, he slept propped up on the couch, mouth agape, a line of drool running down the side of his face. Lost in a peaceful, dreamless black void, it took a full three rounds of *thump, thump thump'* on the front door to wake him.

"Open this goddamn door!" Roscoe shouted. "This is my fuckin' house now!" Gabe's heart began racing before his eyes fully opened. He loved his father as much as it was possible for any ten-year-old to love an adult he knows is a worthless idiot. That didn't mean he missed him or the chaos his presence provoked.

The pounding and swearing continued. Gabe slowly rose from the couch and made his way to the door. Dust flew off the door's edges as it rattled under his father's barrage.

"Daddy?" Gabe managed.

"Gabe?!" Roscoe shouted. "Boy, your little punk ass gone deaf? Open this damn door!"

Gabe took a deep breath, striving to be brave. "Mom said not to let you in!"

"I don't give a fuck what she said! Is she there?! Open this door! Why didn't someone tell me that crusty old bastard Augustus was dead! Just gonna come live in the fancy house by ya damn selves and to hell with Roscoe, right? Is that what you both said, you little punk? To hell with your daddy?!"

"No, daddy! It wasn't like that!" Gabe shouted back. Tears came to his eyes. "It's just that you're fighting all the time!"

"You're about to see some real fighting if you don't open this fuckin' door, boy! Starting with the ass-whipping you're going to get! This is about to be the most fucked-up Christmas you ever had!"

Defeated and confused, Gabe fell to his knees. In his decade-long life, he'd never felt smaller. As desperation and fear set in, Gabe's mind wandered to the one person who would not have tolerated this happening to him. Augustus had always been firm, but far from abusive.

I just want Granddad back! Why did Granddad have to die? He'd put a stop to this! I'm so lonely without him. He was the only one who ever really talked to me or seemed to care. Everyone else is too busy yelling and slamming doors and staring into their phones.

As his tears hit the floor, Gabe heard his grandfather's deep, soul-stirring voice. Even as he agonized over his situation, Gabe noticed the room grew much colder.

"I'm here, Gabe! It's all right! Go to my bedroom! I know I always said you should never go in there, but it is okay now. I'm going to take care of this." Being sensible, Gabe chalked up what he heard to a mixture of fright, indigestion, and wishful thinking. People only came back from the dead in movies. Hell, Augustus himself once said that. Little did anyone know, Augustus often appropriated flippant and cynical remarks of others to keep his true spiritual nature hidden.

"Go to the bedroom," the disembodied voice of his grandfather commanded.

Gabe's troubled mind went numb as he stood and headed for the staircase. His father's voice and the banging at the door faded.

He raced up the stairs, arms unintentionally flailing as he bounded two steps at a time. An eerie awareness filled him as he started up the final set of stairs, a set that until this moment he had never been to the top of.

On the second floor, Gabe was greeted by a warm, welcoming light spilling out of the bedroom like a beacon. The bedroom door had opened, seemingly on its own. As he cautiously crossed the threshold, his nostrils filled with a mixture of scents: dust, candle wax, every hug his grandfather had ever given him. Gabe couldn't have imagined it possible to go from terrified to comforted so fast.

To Gabe's right, a king-size bed was covered by a colorful, worn quilt. The bureau beside the bed was covered with candles, several of which were inexplicably lit. Some were simple cylinders of wax; others were shaped like skulls, naked people, and genitalia.

The peaceful glow called to him, bidding him to forget about his father banging on the front door.

"Everything is going to be okay, Gabe," his grandfather's disembodied voice said.

"But Grandpa, how did this happen? You're supposed to be dead."

"I'm not sure, boy. My best guess is my anger toward your father has sustained me."

"Anger?" Gabe repeated. "Anger is supposed to be bad."

"It is, son. When I died, I was so angry about everything that's been going on with you and your mother that I became anchored here. One minute I was in the hospital, too weary to keep my eyes open; the next, I was watching you and your mother at the crematorium. Ever since I've been drawn to whichever one of you is in most distress."

"Well, things are going to be really stressful when my daddy gets in the house," Gabe replied.

At the mention of Roscoe, every candle on the bureau went suddenly ablaze. A terrible shrieking noise filled the room. Gabe cupped his hands over his ears.

"Granddad! You're going to burn the house down!"

All but one of the candles snuffed out.

"Go to sleep, Gabriel," said Augustus.

"But Granddad..."

123

The candles erupted again. "Do as I say, boy!"

Gabe tried to run from the room. The bedroom door closed and would not budge. Frightened, he climbed onto his grandfather's bed and curled up into a ball. A whimper escaped his trembling lips, and a single tear ran down the side of his face.

"I didn't mean to scare you," Augustus said in a soothing tone. "I love you. I've never meant to scare you. Anytime I yelled at you, it was only to steer you in the right direction. You rest now, boy. I'm going to have a talk with your father."

"No, Grandpa! You can't let him in! He wants to beat me!!"

"No one is beating anyone. Now, settle yourself."

Though Gabe couldn't see the hand, he felt it gently brush his cheek. "Everything is going to be okay, Gabe. I promise."

Gabe opened his eyes. Most of the candles were out again. Thin circles of smoke danced around him. His breathing slowed; his heart stopped racing. Despite his fears, his eyelids suddenly grew very heavy.

"I missed you, Grandpa!" Gabe drifted off.

❋ ❋ ❋

After a full ten minutes, Roscoe decided to circle around to the back of the house and try a window.

Until tonight, Gabe had always had his mother or grandfather standing between him and the punishments Roscoe often felt he deserved. Roscoe's first order of business would be to make up for that once he got inside. Roscoe looked forward to the lashing he would give Gabe.

"Your luck has run out tonight, li'l fucker!" Roscoe stumbled through the snow to the back of the house. After a brief loss of footing, Roscoe found himself staring at three first floor windows, the sills of which came up to his chest. The largest of these led to Augustus's den, one of the rooms Roscoe was never allowed to enter when the patriarch was alive.

Roscoe tried the window. It opened easily. The surprise nearly sobered him. He was about to hoist himself inside when a shove sent him flying backward. Two inches of previously undisturbed snow cushioned his landing.

Roscoe was no stranger to weightlifting. He stood 5'8" with a mostly muscular frame that hit the scale at around 190 pounds, depending on how much he'd had to drink that week. It would take a very strong man to shove Roscoe with any measure of success.

"YOU HOODLUM PIECE OF SHIT!" The voice seemed to come from everywhere and nowhere. *"HOW DARE YOU!"*

Roscoe recognized the voice, despite its new, unearthly timbre. "You old motherfucker! I thought you was dead!" Roscoe rose to his feet slowly. His eyes narrowed, seeking the old man, who, as far as he was concerned, was only another ass he needed to kick. "You're gonna wish you stayed dead, you old bastard!! Helping your skank-ass daughter turn my kid into a little punk crybaby bitch! I'm fuckin' all of you up tonight!"

Roscoe stepped forward and slipped, falling hard on his back a second time. Something seemed to have grabbed his ankle. His inebriated mind refused to process the possibility he might be facing an invisible assailant. The flattened snow was less forgiving this time, as the second landing knocked the wind out of his lungs so hard he could barely scream. "Fuck!" He didn't feel the gash that opened three inches behind his right ear when his head struck the ground or the thin trickle of blood running down his neck onto the snow.

Roscoe lifted his head. Cold, white snowflakes swirled around him. The isolated vortexes accelerated and merged, forming a powdery outline of the face of Augustus Marks.

"Fuck you, old man!" he cried at the apparition. "I'm not

scared of you!!"

But Roscoe was lying, and his fright increased exponent-tially as he found himself lifted from the ground. He wriggled, flailing like a lobster held over a pot of boiling water, rising upward. As the whirlpool carried him past the second-floor windows, his father-in-law's voice filled his ears as clearly as a pair of three-hundred-dollar headphones.

"You're going to die now!"

"Hey… Hey… Can't we discuss this? You know, like fami-ly?" Roscoe was finally humbled.

"What would you like to discuss, Roscoe?" the voice asked. "How you took advantage of my daughter's bad boy phase and tricked her into thinking you'd make a decent husband? Or maybe the lazy, ambitionless example you've set for my grand-son?"

"Come on! You were young once. I was just doing my thing!"

The angry face formed in the swirls of snow again. "Well, 'your thing' cost me a lot of money and may very well have cost my daughter her future. 'Your thing' turned our lives to shit! I will not have you turning my grandson into a smaller version of your dumb ass! I'd pull you apart like a fly if I could. But I'll settle for this."

Roscoe continued rising. Something pushed against his chin. He tried pushing back, but the force was too great. "Wait!! You can't kill me!!" Roscoe screamed. "I mean, come on!! If you kill me, I'll just be a ghost like you! I'll haunt your ass! I'll haunt the kid!!"

Roscoe's ascension stopped just shy of the roof of the house. The unseen power that hoisted him into the air relinquished the upper part of his body and dangled him by his ankle. Au-gustus's disembodied voice filled his ears with a last declara-tion. "You're going to Hell. You're not haunting anyone. Merry Christmas, Jackass!"

The last thing Roscoe heard were the vertebrae in his neck grinding against each other, followed by a definitive "pop." His eyes glazed as of blood spurted out from between his chapped lips.

Augustus released the lifeless corpse and watched Roscoe drop face down to the snow-covered backyard. The body hit with such force that his skull split open like a sledgehammered cantaloupe. A red, star-shaped splatter erupted from the contact point. Mixed with the snow, the blood and gray matter could almost be mistaken for a dessert topping.

Except for the approaching sirens, the neighborhood Augustus Marks called home for more than fifty years of his life was quiet again.

❋ ❋ ❋

"Ma'am, it would appear that your husband attempted to gain entry by climbing onto the roof and then accessing an upstairs window. He lost his footing and fell head first into the backyard. He died on impact."

Alisa threw an arm around Gabe, sobbing. Roscoe may have been an idiot of epic proportions, but he was still someone she had cared for deeply. Gabe snaked an arm around his mother and rubbed her back for comfort. His face betrayed nothing of what he had experienced earlier that night.

"They'll do what they can for him at the morgue, but, to be honest, there isn't much left of his face. When you make the funeral arrangements—"

"Thank you, Officer Albrecht," Alisa cut him off. "My husband wanted to be cremated. It's under control."

"Very well," Albrecht responded. "Sorry for your loss."

"Thank you."

Alisa tried to sniff away tears and mucus. She squeezed

Gabe's slender frame even tighter. "Are you sure you're okay? You didn't see what happened to your father?"

"I know what happened, but I didn't see it," Gabe answered.

"Be sure you never say that again." Alisa glanced at the cops, who were thankfully out of earshot. She seized Gabe in her arms again. "I just don't know what to do. All of these horrible things happening just before Christmas."

Gabe's mind drifted back to the day of Augustus's funeral. There was an incident no one else noticed. As the church was emptying, an old friend of his grandfather's leaned close and whispered in his ear. "It's too bad your grandfather left you while you were so young. There is so much knowledge he could have shared with you."

Gabe continued holding onto his mother, watching as a shadow moved across the walls behind her and disappeared. "Don't worry, mom. Next year, Christmas will be much better."

TRADITIONS AND ROTTEN DELICACIES
S.E. Casey

He squirmed in Grandma Josie's embrace, her breath reeking of holly and candy canes. Unlike the sweet peppermint scent that he sometimes whiffed on his mother's lips during the season, rather Grandma's was a fermented, foul stink. Her unique malodor suggested a wasting, as if she was some yuletide ghoul. Frank twisted to escape her clutch, but he couldn't wriggle free. She whispered in his ear, giving him a healthy dose of that mephitic minty breath.

But you don't want to be alone on Christmas, Frankie. No one should be alone on Christmas.

He didn't want to be alone necessarily, only back home, in his room, playing with his new toys. However, Grandma's house on Christmas was a family tradition to which everyone submitted without question. Despite his short-lived perspective, it was as if Christmas had always been here, in those many years before he was born, and would be forever after.

Christmas Day was the only time of the year he would see Grandma Josie; she too old to drive, and her house too far away for his family to make regular trips, so they would gather here for this one day in the year. Frank wouldn't have minded visiting her at other times, or more preferably, if she were to visit them. His problem was Christmas, or specifically, his Grandma's monopoly on it.

Her own special day.

To make things worse, the gifts she doled out to him and his cousins were fatally practical. She never gave out games or toys, only sensible items like clothes or school supplies. Everything would be wrapped in cheap, brown paper. His mother tried to explain something about her living through a Depression, but he didn't understand the relevance. In red marker, Grandma Josie would write only the recipient's name, no need for her own, the monochrome paper identifying her as the sender.

However, Grandma made up for the blandness of her gift presentation with the seasonal decorations. Her home was festooned with Christmas reds and greens of the many garlands, holly wreaths, and mistletoe she hung. When the sun set, she would turn off the house lights, letting the rooms glow with only the soft yellow of the window candles and the pulse of the red, blue, and green Christmas lights that were strung across the entirety of the house.

Snaked around doorframes and woven through banisters like a jungle vine, Frank doubted the lights were ever taken down, that they were left up all year. In fact, they were so indelibly woven into the architecture that he didn't see how they could be taken down.

He imagined that when Grandma died and the house went up for sale, they would have no choice but to cut them down with an ax.

He hated the lights. At least, ever since he was four. The oversized bulbs were irresistible, tempting to be touched as if they were giant magic jellybeans. However, the enchanted candies burned to the touch. He hadn't understood where the pain came from, was only relieved when Grandma Josie had pried his blistering hands away from the bulbs.

In the years since, Frank loathed the Christmases here, especially that time after sunset when Grandma turned off the house lights. The colorful Christmas lights flashed with a disingenuous merriment, a paradox of beauty and pain taunting him to touch them again in their unholy language of color and rhythm. He could only sink down in his seat as far away as possible and dream that he was home playing with his toys.

Across the room, amidst the pulpy waves of color, Grandma sat in her favorite chair beside the fireplace. She seemed farther away than she was, an illusion of the light show. Frank's attention would narrow until the room became only the two of them, the lone survivors of a shipwreck adrift in a delirious ocean. As if they were in separate life rafts, he would watch her, a wild-haired woman oblivious to the rough seas of a stormy night. In the chaotic blinking, she seemed to flicker like a projection, as if something sinister passed back and forth in front of the lens.

Frank was good at puzzles, superior at all the board games he played against his cousins. Of all people, Grandma Josie noticed, always commending him on his exceptional ability to concentrate. He applied the same unwavering focus onto her fluttering form, figuring out how he could prove her spectral nature. But before he could convince himself that she indeed hovered between this world and some deviant yuletide alterrealm, she would swivel toward him acknowledging his fastidious study.

And with a wicked smile that, despite the crowded room, was somehow aimed only at him, and always she would force him to look away.

✳ ✳ ✳

He gulped down what remained in the glass to alleviate his pounding headache. The bitter sting of alcohol helped to wake him up but did little for the pain. Struggling out of bed, he willed himself down the stairs, orienting himself to the time and date.

The angle of the morning sunlight quickened his heart rate. He would be late for work again. It didn't matter; he was too important to the office for his bosses to say much. Let them try to do without him, what with all the questions and problems thrown at him each day; he was the only one who could solve them. But the adrenaline spike cleared his mind. He wouldn't be late. There was no work today. Today was a special day.

Today was Christmas.

Frank's relief dissolved into an indeterminate dread. He didn't enjoy Christmas, more the specific day than the holiday itself. In his house, there were no decorations or ornaments to celebrate, or to portend, Christmas's arrival.

This year he would receive one gift, however. He was alone. There was no one else in his house, no one invited, and no one coming later. His daughter was off with her fiancé skiing or snowboarding in Vale or maybe Aspen. He didn't remember the details of whatever pointless endeavor at wherever trendy resort.

His ex-wife wasn't talking to him lately. Usually, that meant she had a new boyfriend; he couldn't keep up or care. And his friends wouldn't be by; he had friends, but they weren't *those* kinds of friends.

After all these years, this would be the first Christmas he would spend entirely alone.

Frank decided to celebrate by returning to bed, more than

content to sleep off his hangover. As he turned heel back up the stairs, he spotted a package in front of the fireplace.

He walked into the living room to investigate. He wasn't seeing things; a box wrapped in brown paper had been placed on the floor.

The simple package betrayed nothing about what it could be. The unknown and unwanted gift had no address or label. Despite the fact he didn't see any tags, he recalled those Christmases forty years ago, and Grandma Josie.

Without bothering to pick it up or kick it over to his chair, he sat down on the floor next to it. Unwrapping it quickly, he revealed a plain cardboard box. Tearing away the yellow packing tape from the lid, he unfolded the flaps and peered into its dark mouth.

Frank reached in and pulled out a tangle of wires so knotted that he didn't immediately identify what it was. The distractions of his hangover forgotten, he placed the snarl of Christmas lights in his lap, appraising it in sections, dividing it to conquer the knotted puzzle.

Inside the tangle, he spied the plug. A starting point. He dug in to pry it loose, winding the end over and through the tight labyrinth of wire and bulbs.

It was only a small start to unraveling the mad jumble, a ball so dense that there was little empty space to free the plug. There was nothing else in the box, no hint-book to the muddle. He would have to solve it himself. Using his intuition, he plugged it in. The lights came to life, a flashing pattern allowing him clues to plot an eventual solution.

One thread and unhitch at a time, a repetition of simple operations would solve this problem. He paused to consider the point of this charade mysteriously foisted upon him. Still, the tiniest of momentum generated from slipping the first knot made him forget everything but the work.

The process would be slow, but he had all day, no one for him to entertain, no distractions. He was alone with only the flickering memories of past Christmas days.

* * *

"It'll just be for a few minutes, I promise."

Her husband rolled his eyes. He and her son were miserable, worn out by the long day. However, there were responsibilities that came with Christmas—it wasn't supposed to be all fun. On top of the five o'clock wakeup-call her seven-year-old demanded, they had logged over a hundred miles on the road back and forth between their respective families in two states.

Just one more stop.

Bethany knocked on the front door but got no answer. It was only an hour after sunset. Certainly, it wasn't too late. Also, knowing her cousin, she didn't expect him to out reveling in any Christmas festivities. She tried the door. It opened. She tiptoed in. Her husband and son lagged behind, her cousin Frank not their favorite relative.

"Hello? Frankie? You here?"

The house was silent, filled with a smell of a pork roast that was wholly unappetizing. Bethany put a hand to her nose. Maybe it was the acrid, burnt quality that she found off-putting, or maybe it was the Christmas smell that was out of place given her cousin's wretched attitude toward the holiday. Still, she made visiting cousin Frank a priority, a lesson that had been seared into her as a child.

No one should be alone on Christmas.

The house was dark excepting a red and green glow that spilled from the living room.

"Frankie? Is that you?"

134

The smell was stronger as she entered the room. Before the empty fireplace, Frank sat on the floor with his back to her. He hunched over a cord of half-untangled lights, the large red and green bulbs blazing. The stink of a roast didn't drown out an unmistakable hint of mint and holly, disorienting in its putrescence.

Bethany dry heaved, the cloud of Christmas rot triggering her gag reflex.

Nonetheless, she approached with care. Her hand pinching her nose, she reluctantly craned her neck over his shoulder, wary of whatever secrets he worried over, not wanting to see, but needing to know.

Lost in a soft trance, Frank, as if possessed by some sadistic thrall, paid no heed to her intrusion. His raw fingers, flesh sloughing off in blistered clumps, whittled knot after knot away from the searing coil. His concentration unwavering, he had adjusted to the wounds, taking advantage of newly exposed bone and cauterized scabs as picks and levers.

Lost in the puzzle, he didn't flinch as she started to scream.

✳ ✳ ✳

Numbly, he worked the wire. The strobing lights saturated the room, an oppressive heaviness in the air. Sweat beaded on his brow, but he didn't wipe it away, his flayed hands buried in the tangle.

You don't want to be alone on Christmas, Frankie.

He didn't look up, keeping at the task at hand, but he knew she was there, a wild-haired woman sitting in a well-worn chair grinning wickedly. He could smell her septic exhalations from across the vastness of the room. But maybe it was leakage from some other world she flickered in between, a world that had overwhelmed itself, choked by its own trappings. The disconsolate air was of a festival soured, a yuletide torrent of mirthless excesses and grating rituals.

But he wouldn't look. She had always had that power over him. And he wasn't curious; he had no need to be. After all, he was safe, in his room, playing with his toys, as he had always ever wanted.

Two Years to the Day

Neil Davies

Footsteps in the upstairs office.

The kids should have known better. Just because their father was away on business didn't mean they could run riot in his office. No one was allowed in there without his permission. Even *she* had to knock and wait.

Kim paused in her preparation of Christmas dinner, sighing despite her determination to be more cheerful this year.

Away on business.

What kind of company sends a family man away on business over the holiday? Christmas morning and she hadn't even been able to call her husband because of the different time zones. She didn't dare risk waking him. He got angry when woken early.

More footsteps in the upstairs office.

She would have to get the kids out of there before they did some damage she couldn't hide.

"Kids!" she called as she wiped her hands on the tea towel hanging by the kitchen sink and headed for the hallway.

"Yes, mum?"

That was ten-year-old Karla, her voice clearly coming from the living room.

Kim pushed the door open and her two children, Karla and George, looked up from where they sprawled on the floor among their new toys and twisted, curling wads of torn wrapping paper. On the far side of the room, the Christmas tree sparkled with lights, and the wood-burning stove gave heat to the otherwise cold room. The only thing that spoiled the festive image for her was the ax on the hearth. It made her uncomfortable. She didn't like it in the living room, but Graham had insisted. He used it for chopping wood for the stove and wanted it close by. She looked away, not sure why it sent a shudder down her spine.

"Have either of you been up in daddy's office?"

Her children shook their heads, and she knew they were telling the truth. Fear of an angry daddy outweighed curiosity. She should have known better.

So, what were the footsteps she had heard?

She left the children playing and walked slowly to the foot of the stairs, staring up into the gloom. The heavy overcast sky gave little light through the small landing window, but it was bright enough for her to see there was no one there. She listened, but all was quiet. No footsteps, no noise at all other than the excited voices of Karla and George behind the closed living room door and the growing wind outside.

She should check. She should go up and take a look. Chances were it was just the typical noises of an old house. Or perhaps the office window was open and the wind had blown something from the desk?

She hesitated, one foot raised above the first step.

What if there was an intruder? Someone who'd broken in upstairs, climbed through one of the windows? It was Christmas Day. Burglars knew people had lots of new things on

Christmas Day.

But surely a burglar would have chosen one of her neighbors? Both sides were out at church. Their houses were empty. Why would anyone choose *her* house, with a mother and two children inside?

Unless he wasn't there to steal but precisely *because* she was alone with her kids, her husband away on business.

The thought made her stomach turn, a sweat break out on her forehead, and she gripped the banister hard, knuckles showing white through pale skin.

Perhaps he'd seen her shopping, followed her home, and was even now waiting for her in the upstairs office. Waiting to attack her!

"Mum! What time's dinner?"

The sudden shout startled Kim out of her spiraling dark thoughts. She swallowed, her throat dry, and forced her fingers to loosen on the banister. She even managed a smile. Typical George. Always hungry.

"Not until this afternoon," she called back, hoping the shaking in her voice was not noticeable. "I'll get you some breakfast in a minute."

She was being foolish. George's call for food had made her realize that. There was no burglar, no attacker waiting upstairs for her. Just the house, the wind, and her overactive imagination.

But she had to go upstairs to be sure.

One step at a time. Easy. Listen to the children playing below. Good kids. Seldom argued, and never when Graham was home. He'd had a strict upbringing; his father had been more than ready to dispense discipline with his leather belt for the children, his fists for his wife. Marrying Kim had been Graham's escape from all that and, although he had threatened, he had never hit her. He slapped the children more than she liked, but never anything more. Still, she didn't like to see the fear in her children's eyes when Graham lost his temper, nor the fury in his face, the obvious struggle he had to keep control. Those were the times she saw his father in him. Those were the times she was most afraid.

But she loved him. Despite his temper, she loved him. And when he wasn't angry, he was attentive, caring, a good husband and father.

Why was she thinking about this now? All she had to do was take a few more steps, see the office was empty and get back to cooking Christmas dinner. Nothing more. Christmas morning was not the time to analyze her marriage.

She reached the landing and flicked the light switch to dispel the gloom. Nothing happened. The bulb had blown again. The house needed rewiring, but Graham said it was too expensive and they could manage.

She didn't let the lack of light worry her. It wasn't dark, just gloomy, the sky outside a dark gray, the wind gusting against the window, rattling the glass in its frame. He had promised her they'd get double-glazing in the New Year. She hoped that this time he kept his word.

The doors to the bedrooms, the children's and her own, were open and the rooms untidy but empty. She almost smiled despite her nervousness. When Graham was away on business, she could wake up and leave the room a mess until later without it causing an argument. The children, too. There were advantages to Graham's busy working life.

The fourth room, after the bathroom, was Graham's office. Here the door was closed, as it always was. She paused, listening, but there was no sound.

Her hand was on the handle when she heard the shuffling, definite, unmistakable shuffling of feet from the other side of the door.

She almost screamed.

What should she do?

She glanced behind her, suddenly afraid someone was sneaking up on her, but the landing was still empty. Downstairs, the children were arguing. Nothing serious, just brother and sister fighting over a toy, but it focused her mind, and she knew that protecting them was the most important thing. She had failed them in the past, not stepping in when Graham raised his hand, but not this time. No stranger was coming into her house and threatening her children!

She pushed open the office door, stepping quickly inside, trying not to show the fear that almost buckled her knees. After a moment's fumbling, she found the light switch and, as the room filled with light, glared challengingly around.

Nothing. The room was tidy, undisturbed, and empty.

Footsteps on the stairs!

She turned and hurried onto the landing, leaning over the banister to look down to the hall, but there was no one there, and the footsteps had stopped.

What was going on?

The children. She must check on the children.

Almost slipping, only the banister stopping her from tumbling, she rushed down the stairs, no longer able to hear the children, panic building in her chest.

She reached the hallway at a run and slammed through the living room door.

Karla and George sat quietly on the floor, still playing but in silence, their heads down.

"Are you okay? I got worried when you went quiet."

Karla looked up at her mother and nodded. There were tears in her eyes.

"We're sorry we were arguing, mummy. Now we're being good and quiet, just like daddy wants us to be."

"You don't need to be quiet, sweetheart. Daddy's away, working."

The look of disbelief in her daughter's eyes disturbed her. Her son never looked up from his toy.

The sudden knock on the front door made her physically jerk, her heart pounding.

She was being foolish again. Noises in an old house, children playing quietly, nothing that any normal person would worry about. And now someone at the door. Probably her neighbors back from church, stopping by to wish her a Merry Christmas. Nothing to be frightened of.

Karla's head had dropped back to her toy and Kim, confused more than worried by her children's sudden change, pulled the living room door closed and crossed the hallway as the someone outside knocked a second time.

She recognized PC Burroughs immediately. As the village policeman, he was regularly to be seen patrolling the streets or at the school fairs, always smiling, always happy to stop and chat.

Behind him stood a younger policeman who Kim did not recognize, but she smiled at him anyway.

"Good morning, Missus Charlotte. Sorry to drop by unexpected, but I just wanted to introduce PC Blake."

The younger policeman smiled at this and said, "Good morning."

"He's just started in the area, and I'm showing him around, making sure people know who he is."

"Well," said Kim, wondering just for a moment whether she should mention the noises in the house but worried she would look foolish. "It's nice to meet you, PC Blake."

"Nice to meet you, too, Missus Charlotte."

PC Burroughs peered past her into the hallway.

"Is everything alright, Missus Charlotte? Is there anything

we can do for you?"

"No, no, I'm fine." She forced another smile. There was no point involving the police over her own irrational fears. Graham would be furious if he found out.

"Well, then, we'll be on our way. Lots more people for PC Blake to meet yet. Merry Christmas, Missus Charlotte."

"Merry Christmas," she replied as the two policemen turned and walked down the path.

She waited until they were through the gate before closing the door.

* * *

"Sad case that," said PC Burroughs as they headed back toward the village center. "Always like to check in on her on Christmas Day."

"What happened?" asked PC Blake, curious. He'd heard rumors, but he preferred to know the facts.

"Husband was always a bit of a nasty bugger, terrible temper, that sort of thing. Two years ago, on Christmas morning, he finally snapped. He claimed the children were shouting, arguing, and he just wanted some peace. Took an ax to them. Boy and a girl, eight and ten. Killed them instantly."

"What about Missus Charlotte?"

"She heard the noise, tried to stop him, but he turned on her, too. Hit her three times with the ax. She was lucky to survive. Then he calmly calls the police and confesses, like it was a perfectly normal thing to do. Ended up in a prison hospital. Totally crazy."

PC Blake let out a long breath of air, shaking his head. "Well, I hope they're keeping him locked up in there forever. I wouldn't like to be her if he ever got out."

"No chance of that," said PC Burroughs as they neared

the local church, bells ringing as people exited the doors. "He died just a couple of days ago. Heart attack. Came through in the daily bulletins, but the doctor recommended not telling Missus Charlotte, not just yet. You know, Christmas is always difficult for her, with all those memories."

❋ ❋ ❋

Kim looked in on the children, but they had gone. They'd tidied up, too, taking all their toys and wrapping paper with them. She always knew they were good kids.

She noticed the ax was missing from by the wood-burning stove but thought little of it.

Footsteps behind her. The children? She turned and smiled, surprised at the man who stood there.

"Graham. You're home."

The ax cracked open her skull, cleaving deep into her head, the blade finally stopping just above the bridge of her nose.

She fell, her last gasping breaths blowing bubbles in the blood that flowed down her face and into her mouth.

Her body lay in the hallway, a growing pool of blood around her head, staining the shaft of the ax, its blade still deep in her skull. The house was empty and quiet, the only sound faint footsteps on the stairs, the landing, and the opening and closing of the upstairs office door.

S*ack of S*ouls

Christopher Stanley

He's there for the young man who immolates himself on the steps of the Cenotaph. He's there for the hundreds of terrified refugees whose dinghies capsize in the choppy waters of the Mediterranean. He waits behind the curtain of every flu and cancer victim. For the falls and suicides, the road traffic accidents, and state-sanctioned murders, he lingers in the shadows with his hessian sack held ready. His sack has never felt so heavy.

In Southern Nevada, he attends a Gamblers Anonymous meeting. No one asks for his name, and he doesn't wear a badge, choosing instead to sit alone at the back of the room and sip sherry from a flask. After the meeting, when everyone else has left, he steps up to the podium, sweeps his beard to one side, and leans toward the microphone.

"I have a problem," he says in a solemn baritone. "I like to gamble. Card games mostly. Tarock, Tarocco; anything with Tarot cards." His voice catching, he says "I gambled everything I had. My passion, my purpose, everything. I lost."

In his shades-of-midnight suit, he's there when the plane

crashes in the Indian Ocean, for the gun massacre in Ohio, and the starving children in the Sudan. His sack, which was once filled with the promise of joy, now bulges and throbs like a diseased heart.

He finds Jenny sitting on a bench in Castle Park, staring up through the freezing mist to the ruins of St. Peter's Church. She wears the mismatched threads of the homeless and cradles a can of super-strength lager in the crook of her arm. He sits next to her and sips his sherry.

"Stuff'll kill you," she says.

He spits the sherry back into the flask. It's been fifty years since someone acknowledged his presence. He tucks the flask away in the folds of his suit and leans closer to her. Like so many bench dwellers, she wears a heady perfume of sweat and piss and tobacco. And even when she speaks, she hardly moves at all.

"If you were hoping for a kiss," she says, "you're shit outta luck."

He can't help but laugh. She reminds him of the little girl who spoke to him fifty years ago, the one whose eyes shone like baubles on a tree. She demanded to see inside his sack in case there was something she wanted more than the presents he'd already left at the foot of her bed. When he refused, she folded her arms and scowled.

On the bench, Jenny says "We've met before, haven't we?" Her eyes sparkle when they catch the moonlight. Then she coughs, and it's a violent reflex that tears deep into her chest. A thin line of spittle and blood connects her bottom lip to the frost-speckled concrete below. Carefully, he touches his hand to her shoulder.

"Last time I saw you," she croaks, "you were wearing red. You were happier then."

He helps her to lie down on the bench, her frail body seeming to collapse inside her sleeping bag. There are other places he's supposed to be, but they can wait. Boats will sink, and schools will burn, but how long will it be before he meets another Jenny?

"I lost everything, too," she says.

"One thing I've learned," he replies, "you can't cheat Death." He kisses her on the forehead and whispers "You can see inside my sack now."

As Jenny's spirit leaves her body, a sleigh passes overhead, pulled by a dozen hooved and snarling animals. It's filled with presents wrapped in every color of the season, anchored in place by the blade of a scythe. The sleigh's rider holds onto the reins with long, bony fingers; a pack of Tarot cards tucked up one sleeve and a smile permanently carved into his face.

For any children who are still awake tonight, Christmas will never be the same again.

S*anta S*lay

Terry Miller

The first flake fell that Christmas Eve
　　As children slept in their beds.
　　From house to house, a stranger crept
With an ax to chop off their heads.

　Mommies and Daddies slept unaware,
　　Their bodies tired from the day.
　Smiling faces danced in their heads,
As this man dressed as Santa did slay.

　Silent footsteps from room to room,
　　His hand gripped tight on the ax.
　He carefully moved from bed to bed,
　　Smiling with glee at his whacks.
　　A silent night then a silent morn,

　Headless corpses all quiet and still.
　　One man walked the snowy streets,
　With fresh meat for his holiday meal.

CHRISTMAS LIGHTS ON BENNER'S MOUNTAIN
David Bernard

Tom Harley was tending bar at Dienny's pub, wearing the same ratty Santa hat he wore every year. It was assumed that sooner or later the threadbare relic would either disintegrate or the Biglersville Health Department would make him burn it.

Old Man Withers limped into the bar with a troubled look on his face. Bad leg and all, Old Man Withers was usually the type that was happy to the point of being suspected of being a tad touched in the head. As the old farmer slid onto his usual stool, he nodded over his shoulder.

"I just saw the lights up on Benner's Mountain."

Harley nearly spilled the beer as he handed it to Withers. The bar had gotten very quiet. Only the Christmas music on the radio broke the silence. Finally, Frankie Fenmore swallowed the rest of his beer and reluctantly peeked out the door. "He's right. The Christmas lights are back."

It's hard to spook an entire bar of old Yankees in the Northern Kingdom, but the appearance of the lights on Benner's Mountain was the easiest way. Ever since Ethan Allen was a

149

baby, their appearance in December had been an omen. They didn't appear every year, but when the lights shone brightly, a calamity was about to befall Biglersville. The story dated back to the earliest history of the town during the Revolutionary War, ever since that bloody Christmas Eve when marauding Indians massacred a party of Tories heading to Canada that had camped for the night on Benner's Mountain. Basically, if it was around the holidays, and there was blood about to be shed in Biglersville, the ghost lights were seen glimmering through the trees. Back in the 1940s, Sam Grove, the editor of the *Biglersville Bugle* coined "Christmas Lights" to describe the ghost lights tradition about a year before a freak mishap with the printing press ended said editor's propensity for witticism. Most Biglerians hate the phrase, and more than one has ex-pressed a certain grim satisfaction that his drowning death in a barrel of ink had in itself become one of the ghost lights' tales.

Harley casually checked the sawed-off shotgun he kept under the bar. "I wonder who it is this time?"

Frankie kept glancing out the window. "It's a prank. No such thing as ghost lights. Probably those idiots from Saunderton tryin' to spook the whole town."

Curly looked out the window. "My Grannie used to say it was the Devil lightin' a path for the new souls goin' to Hell."

Barney chimed in, "My Paw says it was spaceships usin' the powah up on the mountain." Everyone just looked at him. "My paw says that ley lines intersect up theah, creatin' a grid the aliens use to fuel the flyin' sausahs. The star over Bethlehem? That was a UFO—everyone knows that."

Old Man Withers sipped his beer. "I hear it's a warning about the ghost of a witch who hates this town so much that she kills off the townsfolk one or two at a time, just for fun."

"I still say if we figger out what them ghost lights is, we

can figger out how to stop 'em. I say we grab rifles and go see what's up theah." Frankie looked out the window.

After several hours of heated debate over the origin of the lights and an inadvisable number of rounds of beer, it was decided to take a vote. Bigfoot came in a close second, but the final decision was that it was a hoax. It was then decided that an armed party would head up Benner's Mountain, find out the source of the lights, and confront the joker spooking the town.

Frankie Fenmore, being the closest to sober, was appointed leader. Rifles were retrieved from trucks, and the party prepared to confront the troublemaker on the mountain. Frankie led the fearless heroes to the door. Curley and Barney, in worse shape than the rest, would keep their rifles slung over their shoulder until needed. Even so, Charlie, Teddie, and Fred didn't look real happy about stumbling around in the dark with people who were even drunker than they were.

Frankie turned to the bartender. "What about you Hahley? You comin'?"

Harley just shook his head. "You know I can't. Dienny will have my ass if I shut the place down this close to the holidays just to go huntin' spooks. Good luck fellas." Harley didn't sound particularly upset about missing the hunting party.

And with that, Harley and Old Man Withers watched the fearless warriors stagger off into the dark. Harley looked at Withers. "I'm not a gamblin' man, but I'd bet that the only thing those clowns will find up theah is how much it hurts when a drinkin' buddy shoots you in the foot."

Old Man Withers just sighed and shook his head. "I think shooting each other is the least of their worries out there."

Harley wiped the bar. "You know, I thought I'd heard every crackpot theory about the lights up theah, but I don't recall that one about a ghost witch killing off folks. Where'd you heah that one?"

Withers just sat there, staring into his beer. "I've known that story forever. It started back in 1777. A group of Loyalists heading north to Quebec made camp on the mountain. A couple of folks came into town looking for medicine and got chased off by the local patriots. As we both know, Biglersville has never been really friendly to strangers, and although the good folks around here believed in charity, the Tories were Tories, and we were at war. So these poor folks, who were exiles because they thought a British colony should be loyal to their king, were chased out of town like vermin, and on Christmas Eve on top of it."

Old Man Withers turned on his stool to look toward the window. "You've heard of Zaccheus Laudon?"

Harley paused. "Zaccheus Laudon? Sure. The fellow they named the library after. He owned the first mill in town. I think he was a state senatah, too."

Old Man Withers spun back to the counter. "I forgot about the library. Anyway, Zaccheus Laudon, in his younger day, was a drunken, swaggering bully, and the ringleader of a group of bored farm hands with time on their hands and trouble on their minds. Laudon got the notion that Connecticut Tories were probably carrying all their valuables with them. So later that night, after the town's Christmas festivities died down, he and his little gang of thugs got together, dressed up like Indians, and snuck up to the Loyalist camp on Benner's Mountain. They slaughtered the whole lot of them in their sleep. No gold or silver, of course, but it was a little too late to apologize. The good, God-fearing scions of Biglersville's founders buried them all in shallow graves and then burned their wagons. The lights up there are ghost fires from the wagons burning all those years ago."

Harley just stood there. "I have nevah heard that tale, and my family were foundin' fathers."

The old man just kept staring into the beer. "Laudon's grand-sons were at the mill when it exploded and wiped out the entire Laudon line. And when Frenchy Bergeron went mad and killed his family with an ax, the victims included his moth-er, who, if I recall, was a Peaslee, another line of founders that ended that night."

Harley looked at him. "So you reckon these ghost lights up theah kill off the descendants of the founding fathers?"

The old man sipped his beer. "Me? I think the lights are the other Loyalists trying to warn the town from beyond the grave that the witch is among the living again. Or it could be a coincidence that the lights appear when one of the original bloodlines dies tragically. Biglersville never really grew. Quite a few folks are related to founding fathers."

Harley shook his head. "Not really. My old man's been working on a book for the town's two-hundred-and-fiftieth anniversary. Most folks can only trace theah family trees back to the Revolutionary War, when veterans got land grants for theah service. There aren't a lot of folks left that can claim to be descended from a foundin' fathah."

Surprisingly, the old man looked pleased with that infor-mation. "Maybe the witch is more efficient than she thought."

Not sure what to make of the statement, Harley picked up another glass to wipe. "So Withahs, tell me about this witch. You seem to know an awful lot about her."

Old Man Withers put his beer down. "Well, the story I've been told is that her name is Patience Fallow. Her grand-mother was Alice Young of Windsor, Connecticut, the first woman hanged as a witch in New England—forty-five years before the Salem Witch Trials. Patience was a harmless old lady, who only used her gifts to help her friends. I guess we'd call her a white witch these days. None of that possessing children or killing cattle nonsense you saw up in Salem. She was one of the Loyalists heading to up to Quebec when Biglersville's upstanding citizens attacked. Patience watched her grandchildren killed before her eyes, and, well, the only thing harder to kill than a witch is an angry witch."

Old Man Withers glanced toward the door and held up a finger to pause the conversation. In the distance, there was a low rumbling that echoed through the night. Harley rushed to the door. The ghost lights still blazed in the night, but now a massive cloud of dust was rising from the mountain, hiding the Christmas full moon as dust roiled across the sky.

Harley just stared. "What the hell just happened?"

Old Man Withers hadn't left his stool. "Sure sounded like a landslide to me. I hope that hunting party is okay. Say, Frankie Fenmore's kin were founding fathers, too, weren't they?"

Harley watched as police lights went tearing up the road. Somehow he knew what they'd find on the old mountain road.

Withers joined him at the window. "The devil lights are still burning. I guess old Patience isn't quite finished tonight."

Old Man Withers just stood at the door, looking outside almost expectantly. A fire truck went racing by but in the opposite direction. Harley stepped outside and looked up the street. He came back in shaking his head.

"Looks like a fire downtown, maybe around Town Hall," Harley paused. "Or is it the library?"

Old Man Withers shook his head. "What an odd coincidence that we were just talking about the library." He limped back to the bar. Harley watched. In the mirror behind the bar, Withers had an oddly smug look on his face.

Harley went back to the bar. He felt he was forgetting something.

Old Man Withers finished his beer. "Patience is having a busy night. I bet she sleeps for another ten years after this."

"Withas, why are you talking like that?" Harley was still

trying to shake the feeling he'd forgotten something. "It's like you know her."

"I guess I've heard the story so often, I feel like I know her." The old man smiled and looked back out the window as the flashing lights of another fire truck sped past, the siren fading into the darkness.

Harley poured himself a shot, something he rarely did on the clock. "So Withahs, anything else about this witch I should know?"

Withers just stared out the window. "I don't think so. Just the ghost of an angry old witch looking for revenge centuries after this town killed her and everyone she loved. It's not like she can make libraries catch fire, trigger landslides, or possess old men."

Harley paused in the middle of pouring a second shot. He knew what was bothering him. "Withahs, you have a Yankee accent thickah than mine. When did you lose it?"

Withers just stared at the window. "Oops. Tis more difficult to maintain an accent than thee might imagine."

Harley grabbed the shotgun out from under the bar. "Who the hell are you?"

Old Man Withers cocked his head but never stopped gazing out the window. "I told you—just the ghost of an angry old witch looking for revenge."

Harley pulled the trigger. The shot ripped through Old Man Withers. The old man wordlessly collapsed on the floor. There was no blood, and Withers suddenly looked like he'd been dead for days. A shimmering cloud left the body. Harley could only watch in horror as the cloud coalesced into the translucent form of an old woman in colonial garb. The form solidified as it took a step forward.

"Thomas Harley, thou art a fool to think a mere musket could stop the vengeance of the righteous aggrieved." The old woman walked over to the door and locked it, then flipped the sign to CLOSED. Almost as an afterthought, she stopped to unplug the Christmas lights framing the window. Only then did she turn with a smug, little smile on her face.

"Thomas, thee are last of the murderous Harleys. Thy ill-begotten ancestor Caleb Harley was the man who killed my darling grandchildren. Thy ancestor was the first to feel my wrath. Allow me to show thee how slowly and painfully thy great grandfather died. Thou shan't enjoy it, but I most assuredly shall."

On Benner's Mountain, the lights began to slowly fade even as distant shrieks echoed through the woods.

The Winter Coat
Dan Foley

Bernie was cold, really cold. He had survived the first few weeks of winter without his coat by huddling around burning 55-gallon drums filled with scrap wood during the day and sleeping next to steam vents during the night. Now there was a storm coming, with a foot or more of snow predicted. People had been talking about it all day. Most of them were excited because it would finally be a white Christmas—the first one in years.

Bernie wasn't happy about it. If he couldn't find his coat today, he was going to have to sleep in the shelter tonight. Bernie hated the shelter. The beds were too small, people stole his stuff, and it smelled wrong. That was the part he hated the worst. Bernie didn't like things that smelled wrong.

Last spring he had left his coat—a big, long, old wool coat he had found at the Good Will—at a dry cleaner because the sign in the window said "Free Storage." Billy Turner said that it meant they would keep his coat for him during the summer, when he didn't need it, and give it back to him in the winter. And they would do it for free. He really didn't want to leave it, but Billy had reminded him he had lost the last one because, when summer came, he had hidden it somewhere and then forgotten where it was. Bernie finally left it because he didn't want to lose this one, too. It fit, and it smelled right.

It had been a good idea at the time, but now he couldn't find the place where he had left it. Billy would know where it was, but Billy was dead. Some kids had pissed on him and set him on fire to get his wine. And now he needed that coat, really needed it, and he couldn't find it. He had been looking for it for weeks, presenting the silly little tag they had given him in every dry cleaner in the city trying to find it. Was it his fault that he couldn't remember where he had left it? No. They were all the same, weren't they? But they all said he had to get it from the same cleaner he left it with. He couldn't understand why they just wouldn't just give it to him. And now… Now that he had found the right place, the coat they wanted to give him wasn't his.

"This is not my coat," Bernie insisted.

"It has to be," the clerk replied, just as insistent. "It's the right tag. Check the numbers. It's the right size—fifty-six, extra long—and the right color, dark gray. Look, it's even got your name sewn in the back."

Bernie looked. Yes, it was his name all right, Bernie Black, right there on the collar. Right were Sister Agnes had sewn it on his coat. But this one wasn't his. This one was somebody else's.

"This isn't my coat," he told the clerk one more time.

"Look, I'm going to get the manager," the clerk said, and left him standing at the counter.

While he was gone, Bernie stared out the window at the falling snow. There was an inch on the ground already, and it didn't look like it was going to stop. People were hurrying by, but a few stopped to drop a few coins or a bill in the red Salvation Army kettle with the costumed Santa ringing his bell. Those same people would turn their eyes to the ground and hurry by if Bernie asked for a handout. Oh, sure, one or two might give him something, but nothing like the red kettle was getting.

"Is there a problem, sir? Sir? Sir? Sir, is there a problem?"

"What?" Bernie said when the manager finally managed to get his attention.

"Is there a problem?" the man asked again, his impatience showing in his voice.

"This is not my coat," Bernie insisted again.

"Why don't you think it's your coat?" the manager asked, taking a different tack with the very large, very agitated man standing across the counter.

"It doesn't smell right," Bernie said. "My coat smells good. This coat smells like lighter fluid."

"Sir, the coats been cleaned. If you smell anything at all, it's cleaning solution. I guarantee, once you wear it for a few days, it will smell different."

Bernie noticed the clerk choking back a laugh. He knew the manager was making fun of him; he just didn't know how. A lot of people made fun of him, but there was nothing he could do about it.

Bernie looked closer at the coat. It was clean, so it could be his.

"Why did you clean my coat?" Bernie demanded. "I didn't want you to clean my coat. I just wanted you to keep it for the summer."

"Uh, Mister Black, I don't think you understand. We're a dry cleaner. That's what we do when you leave something here. We clean it."

"Well, I didn't want it cleaned," Bernie yelled. "I just wanted you to keep it for me."

"I'm sorry, sir, but you do agree this is your coat? Right?"

"I guess," Bernie finally agreed, and slipped the coat on. It was a loose fit, even over his sweatshirt and two sweaters, but that's what he liked about it. It was big.

"That will be twenty dollars, sir," the clerk said as Bernie turned to leave.

"What?" Bernie asked.

"Twenty dollars, sir, for the cleaning and the repairs."

"The sign said free," Bernie said, confused that they were asking him for money. He didn't have any money.

"The storage is free. The cleaning and repairs were twenty dollars," the clerk tried to explain.

"No," Bernie insisted again. "The sign said free."

The clerk started to argue with him, but the manager stopped him. "Let him go. Just get him out of the store," he whispered. To Bernie, he said, "It's all right sir. Consider it a Christmas present from me to you."

Bernie nodded but didn't answer. He just left with the coat.

Outside, when Bernie shoved his hands into the coat's pockets, panic clutched at his heart. Inside, both pockets were whole. The right one wasn't supposed to be whole; it was supposed to be ripped. He was supposed to be able to put his hand between the outside and the liner. If the pocket wasn't ripped, where was he going to keep his treasures?

With an urgency born of fear, Bernie crossed the street and huddled in a doorway. Sheltered from the snow, he shrugged the coat off and ripped the inside out of the right-hand pocket, then plunged his hand into the coat's recesses. After a minute of frantic searching, he found something that felt right. Holding his breath in case it wasn't what he was looking for, he extracted a desiccated human finger from its hiding place. He didn't remember where it came from, but he had had it for as long as he could remember. Now he knew for sure this was his coat, but that still didn't mean he could wear it. It still didn't smell right. To ease his mind, he held the finger to his nose and smelled it. His spirits fell even further. It was ruined. It didn't smell like his finger; this one smelled like chemicals.

Bernie was huddled in the doorway, his mood darkening when the lights went out in the dry cleaner. The Salvation Army Santa was long gone, along with everyone else trying to get out of the storm. A second later, the manager emerged. He quickly locked the front door, stepped onto the sidewalk, turned left, and walked off into the snow. Without knowing why — Bernie did most things without knowing why — he left his doorway and followed the man.

The manager walked through the falling snow, shoulders hunched and head tucked into his collar, trying to keep his head as dry as he could without a hat. Bernie had no such compunctions; snow piled up on his head and shoulders and the coat slung over his arm. He also had no concept of stealth and was soon following no more than five feet behind the manager. If it hadn't been for the sound-deadening snow, the man would surely have noticed him.

Bernie followed the man for three blocks. He didn't know why, he just did. Somewhere along the route, it dawned on him that if the manager was responsible for making his coat smell wrong, he should be the one to make it smell right again. He was about to grab the man's shoulder to tell him that when the manager turned and walked up the steps of an apartment building, an old brownstone. Bernie followed.

With his head scrunched into his collar like it was, the man never noticed that Bernie was behind him until he followed him right into his apartment.

"What the hell are you doing here?" the manager demanded after he got over his initial fright at seeing Bernie standing in his door.

"I want you to fix my coat," Bernie said, following the manager into the room. "I want you to make it smell right."

"Get out of here or I'll call the police," the man threatened.

"No," Bernie said, and pushed the man away from the telephone. Bernie didn't like police, and he hated jail more than he hated the shelter. In jail, they hurt him.

Failing to reach the phone, the man bolted toward the door. Bernie got there first, slammed it shut, and pushed the man back into the apartment.

"Make my coat smell right," Bernie insisted, holding the coat out to the man.

"Get the fuck out of my apartment, you retard," the manager told him, getting bolder. "No one pushes me around in my own apartment."

When Bernie ignored his demands, the man went to the kitchen area and got a large knife out of a kitchen drawer.

"Get out now," the man demanded, "or you'll be sorry."

Bernie ignored the knife and thrust the coat at the man. "Make my coat smell right," he demanded, anger starting to replace the frustration in his voice.

Cut off from the door and faced with a large, angry retard, the manager panicked and lunged at Bernie with the knife. He managed to slice into Bernie's hand with his first thrust. His second try barely missed, slipping by less than a quarter of an inch from Bernie's face.

As soon as the knife cut into his flesh, Bernie was a different man. His body took over. Instincts learned in a different time, in a more dangerous place, controlled his movements. He ignored the pain, feinted left, and moved right to avoid the blade. When the knife whistled by him, he struck out and smashed the heel of his hand into the man's nose, crushing it. Stunned, the manager stepped back but didn't drop the knife. Bernie's next blow, a slashing karate chop, caught him in the throat, and he dropped to the floor like someone had pulled a rug out from under him. Bernie watched curiously as the man thrashed about like a fish out of water until he died, his windpipe crushed by Bernie's blow.

"Uh, oh... Uh, oh," Bernie said, looking at the man. He was in trouble now. No time to think about that, though; first, he had to take care of his hand.

The first thing he did was wrap the coat around it. When that didn't stop the bleeding, he wrapped it in a dishtowel.

With his hand wrapped in the towel, Bernie turned his attention to the body on the floor. He really didn't want to deal with it, so he covered it with his coat. A single hand stuck out from the bottom, but Bernie ignored it. Once the body was out of sight, he could pretend it wasn't there. But now Bernie had another problem: his coat was gone again, and it was still snowing. Where was he going to spend the night? He fell asleep on the couch worrying about it.

The morning sun filtering through the unshaded living room windows woke Bernie from a dreamless sleep. He didn't know where he was, but that didn't bother him. He often woke up not knowing where he was.

Bernie found the bathroom, relieved himself, and rummaged through the medicine cabinet looking for drugs or anything else he might find. The best he came up with was a new bottle of aspirin and a half-full one of ibuprofen. He wasn't sure which was best, so he took two of each for the pain in his hand.

His next trip was to the refrigerator. On his way there, he passed his coat, which was lying in a pile on the floor. He knew what was under it, but if he couldn't see it, it wasn't really there. But when he looked down, he saw the hand, a telltale reminder of what was hidden there.

Bernie didn't want to see the hand sticking out from under the coat, but he couldn't bring himself to lift the coat and push it under. If he did, he might see what was hiding there. So instead, he lopped it off with a cleaver he found in one of the drawers. It took three good whacks, but he finally managed to cut through the bone and tendons and separate it from the body. Then it was easy to just kick it under the coat.

Bernie sat at the window watching the snow fall. He didn't know it, but it was the worst blizzard the city had seen in years. Fourteen inches had already fallen, and another eight to twelve was expected before it would stop early the next morning. As a result, the entire city was shut down.

Bernie stayed in the apartment for two days, listening to Christmas carols on the radio. On the morning of the third day, the phone rang. Bernie didn't answer it because it wasn't his. After the fourth ring, however, the machine picked up.

"Hello, this is Robert. I'm not in. Leave a message."

"Hey, Rob, where are you. I'm at the store, and it's closed. Are you okay?" a disembodied voice announced to the room.

After the caller hung up, Bernie looked at the coat piled on the floor. He couldn't ignore it anymore. Now the thing under there had a name. Now it was real. Now Bernie was going to have to leave. This was not a good thing. And as much as he didn't want to, he was going to have to take the coat. The coat that didn't smell right.

When Bernie lifted the coat off the thing hidden under there, he refused to give it a name even though he knew it was Robert, the unmistakable odor of a body in the early stages of decay greeted him. He sat on his haunches, breathing it in, reliving the memories hidden in its fragrance. It reminded him of places long ago and far away. Places where he fit in. Places where he was happy.

Except for the dried blood from Bernie's cut, the coat didn't look any different. It wasn't until he was outside and tried to put his hands in the pockets to protect them from the cold that Bernie realized he was holding the severed hand of the manager. He raised it to his face and carefully sniffed at it.

Not exactly right, but close, he thought as he stuffed it into the lining of the coat. Perhaps in a few days it would be better. It seemed the manager had given him more than the coat for Christmas.

When he passed the Salvation Army Santa ringing his bell on the next corner, Bernie dropped the ruined, chemical-smelling finger into the red donation kettle.

A CHRISTMAS STORY

Kurt Newton

Snow.

Yup, there has to be snow. Christmas just wouldn't be Christmas without it.

What else?

Music.

Yes, music. Jingle jangle. Happy music. Soft, snow falling music. Crooning, caroling, sleigh ride music. Yesiree. Gotta have it.

What else?

Food.

You got that right. Eats. Ginger this and ginger that. Hot apple cider. Cookies, pies, candy canes. Yummy yum yum.

Okay, what else?

Presents.

Uh-huh. Nice shiny presents. Big colorful presents. Ribbons and bows and stacks upon stacks of credit card charge after credit card charge, and overcharge, and can't pay this month's oil bill charge... or the light bill... or the car payment… or the… you name it! But there are presents. Boy, are there presents. "For the last time" presents. And "Didn't I tell you not to spend all our fucking money" presents. And "Since when is it okay to mouth off to me when all you do is sit around and complain about how I never take you anywhere or buy you anything when you know damn well I work all day and we still don't have a pot to piss in you ungrateful bitch" presents.

Okay, what else?

Blood.

Now we're talking. Bloodshot eyes. Bloody lips. Bloody knuckles. The blood splatter on the window curtains from the double-barrel shotgun blasts. Not to mention the blood trail leading from the Christmas tree out the back door, through the snow, to the backyard shed, red as cranberry sauce on a bed of mashed potatoes.

Okay, what else?

Santa Claus.

Of course. The old fat bastard himself. Ho, ho, ho, work one day a year lazy-assed heart attack waiting to happen, filling everyone's heads with presents, nice shiny presents, big, colorful, blood-soaked presents. Fucking Santa.

And since when does Fucking Santa come knocking on the front door demanding to be let in?

And since when does Fucking Santa drive a sleigh with red and blue flashing lights? I mean, c'mon. Really? Fuck me.

Fucking Santa needs to learn a thing or two about patience. Fucking Santa needs to learn to keep his fucking nose out of other people's fucking business. Guess I'm going to have to teach that fat fucker a lesson!

Here I come, you fucking overgrown elf. Hope you like both barrels between those rosy fucking cheeks of yours…

Family Heirloom
Karen Thrower

artha sat on the couch, her second glass of wine in her hand. The Christmas lights on the tree reflected on the half-empty glass. She wasn't sure she'd be up to decorating this year, not after her daughter, Sophie, died. But her husband, Joseph, insisted it would help them remember their little girl. Except...all Martha thought about was how much Sophie seemed to hate Christmas. Ever since she was tiny, she fussed and cried and had nightmares the entire month of December. Joseph said she'd grow out of it, but year after year it was clear Sophie was a rare kid who hated Christmas.

She turned nine in July, but the cancer had spread so fast, there was nothing they could do. Martha remembered sitting on the hospital bed, holding Sophie's hand. She thought about how brave her daughter was; she didn't seem scared at all. Relieved, almost. Martha felt morbid when she thought about it. But she had never been that close to death; it might have indeed been a relief.

Joseph walked back into the living room and put candy canes on the tree. "Guess we're going to have to eat them ourselves this year," he said.

Martha rolled her eyes. They ate them every year. Sophie wouldn't go near the tree, even to get candy. "You can have them." She got up and sipped her wine as she walked down the hall. As she passed Sophie's room, she noticed something red on her bookshelf. She stopped and saw that old elf doll that had belonged to Joseph when he was a kid. If there was one thing Sophie hated about the Christmas season, it was that elf. She'd beg and scream for her dad to put it away, but he never did. As usual, he'd ignore her tantrums and say she'd grow out of it instead of heeding her wishes. The truth was, Martha didn't like it either, but it was part of her husband's childhood, so she put up with it. Its plastic face was creepy and cracked. The way the paint chipped made the smile turn into a grimace. Plus, it smelled funky. Like dirt and sweat. Joseph said it smelled that way was because it was old, but Martha still had dolls from when she was young, and they didn't stink! Martha tried washing it once, using special soap so the red outfit wouldn't turn pink, but nothing worked.

Martha walked into Sophie's room and picked it up. "Ugh." She couldn't hold in her shudder at how squishy the body felt in her hand. She walked back into the living room and held the doll out to her husband. "Sophie hated this, why did you put it in her room?"

He shook his head and went back to putting candy canes on the tree. "She didn't hate it," he said, dismissing her concerns. "She just wasn't used to it."

Martha scoffed. "You're forgetting the time you caught her trying to cut it in half with my sewing sheers."

"Bah!" He waved her off. "She was four. Four-year-old's do that."

"Yeah, to their hair. Not dolls!" She threw it at him. "Keep it out of her room." Martha stomped back to the master bedroom and slammed the door. She couldn't understand her husband's behavior. If he was in some sort of denial over their daughter's death, she didn't know how to deal with it. Two weeks after they put Sophie in the family plot, he mentioned having another kid. She had glared at him and walked out of the room. How dare he try to replace their little girl like that—and so soon! Martha downed the rest of the wine and lay on the bed. At least in her dreams she got to see Sophie.

❄ ❄ ❄

Martha woke with a start. The clock read 3:00 a.m., and she realized she was still wearing her clothes from the day before. Without looking, she knew Joseph was asleep next to her. His snores were like a chainsaw in her ear. He never had trouble sleeping, but she still needed wine. She slipped out of bed and managed to find a nightgown in the dark. When she opened the door into the hallway, she looked across the hall and once again saw the creepy elf in Sophie's room. She growled and hurried into the room.

"God damn it, Joseph, what the hell!" She again snatched up the toy and stomped into the living room. The lights on the tree were still on, as was their custom, and she threw the elf at the tree. It landed about halfway up, and its arm got tangled in the lights. "If he moves that thing again, I'm throwing it away!" She stomped back to the bathroom and changed into her nightgown. It took a minute because, in her anger, she kept getting tangled up in it. When she was finally dressed, she opened the door and walked back to her room. She reached for the door handle but paused. She didn't feel like sleeping next to her husband when he snored; she could hear him just standing in the hallway. So, she grabbed a blanket from the hall closet and went back into the living room. She turned off the lights on the tree and settled onto the couch. *At least I won't have to listen to Joseph snoring*, she thought, and closed her eyes.

❄ ❄ ❄

The smell of coffee woke her, and Martha remembered she slept on the couch the night before. She opened her eyes and gasped when she saw the creepy elf on the couch, staring at her.

She gasped and sat up. "Joseph, what the hell?"

"What the hell what?" he called from the kitchen.

She knocked the elf on the floor and flung off the blanket. "Why did you put that damn thing on the couch? It scared the hell out of me." She walked into the kitchen. Joseph was at the little table in the breakfast nook. He was still holding up the newspaper, so he definitely wasn't paying attention. Martha smashed the paper against the table.

"Martha, what the hell?"

"Why did you put that creepy elf on the damn couch? It scared the shit out of me!"

"I didn't move it! It was there when I woke up, jeez." He picked up the paper and snapped it out, hoping to put it back to its original shape, but Martha had smashed it good, so it fell forward like a limp noodle into his coffee. "Damn it! Thanks a lot!"

"You're fucking welcome, ass." She stomped to the bedroom and slammed the door. They knew losing a child would be hard, but she hated fighting and snipping at Joseph so much. She had hoped the Christmas season would bring them together, but it was obvious that gross elf was going to get in the way.

❄ ❄ ❄

Three days later, Martha was walking to the trash, the elf in one hand, her sewing sheers in the other. Joseph wouldn't stop moving the damn thing and scaring her. She found it on top of the toilet when she got out of the shower. She had no idea how Joseph pulled that one off, especially since he was at work. He even put the little bastard in her car, which, of course, she didn't notice until she was on her way home from the grocery store. Looking in the rear-view mirror and seeing that little shit buckled up in the back was the worst. It had scared her so badly, she'd almost had a wreck. She figured Joseph wasn't going to stop or admit to what he was doing, so she decided to take a page out of Sophie's book and get rid of it. She held the doll over the trash and, with one satisfying snip, cut the elf in half. The two halves fell into the trash, and she covered it with a stack of newspapers.

"That's that, you creepy little asshole." As she turned around, a high-pitched scream filled the air, making Martha jerk in shock. She dropped the sewing sheers and started looking around, her eyes wide and her heart in her throat.

"You stupid bitch! You cut me in half!"

Martha gasped and looked down. *No, it can't be she thought.*

"Get me out of the trash, you dumb bitch! Sew me back up!"

She looked into the trash and saw the stack of papers moving around. The voice was wailing and growling, and Martha screamed as she saw a little white-gloved hand move from under the paper.

"Get me out of here!"

Martha screamed again, and Joseph came running into the kitchen.

"What, what?" He stopped when he saw the elf's arms sticking out from under the papers. "Are these..." He lifted the papers out of the trash. "You didn't! How —"

But she didn't let him finish. She grabbed his arm. "That fucking elf is talking!" she screamed, pointing at the elf. "Kill it!"

Joseph jerked his arm away free and looked at her like she was insane. "Martha, think about what you're saying."

"Listen to the bitch!"

The words came floating out of the bin, and the color drained from Joseph's face. He looked down and saw the top part of the elf pulling itself over to its legs.

"What the hell?" He got closer, and the elf took advantage. The top half of the doll sprung out of the bin and wrapped its little arms around Joseph's face. He screamed and started running around the kitchen, his arms flailing around his head instead of trying to pull off the elf.

"Joseph, stop it!" Her words seemed to help because he finally stopped running. He pulled the elf from his face and held it at arm's length.

"What the hell is going on?" he said.

"Where is Sophie?" the elf asked. His voice was low and disturbing. It didn't help that the stuffing inside the doll was red and kept randomly falling out onto the floor.

"S-Sophie? How do you know Sophie?" Joseph asked.

The elf hit his head on Joseph's hand. "You're kidding, right? You put me in her room every Christmas since she was born. Why the hell wouldn't I know her?"

"But...you're a doll!" Joseph yelled and dropped the elf's torso. The head smacked against the kitchen floor, and he and Martha both backed away. They watched it crawl over to the trash and point up at its legs, now dangling over the edge.

"Sew me back together and take me to Sophie!"

Joseph gasped and scooped up the torso and threw it in the bin with its legs. He picked up the flaps of the trash bag and tied it closed. As he ran outside, he could hear the elf screaming obscenities at him. He dumped the bag into the garbage can outside. Martha followed behind and piled on a few stray bricks for good measure. They stood still and could hear the elf growling and thumping inside, trying to escape.

"Do you think it'll get out?" Joseph asked.

Martha shrugged. "I hope not." They waited until the noises stopped before they walked back inside. Joseph shut the door to the garage, and Martha whacked his arm. "I *told* you there was a reason Sophie didn't like Christmas! I bet that thing tortured her for years!"

He turned, his hands on his hips. "Impossible! She would have said something!"

"Sure about that? I'd ask her every year what was wrong, why she hated Christmas, but I couldn't get anything out of her. I bet she didn't think we'd believe her is she said that little elf shit was real."

Joseph sank to the kitchen floor, his back against the garage door. "That never happened when I was a kid. I would have remembered!"

"Or you blocked it out." Martha sighed and got on the floor next to him. "I can't believe you weren't the one moving it. I'm so creeped out right now." She rubbed her arms and felt goosebumps. "It can't get out, right?"

Joseph tapped his fingers rapidly on the linoleum floor as he shook his head. "There's no way."

"Good. You don't think we should get it out and maybe throw it in the fireplace?"

"Nah, it can't get out. The trash man will come in the morning and take it away. We'll never have to see it again."

"Good." Martha shuddered again and was glad it was over.

✳ ✳ ✳

"Oh moooom!"

Martha's ear twitched, which is what woke her. It had been months since she'd heard anyone call her mom, and she felt her heart race. Her eyes flew open, and she saw the elf holding a knife to Joseph's throat. He head was on his pillow, and he was awake. His eyes were wide, and Martha could see him shaking a bit. She gasped and sat up, pulling the covers up to her chin. It looked like the psychotic little elf had sewn itself together using bits of noodle and bones from a chicken.

"I want Sophie!" it yelled and pressed the knife against Joseph's skin.

"You can't have her! She's dead!" Martha yelled, tears streaming down her cheeks. "She's dead, all right, she died this summer! So just leave us alone!"

"No! I want Sophie. Take me to her now!"

Martha shook her head. "I can't!"

The doll put the tip of the knife against Joseph's throat. "I. Want. Sophie!" The elf pricked Joseph's neck, causing him to gasp. "Put me with her."

Martha shook her head. "We can't. She's buried, gone. Just leave us alone! Find another family please."

"Put me with Sophie!"

"No!"

Joseph yelled and stretched his neck. "Okay, okay!"

Martha gasped. "Excuse me?"

The elf giggled maniacally while crawling down to Joseph's lap, the big knife still in its hands

"Let's go! Here I come, Sophie!"

"Joseph, you can't seriously be considering this!" she yelled at him as Joseph got out of bed. She gasped as she felt something fly by her face, and the elf laughed. She turned and saw the knife embedded deep into the wall next to her head.

"Oh, he's considering it," the elf giggled. "'Cause he's a good boy, aren't you, Joseph?"

Martha was glad he didn't answer, but watching him put on a coat to go dig up their baby girl made her wonder if he'd gone insane.

✳ ✳ ✳

Martha stood at the edge of her daughter's grave, shivering in her coat and nightgown. Joseph's head was the only thing visible above ground now. It was the first time in years she wished they didn't live in Florida. If the ground were frozen, they wouldn't be at the mercy of this possessed toy. She tried hard not to watch it dance around the grave, holding another knife from the kitchen and flopping around like it was being worried at by a dog; it was disturbing. Chicken bones and noodles don't make the most solid sewing materials.

A *thunk* made her ears twitch, and Joseph heaved himself out of the hole. "There, now what?" He was exhausted and covered in dirt.

The elf giggled and looked down into the hole. "Ooh, there she is!" It dropped the knife, and Joseph quickly picked it up as the elf leaped into the hole. It landed with a light *thud* on the casket, and Martha heard a loud creak.

"What the hell are you doing?" Joseph yelled at the little elf. "Get out of there!"

"No!" it screeched, and there was another *thump*.

"It...it got in there with her," Joseph said.

Martha could hardly believe she heard those words. "Over my dead body." She jumped into the hole and landed on top of the casket. "I don't care if it kills me. I won't make Sophie suffer that thing a moment longer!

"No, Martha don't, let's just go," he pleaded with her, but

she ignored him.

"That thing won't get—" She opened the lid, and she started choking on her words.

"What? What is it?" Joseph ran to the other side of the hole and looked down. He saw the evil little elf snuggled under Sophia's decaying arm, like it had been there all along.

"Disgusting piece of shit," Martha whispered.

"Here, get out of that hole." Joseph reached down, and she heaved herself back onto the ground. They stood there, looking at the decomposing body of their daughter, which was now at the mercy of an insane, possessed toy.

"We can't let that thing have her," she said.

Joseph sighed. "What else can we do? We're not exactly equipped to handle something like that."

Martha looked around and saw a small excavator by the tree line about fifty feet away. Something popped into her head, something she'd never do if it weren't for this shitty little elf. She stomped over to the yellow digger and wrenched open the door. Behind the seat was a red gas can, and as she picked it up, the liquid inside sloshed. *Good*, she thought and started rifling through the cab's multiple compartments. Finally, hidden over the driver's seat in the sun flap was a pack of cigarettes and a book of matches. She snatched them up and stomped back to Sophie's grave.

"Whoa, Martha, what are you doing?" Joseph held up his hands, but there was nothing that spineless man could do to stop her.

"Going to give her peace." She shouldered her way past him and poured the diesel over Sophie and the evil elf. The nasty doll opened its eyes as she lit the match with a flick of her thumb.

"You dumb bitch. Don't even—"

She didn't let him finish; she dropped the lit match into

the coffin. It screamed as the fire burned its red clothes and its face melted from the heat.

"Now you won't have to spend eternity with that thing, baby," she whispered to herself.

"Martha, what the hell!" Joseph was staring at the fire. "That's our daughter!"

"And now she'll be at peace." She reached into her coat pocket and felt the car keys. "No thanks to you." She started walking back to the car.

"No thanks to me? That thing was right. You are a crazy bitch!" Martha stopped and turned back to her husband. "You're burning our daughter!"

"Which we should have done in the first place! I didn't want to bury her where the worms and bugs would eat her! I wanted her cremated and with us!" She rushed at him. "But I let you have your way, but now? You just agreed with that evil thing that tortured our daughter so much she preferred to die than tell us about it. Go fuck yourself!" She shoved Joseph, and he staggered backward, almost falling into the grave. He could feel the heat at his back as he struggled to maintain his balance. She shoved him again, and this time he stepped backward and fell into the grave. He screamed and flailed, tried to get out of the hole, but the fire worked quickly. She watched his eyeballs and flesh melt as his screams grew weaker.

When there was no other sound except the crackling of the flames, Martha started filling in the grave; the smell of burnt skin and hair hung in the air but slowly dissipated. She didn't think it was fair that Joseph got to spend eternity with Sophie, but at least she'd have one parent with her.

When the hole was filled in, Martha walked over to a nearby grave and plucked a dying rose from a bouquet. She laid it on Sophie's grave and bit her quivering lip.

"Goodbye, baby. Mommy loves you."

GOING HOME

Alan Derosby

While many Mainers might be pleased when they woke up to see they'd have snow for Christmas, Charlie Wilkerson would not be. It made him unhappy. In fact, it ruined what had started out as a pleasant evening, making a drive home quite difficult. Charles had seen the first tiny flake fall on his window as he made his way to the party. By the time he was forced to leave, there were several inches on the ground. It was all about timing. Tonight, Charlie's timing was poor.

Charles Wilkerson was what most would call a functional alcoholic, and he had been for decades. The drinking rarely interfered with his professional life. Many of his coworkers knew Charlie liked to have a good time, but few understood how deep his problems were. At work, Charlie was as clean as a whistle, but once he got home, drinking was his life. From the moment he closed and locked his front door, Charlie had a drink in his hands. His drink of choice was almost always Crown Royal on ice. He would pour himself a small glass with three cubes of ice while he changed out of his work clothes. By the time he was back downstairs and making some dinner, the cup would have been filled a second time. With dinner, Charlie would usually have himself a tall glass of water but would always have his bottle handy in case he developed a hankering for a few shots. After dinner, Charles would retire to the living room, watching television with the bottle of whiskey and his glass on a folding table next to the recliner. At this point, depending on how much he had consumed, Charlie could take it with or without ice. Most times, the entire bottle would be empty by the end of the night. Any remains would be topped off with the new bottle the following evening.

Since the late 1960s, Charlie Wilkerson's employer had been, and still was, the Newport Tree Farm. The Newport Tree Farm was the largest nursery for trees in New England and provided Christmas trees for people all across the United States. In 2008, the Farm was on the news, supplying the ceremonial tree to Central Park. At the beginning of December, the farm would always ship their best tree to Washington for the presidential family. It was a little reminder to the President not to forget the people of "Vacationland." The company had opened back in the 1960s, selling not only real trees but an assortment of fake ones as well. It quickly became the largest nursery in Central Maine, employing close to fifty workers at the pick-it, cut-it, and buy-it tree farm. As quickly as they expanded, Newport Tree Farm was forced to hire workers to run the business year-round. In 1969, Charles Wilkerson, fresh out of Thomas College was hired as the first salesman to cover states that sat below Maine. It wasn't long before Charlie was traveling six days a week, sleeping in cheap motels on the outskirts of tiny Massachusetts' towns. Life was good for the tree farm, and life was good for Charlie Wilkerson.

Marriage, however, was never a successful venture for Charlie. He had been in and out of love numerous times, and on a few occasions, he'd taken it as far as the altar. Of course, in the end, the bottle had stepped in between him and a successful relationship. It always cost him, which resulted in Charlie still renting a run-down duplex apartment. It wasn't much, but it was always home to him. He viewed a house as an investment he couldn't keep up with. Why buy a house that might need repairs he was unwilling to spend the time or money to fix on his own. With an apartment, the owner of the building took care of all the repairs. More income could be put to where Charlie wanted it. In his case, it was directly to the Canadian distillery that made his whiskey.

The past year had been a very successful one, at least economically. Charlie had finally passed a five-figure income, made his last alimony payment, and was able to go on a vacation. It was funny how close it all came to his retirement. He had hoped to have fun well before, but spending was a problem. Even with all that money, he always seemed to be scraping by at the end of the month. It was all spent on things he didn't need, including his newest baby. Earlier in the year, as a present to himself, Charlie bought the one thing he always desired—a fancy car. He now was roaming the city in style in his 2012 Jaguar XK. It was a sleek royal blue with caramel seats. Everything was top-of-the-line, with all the bells and whistles, and his wallet certainly felt it. The final price was over forty thousand dollars, but it was his dream. Even when it came to barely making ends meet for the vehicle, Charlie thought the appearance of driving a Jag was too good to pass up. Now that particular purchase sat in the driveway of his low-end apartment each and every night. Charlie never thought about how the car would handle in the winter. The Jaguar wasn't meant for snowy weather. Still, he didn't care.

Every Christmas Eve, Newport Tree Farm would celebrate their annual Christmas Party for employees and their families. It had become quite a tradition. There was good food, good drink, and great prizes handed out. Three years ago, Charlie had won a thirty-two-inch, flat-screen television that currently sat in his bedroom apartment. This year the top prize was a week's vacation at a local ski resort, donated by the lodge itself in exchange for some Christmas cheer. The tree farm always took good care of its workers, and Charlie loved them for that. He also appreciated the free booze. On and off throughout the evening, he had refilled his red Solo cup with beer. He wasn't usually a beer man, but the choices were that or wine, and wine gave him a headache.

Charlie seemed to lose track of time. The beer quickly disappeared from his Solo cup. By his eleventh glass, Charlie was feeling pretty good and decided it was the perfect opportunity to talk with the new receptionist, Lisa Quirion. At first, Lisa was very nice, but she soon turned sour. The woman told him several times she was engaged, but that didn't stop Charlie's advances. When Lisa finally gave up and turned to leave, she was met with a hard slap to her behind. Her loud scream brought both owners and a few co-workers over to hustle Charlie out into the night air. The boss walked him out, yelling that Charlie better sober up before he got himself into more trouble. The door slammed behind him, leaving Charles Wilkerson standing alone on the front steps of the Newport Tree Farm, only his red cup and cloudy memories to remind him of the evening's events. He threw the empty container back toward the door and walked down the pathway to where his car was. At first, he couldn't find it. All the cars had been blanketed by several inches of snow. Only when he fumbled for his keys and hit the unlock button did he hear the signature beep and see the flashing brake lights, making it easy to find his car. When Charlie got to his Jaguar, he opened the door, forgetting to clean off the handle. A small clump of snow slipped inside, hitting the front seat. Charlie ignored it, instead leaning in to start his car while he cleaned the remaining snow off the vehicle. By the time he finished clearing off the snow, it was already piling up again. It was going to be one of those nights. Charlie just hoped the roads were plowed.

Charlie never once questioned if he was sober or not. On many nights, he'd driven drunk and had never been stopped. He attributed it to the fact that he was just a good driver and was always in control. No matter how much he drank, he always got behind the wheel. One of his three ex-wives had even divorced him over his constant drunk driving. She had left him, saying she wouldn't be a part of his life when he finally killed someone. Charlie told her that was unlikely, but she, like every other wife or girlfriend, came second fiddle to the bottle of whiskey. That was the way the world worked for him. He was happier that way.

The Jaguar slowly backed up the Farm's driveway, the tires rubbing up against snow that had piled behind it. If he hadn't been forced out, Charlie might have made the decision to leave his car here and call a cab. However, he didn't want to do that and took his chances on the slippery road. He'd just need to drive slowly tonight and take the highway. That was usually cleared before any of the side roads. Forgetting to put his seatbelt on, Charlie pulled out of the Newport Tree Farm parking lot and hit the road. He drove very slowly down the street, passing many houses filled with love during the holiday. Sometimes, Charlie wished he had that, but alas, no one cared to get together with him anymore. That was why he was attending a work party on Christmas Eve because no one in his family cared about him anymore.

For a moment, he never noticed he was veering off the road. When he did, Charlie quickly yanked his wheel to the left, taking out some stranger's mailbox. He let out a loud sigh, knowing he needed to be more focused. This time he unrolled his window. Maybe some fresh air would help keep him level-headed.

Charlie saw the highway sign and put his blinker on early. There was no need to draw attention to his driving, not in his present state. When he first sat in the car, he knew he was buzzed, but now he realized he was a bit more than buzzed. He was drunk. He stuck his head out the window, letting the cold air and snow hit his face. It woke him up briefly, but his head was swimming. He could always pull over on the inter-state rest stop and sleep for a while, but it was Christmas Eve. Plus, if he ran out of fuel, he would freeze to death. It was best to drive slow and get home. By highway, his apart-ment was a mere eight minutes away. Driving at a slower speed, he could be home within a half hour.

As soon as he pulled on to the highway, Charlie could see in the distance that someone was standing on the side of the road. With the snow continually flying in front of the wind-shield, it was hard to see who, or what, it was. Someone must be looking for a ride home for the holidays. Charlie briefly thought about picking up the person, being that good Samaritan on Christmas, but did he really want another person in the car with him given his condition? He was drunk. He didn't need someone calling the cops on him.

As thoughts ran through his head, Charlie felt his mind drift. He was extremely drunk. He leaned close to the dash-board, squinting at the radio and trying to turn it on. Perhaps some music would help clear his head. He smiled when Perry Como came on the radio, blasting the old Christmas classic "Home for the Holidays." Charlie loved that song, and he tapped his hand on the steering wheel in time to the music. It seemed to be working, but he still needed something in his belly. Remembering a bottle of water that sat on the back seat, Charlie took his eyes off the road to grab it. He never realized that his car was drifting off the road until it was too late. The tires slipped, and the Jaguar started to spin until it was facing a young man holding a sign. The hitchhiker dropped the sign but had no time to move out of the way. Everything went into slow motion. The stranger hit the hood of the Jaguar, flying over the car itself. The car continued, not slowing after impact, but continuing to spin, finally slamming into a ditch. Everything happened so fast that Charlie didn't have time to react. His thought process had become so slowed by alcohol that he had no chance to turn the wheel and avoid the hitchhiker. The car hit a road sign head on and spun off into a ditch, where it came to a dead stop. Everything went black.

Moments later, Charles Wilkerson came to. His head was pounding. He attempted to open his eyes, but he couldn't see. Something covered his view, and when he wiped his hand across his face, it came away with blood on his palm. His face must have hit the steering wheel. There was no blood anywhere else but on his hand.

Charlie looked out the rolled-down window and took in his surroundings. He was off the road and jammed into a large bank of snow. Off in the distance, lying near the side of the road, was the hitchhiker he hit. The man was not moving at all. Whatever sign he was holding had flown off, the impact sending it into the snow.

"Shit, shit, shit." Charlie slammed his hands against the steering wheel. He dug into his pockets to search for his phone. He needed to call the cops. Charlie held the phone out and looked at it. The highway was completely dark, except for his car. If he could get it out of the snow, he could drive off. No one would ever find out. For the first time this evening, he knew he was thinking clearly. Who would miss this guy? He obviously was alone. Without second-guessing the decision, Charlie put his car in reverse. It came out of the ditch quite easily, and before he knew it, the car was back on the highway. Before Charlie put it in drive, he looked in his rearview mirror. The man was still on the ground. He thought of getting out to at least check on him, but that was dangerous. If the injured man saw his face, then he'd be able to identify him. Charlie took the only option left to him; he drove away.

The car broke through the snow, the lights shining and cutting a limited path of visibility through the falling snow. Charlie kept his foot on the gas, not caring about the speed. He had already escaped death once. If the police stopped him after hitting a man on the highway and leaving the scene of the accident, speeding would be the least of his worries. Nothing around him mattered right now. The only thing he needed to do was to get miles away here. Then maybe he could pull over to look at the damage to his car; his brand new Jaguar that cost more than anything he owned. Because of his drinking, he ruined his car. There was no concern for the dead man in the snow.

After several miles, Charles pulled the car to the side of the road. He was fairly confident it was safe enough to check the damage. He hadn't seen any flashing lights, and no one had even driven by him since he took off. He had the highway to himself this Christmas Eve. And it was a good thing. That meant no one saw him.

For the first time since he turned onto the highway, Charlie noticed that the window was still rolled down. In the stress of the moment, he had driven off without giving it a second thought. Now, as he sat on the side of the highway, he realized how cold it was. He found the window button on the car door and pulled up on it. But nothing happened. The window was stuck. Charlie waited a moment and tried it again. Nothing. The window stayed down.

"Damn overseas electronics!" Charlie said as he banged his hand down against the door panel. The accident must have jarred something loose when the man hit the hood. Not only would he have to repair the physical damage to the exterior of the car, but he'd also have to pay to get the window fixed. That would cost a lot of money, and he didn't have that.

Attempting to check the damage to the car, Charlie leaned out the window. However, as soon as he did, the snow picked up, and the visibility dropped to zero percent. Charlie's head began to pound from the cold, so he pulled his head back inside the car. He waited a moment before pulling back onto the highway. If he sat here too long, someone would catch up with him and notice the front fender. This time Charlie cut down on his speed a bit, though his car seemed to be driving smoother than he imagined it would. His mind wandered but quickly refocused. For some reason, he did not feel all that drunk anymore, which made things like a broken window that much more annoying. Snow was flying into the car, getting the leather wet. Not that it mattered; he would have to sell the car.

After another forty-five minutes, Charlie cut his speed even more. He was making good time; weather conditions were still rough, though, and he had no idea where he was going. He thought for a moment before finally making a decision. At the next exit, he would turn the car around, head back north, and go home. This time he would take the side roads. He couldn't go back on the highway. The cops might be out looking for whoever hit the hitchhiker.

Charlie knew he needed to calm down; his heart was still racing from the accident. He turned up the radio, which for some reason worked, and began to hum. Perry Como's "Home for the Holidays" blared from the speakers. Though it was just a holiday song, it helped calm Charlie's nerves. He tapped his fingers on the steering wheel as he watched for the exit.

"Just in time," Charlie said. His bladder was full, and he needed to empty it before he pissed on his front seat. He put on his blinker, which surprisingly still worked, and slowed down. However, right when he went to turn, his wheels locked up and the car sped up, passing the exit.

"What the hell?" Charlie wondered aloud as his car pulled back onto the main drag. The repairs would be more costly than he thought, all because some asshole couldn't find a ride home. Not only would he need work on the body of the car, but he would also need an alignment as well.

Charlie started to whistle to himself before suddenly stopping. He was whistling the song on the radio, which happened to be "Home for the Holidays" by Perry Como. He had been on the road, driving away from the accident, for what seemed like two hours, and he realized now that this song had been playing continuously. He tried to turn the radio down, but it didn't work. The knob would turn, but the radio itself stayed as loud as before. He turned the power off, and for a brief minute, it was silent. As soon as he started focusing on the road again, the radio turned on again, and the same Christmas song started to play again. At first, he thought it was an issue with the radio station. Charlie took out his phone and tried to call the station. Everyone who was anyone knew that 94.9, WHOM, was home to Central Maine's soft rock. The station covered New England and parts of Canada. Starting the day after Thanksgiving, WHOM started to play Christmas music and would until December 26th. It had become a tradition that he cared little for. For some strange reason, though, he'd been feeling festive since leaving the party. But now the station was screwed up, and he was rapidly losing his holiday mood. Charlie dialed their toll-free number and waited as it rang. Finally, someone picked up on the other end, most likely the only person working there on a Christmas Eve. Back in the '80s, disc jockeys played the music. Now the stations had all gone digital, and songs could be changed with the flip of a switch.

"Hello? WHOM hotline. Merry Christmas, my loyal listener. How can I help you?" The man's voice sounded like any other radio DJ. It was deep, and he accentuated certain words. He also sounded like he'd been dipping into the holiday cheer at work.

"Yes. Charlie Wilkerson here. Riding home alone on a snowy highway. Your station seems to be broken. Can we change up the tunes?"

There was no response from the DJ. In the background, Charlie could hear music, so he knew someone was on the other end, but what was coming through his phone was "O Holy Night."

"Hello? WHOM? Anyone there? One more chance, chief," the DJ said, leaving out the cheery attitude.

"Yes, Charlie Wilkerson here. Hi. Can we switch the music?" Charlie yelled into his phone, now hoping for a response.

"Okay, buddy. Don't call if you aren't going to talk. Merry fuckin' Christmas, douchebag." The man on the other end of the line hung up.

Charlie looked at his phone. It seemed to be in working order, yet across the top of the display screen, it said: "Out of Service."

He saw another exit coming up. He dropped his phone on the passenger seat. He would find a pay phone and call from there. He suddenly felt alone and needed to talk to someone, even if it meant calling the police to report an accident.

When he went to turn off the highway, his car steered him

back onto the highway. "Jesus Christ," Charlie said as he felt the wheels yank back into place. He tried to turn the steering wheel again, but now it was stuck. The car picked up speed, and when Charlie looked at the dash, he saw he was doing well over a hundred miles an hour—and the fuel needle was still pointing to full. He'd been driving for at least two hours, and the fuel gauge hadn't moved at all.

Snow was blowing into the open window and covering the windshield. There was no visibility. Charlie couldn't see beyond his lights, which was odd since he could see the exit signs as they passed by. Nervousness passed quickly when a more pressing problem made itself known. His bladder was near to bursting, and he felt cramped. He tried to pull over to relieve himself but couldn't. Charlie looked in the back seat and saw the water bottle, but when he reached for it, the container rolled off the seat and onto the floor, well beyond his reach. Charlie quickly unbuttoned his pants to take the pressure off of his stomach, but that did little to relieve the pressure in his bladder. Sticking his head out the window, he hoped some cold air would take his mind off his current situation, but it didn't work. It only added to the pain. He could feel the pressure building as Perry Como voice sang louder and louder. Charlie joined in, singing as loud as possible, trying to block out the pain, but before he knew it, everything came together, and his bladder exploded. He cried out as hot piss soaked front of his pants and seeped into the seat. Charlie tried to sit up and readjust, wanting to stop the warm fluid from running down his legs, but the heavy snow blowing in through the window and the need to keep the car on the road severely restricted his ability to maneuver in the seat. He could do nothing as the urine turned to ice in his lap, against his leg, and on the seat.

The car began to speed up, the needle pushed to the limit.

Charlie pressed down on the brake, but it wouldn't budge. The radio got louder and louder as the car roared past exit after exit, faster and faster.

"STOP IT!!!! STOP IT!!!!" Charlie screamed as he banged his hands down on the dashboard. Perry Como sang louder and louder, telling people there was no place like home for the holidays.

"SHUT UP!!! I'M SORRY," Charlie yelled.

The car started to decelerate. The radio fell silent, and everything in front of the windshield cleared. The snow seemed to melt away on the road ahead. Charlie grabbed the door handle and tried to turn it, but it was still stuck. At least now anybody passing by could stop and help.

Charlie sat in total silence, thinking about his entire ordeal. His pants were completely dry, and if he hadn't felt his bladder empty itself all over him, he would doubt it had ever happened. The inside of the car was dry, and the fuel gauge slowly ticked down to empty. The car sputtered to a halt and shut off.

"Damn hitchhiker," Charlie said, not noticing he was crying. "I'm sorry that son of a bitch felt it was fine to stand on a snowy highway on Christmas Eve. If it weren't for that bastard, I'd be home right now. My holiday is ruined, and my fuckin' Jag is ruined."

No sooner did those words leave his mouth when the car started up again. It roared, and the fuel gauge shot up to full again. Snow poured in through the window, filling his car. Charlie fumbled for his seatbelt. Piles of fluffy, white snow blocked his attempts to lock himself in, and after a few revs of the engine, the car shot off like a rocket. The front windshield was covered with snow, making it impossible to see. The Jaguar jumped to sixty, then to a hundred, a hundred and twenty. Soon the needle had traveled as far as it could go, but that didn't stop the car from continuing to pick up speed. The dash broke, sending plastic flying into Charlie's face as the radio cranked up all the way, as loud as the speakers could handle. Perry Como's voice screamed out ways to get home for the holidays as the car sped down an empty highway. Smoke poured from beneath the hood, and a loud banging came from the engine.

Charlie screamed as the cut from his forehead opened up, and blood poured down, obstructing his view. He wiped his hands across his face just in time to see the snow move around the sides of the car to create a clear view. Directly in front of the car, a huge, green highway sign was situated in the center of the road. The exit coming up was numbered "666," and the destination was "END OF THE LINE." Without slowing down, the car slammed into the sign, sending Charlie through the windshield. Everything went black.

Charlie opened his eyes, completely in shock. He was still alive. He remembered flying out of the car, but when he was able to wipe the blood from his eyes, he realized he was back in his car. The driver's side window was rolled down and "Home for the Holidays" was playing on the radio. After clearing his head, he looked up and caught an awful view in his rearview mirror. He saw the hitchhiker lying in a snow bank, his sign upside down. Charlie began to cry as his car took off, snow falling and music blaring. His Christmas Eve was beginning yet again.

On Christmas morning, police were alerted to an accident just past the entrance ramp to the highway. When they arrived, they found two bodies. One was a young adult male between the ages of twenty-two and twenty-five. He'd been hit by a car and killed instantly. A sign that read, "Going Home for the Holidays. Need a ride" was stuck in the snow. In the ditch, curled around the highway sign, was a 2012 Jaguar

XK. The front hood was destroyed. The windshield was shattered, and the body—later identified as Charles Wilkerson, 63, of Portland Maine—was found about fifty yards from the car. He had also died instantly, the top part of his skull completely shorn off as he flew through the windshield. His legs were practically severed from his body, and large gashes ran the length of his thighs. Blood had soaked his pants and stained the snow, freezing the driver of the Jaguar to the ground. He had also died instantly.

This Christmas morning would be a difficult one for the police. They now had the job of ruining the holiday season for a family who would no longer celebrate Christmas the same way again. Drunk driving ended the life of one man, but for another, it created a never-ending drive on the Highway to Hell.

THE FEAST OF STEPHEN
Lee Glenwright

"*Good King Wenceslas looked out…*" Max was already within arm's reach of the door by the time he heard the voices, their reedy, collective warble carrying through from outside, as if to actually warn him away from the door handle, the only thing that separated him from what sounded like the usual tunefully inept rabble. They no doubt expected some sort of reward for their efforts, if the word "effort" could actually be used to describe what sounded like some blatant crime against singing. He had made the first mistake of approaching the source of the sound in the first place, its true nature disguised by the steady cooking noises that had surrounded him in the kitchen, blanketing him in a cocoon of false protection. His second error was to flick on the hallway light without a second thought, making it just that little bit too obvious that he wasn't away visiting non-existent relatives for the weekend after all. The number of times in the past when he had claimed to be heading off to spend some time at Uncle Henry's place had been so many now that he had almost managed to convince himself that the old sod really did exist somewhere outside of his imagination. As long as other people fell for it, that was the main thing. Good, old Uncle Henry had never let him down before, getting him out of all manner of social situations.

In his defense, he honestly hadn't heard them, to begin with. Their discordance had been masked by the simmering bubble of the heavy, cast iron pot on the stove, along with the slightly crackling hum of the oven, the light from within dancing with a feeble flicker that cast a warming ambiance across the small kitchen. He had never had the time for the season, spending it in his usual solitude, just the way he had always preferred. However, even he had to admit, albeit grudgingly, that the short days and long nights around the holiday time lent themselves to a certain something that he couldn't quite describe. Something that led even him to make just that little bit of an extra effort.

"Deep and crisp and even..."

By the time he had realized that the wooden barricade of his front door was all that separated him from the ragtag gaggle of singing beggars, it was too late. As though smeared with glue, his hand had refused to lift away from the door handle, pushing it down with an almost unconscious movement and simultaneously drawing the door in toward him, almost feeling the warmth rushing from behind him in its effort to escape.

"Gath'ring winter fu-u-el..."

He didn't even really see them, to begin with. Instead, his attention was drawn first by the snowfall, fat flakes of white that drifted down in random, cascading movements, falling to the ground where it lay in a blanket of white, the sort of which he thought had stopped existing once he had grown into adulthood. Of course, he knew that it still snowed sometimes, just not at Christmas, not anymore. He never had liked the snow. It was far too much a reminder of his childhood, of being pelted in the face by well-aimed ice missiles masquerading as harmless snowballs, of being scrubbed with a gloved handful of slush, freezing-cold rivulets of dirty water running down the inside of his coat collar and down his back as it melted against the bare warmth of his skin. The snow reminded him of the telling offs that he had gotten from one or both of his parents whenever he hadn't quite looked closely enough and had trodden in some partly frozen dog dirt as a result. So many memories, none of them filling him with any sense of the joy that was supposed to be in such abundance.

"Fa, la-la-la-la-la-laaa..."

They were still going, pausing only for a brief collective moment, singing replaced with a scattering of winter sniffles and clearing of throats before moving on to the next song in their amateur repertoire. Too late, he had answered them, and now, as much as he wanted to, he couldn't ignore them any longer. They were like the vampires and he was their latest victim, having invited them into his life without due thought.

"In Heav'n, bells are ringing..."

He looked across the assembled group as though trying to pick out a suspect from a particularly imposing line-up, unable to distinguish individual faces. The external light by the door had clicked on at their arrival, but it was one of those older energy-efficient things and always seemed to take about two hours before it was warmed up enough to actually be of any use. Rueful, he turned his head and glanced back over his shoulder. He had left the kitchen door open behind himself, just enough to see the lid on the pot, jiggling and rattling as the bubbling from within tried to push it away, thin wisps of steam and spittle-like spats of water forcing their way out. He really should have thought to turn the heat down. That would be an excuse, that would be a good excuse; *sorry, but I've taken ages to get my dinner ready, now it's simply going to be ruined*. His hand still holding the edge of the door actually tightened its grip, the palm pressing against the slightly rough wood as he thought of swinging it shut, of just blocking them out to go off and pester someone with far more in the way of the spirit of goodwill than himself. Then his heart sank as he spotted the vicar at the back of the group, his face almost obscured beneath a combination of woolen hat, brightly-colored scarf, and heavy beard that he liked to call "seasonal," everyone else preferring the term "scruffy."

Damn, if he shut them out, his would be the name on everyone's lips, you could pretty much guarantee it. *Max, yes, I know who you mean. He's that bloke that lives by himself, isn't he? I always thought he'd probably hate the time of year, but he actually chased off Reverend Martin and a group of carol singers, right before Christmas Eve. Miserable sod.* Of course, he wasn't *really* miserable, at least *he* didn't think so anyway. He didn't understand what was so gloom-and-doom about just enjoying your own company and liking a bit of peace and quiet. He wasn't one to be getting in other peoples' faces all the time, and he never had been either. Nor did he appreciate it when people went sticking their long noses into his business. But for some reason that he couldn't quite fathom, that translated nowadays as misery.

"Oh what fun it is to ride in a one-horse open sleigh-ayy..."

He hadn't even noticed that they had decided to try their luck with a third song, his lack of a favorable response failing to send them packing.

His stomach rumbled with hunger as he thought about the food just feet behind him, yet as good as a mile away. The small fizzing and popping noises were like someone shaking a can of cola then opening it up, but they still weren't enough to dull the mix of voices coming from in front of him. Unable to put it off any longer, he looked from person to person, men, women, and children alike, all standing together in what they honestly believed to be some sort of proclamation of joy, of thanks to some heavenly being that Max had given up believing in a long time ago. He remembered just when it was when the magic finally died, taking a large chunk of his innocence away with it. It had been just a few months after his twelfth birthday, that age when his parents finally felt comfortable enough, trusting enough, to leave him in the house unsupervised, just for an hour or two at a time.

❄ ❄ ❄

"Mind you don't get up to anything." His dad had spoken in that usual garrulous way of his that made it obvious that he believed his words carried enough weight to keep the boy from doing just that. A tall, round barrel of a character, Maxwell Senior was always—on the surface at least—a straightforward man who liked everyone to know that he was such. In contrast, his mum was a small, timid creature, someone who never seemed to raise her voice above a whisper, not that Max ever heard. Opposites, but at least what you saw was what you got, or so he once believed.

"We'll be a couple of hours mind, so behave yourself 'til we get back," his dad had said again, wrapping his favorite long, Tom Baker-style scarf twice around his neck before ushering his tiny, shrew-like wife in the direction of the doorway. Her head bowed as it always seemed to be, to the point where Max wondered whether she had a permanent crick, she mumbled something that might have been goodbye, but Max couldn't quite be sure.

Then the door had closed behind them, and they were gone. For a precious short while, the house and everything in it had belonged to him.

He had been planning it for several weeks, just waiting for the right time. Christmas was only a couple of weeks away, and although the cheap Woolworths plastic tree, baubles, and tinsel were yet to be strewn about the house, transforming it into a gaudy, multi-colored grotto, his Christmas list had long been scrawled in finger-smudged ballpoint and sent away to whoever it was who received such things.

Yes, he had been planning for weeks, just biding his time with the sort of patience that he rarely possessed, but that was still rare in someone of his age. He had just been waiting for the right time to put his budding theories to the test.

A couple of hours, they had said as they left, leaving him with plenty of time, plenty. They had only been gone less than ten minutes. All the same, he couldn't help but glance back over his shoulder with every few steps up the staircase that suddenly seemed to stretch on forever. What if they had changed their minds? What if mum had forgotten something that she felt she simply couldn't last two hours or so without? Every creak of footstep against stair tread was amplified in the quiet a hundredfold, announcing his intent to everyone within a mile radius, as his palm grew slick with sweat against the banister, threatening to lose its grip and send him plum-meting down in an endless spiral into some dark place far, far below.

He planted both feet on the landing with the firmness of an Arctic explorer before giving up his hold on the handrail. His breathing was fast and shallow, his head lighter than it should have been. His dad would sometimes shout at him, telling him that his skull was filled with sawdust instead of a brain. Right in that moment, it actually felt as though that really could have been true.

He was sure to look both ways up and down the long platform of the landing. All of the doors were closed, and he narrowed his eyes through the gloom even though he knew exactly what was there. His bedroom was off to the right, the bathroom and toilet just next to it, handy in case he needed to pee during the night. Mum and dad's room was on the left-hand side, supposedly far enough away so as not to disturb his sleep, or so they liked to believe.

"It's only a room," he told himself, the voice that sounded so full of confidence inside his head coming out more like a strangled stage whisper to his ears. "I'm just going to quickly check, so I know for sure. It'll stop the other kids from making their jokes about me." His Christmas list had been just as long as always, but not quite so over the top as it maybe could have been. He had been very specific. The aim was to prove a point, that was all. Just a quick peek inside the room in an attempt to catch the smallest glimpse of some recognized item, to prove what he already half-suspected; that he was too old for the magic to be real any more.

He pushed the door open slowly on hinges that creaked as they reached the limit of their movement. He knew about the noise, having heard it on many a night when his parents decided for some reason or other that they wanted a little more privacy. He had stepped forward into the room, the thick pile of the carpet beneath his feet far more yielding and luxurious feeling than the hard-wearing covering in his own room. Decorated in simple beige and magnolia, with the contrast of dark curtains and bedcoverings, his surroundings looked far too clean, almost sterile, at odds with what he imagined of either of his parents. The floor was clean, free of any tell-tale signs of Christmas presents, free of anything for that matter. How did they manage to spend any time in there without even the slightest bit of clutter? Grown-ups were so weird sometimes. He shook his head, partly in disbelief but also to clear it, to refocus instead on the task in hand. A bedside alarm clock blinked its green LCD just out of the corner of his eye. He couldn't remember the exact time that they had left, but it couldn't have been any more than twenty minutes ago. Still more than long enough to find out what he needed to know.

In the far corner of the room, next to the bed, was a walk-in cupboard door, painted a shade of white that age had turned a pale straw color. The chrome-look handle glinted and winked at him with the reflection of the clock, like an all-seeing eye or a camera record-ing his every illicit move and sending it back to some remote witness gathering evidence to be used against him at some future time. He reached out a hand that trembled in anticipation, feeling a static charge coming from the handle, reminding him that it wasn't too late to retreat, to just go to his own room or, even better, back down-stairs, as far away as possible from temptation. There was still the opportunity to keep the dream alive for a precious few weeks more, at least until next year. Then he could do it all again, a little older and a little more knowledgeable in the ways of the world.

Then he told himself that no, he couldn't wait that long. He leaned in and grabbed at the handle, squeezing his fingers and palm around it as if trying to force sound from it. As he did so, he pulled his arm back, almost able to convince himself that—Whoops!—it was all an accident and he wasn't really thinking of what he was doing anyway.

He stood, breathing in the slightly musty odor that escaped from the back of the cupboard, like an archaeologist gazing upon the en-trance to a newly discovered tomb for the first time. Except instead of the gleam of treasure, there were just clothes. Twin rails of shirts, trousers, and sweaters packed into that small space. At one side he could see an old full-length coat that looked like it was barely fashionable in the sixties. A long, velour thing with a fur trim collar, probably the source of most of the smell. Moving his gaze down to the old mothball-strewn floor of the cupboard, he saw something new that caught his attention. A pile of papers poking out of the corner, partly covered by an old towel, that looked like a collection of comics or something. He had heard stories of old comic books selling for much more than they had ever been worth when they were printed. Perhaps his dad was hoarding a small fortune, maybe without even realizing it. Grinning, Max squatted onto the floor, the carpet squirming beneath his stockinged feet as he reached out to move the towel.

His jaw dropped and froze into place as he looked at what he had just uncovered.

Jack Mason, one of the older kids at school, was one of those types who wanted people to think that he knew everything about everything. He had once told a group of classmates, including Max, during a free lesson about something that he called "titty magazines." They were, he had said with hushed, almost grave tones tempered with his typical eagerness, something that grown-up men read, with lots of photos, mostly of women wearing not many clothes and sometimes no clothes at all. Jack had once found just such a titty magazine poking out from the neighbor's dustbin on collection day, the cover torn and partly removed. What Max had found in the cupboard had nothing to do with presents or Christmas, but was his dad's very own collection of titty magazines. He leafed through them, dragging his thumb against the spines from bottom to top of the pile like a dealer shuffling a deck of cards. Magazines with strange-sounding names like Fiesta, Razzle, *and one with the self-explanatory name* Men Only. *The women on the covers all wore smiles and very little else.*

Without even thinking about anything like what he was doing or what the time could have been, he pulled an issue from the middle of the pile. According to the cover, it was called Mayfair and promised that RED HOT AMANDA WAS GOING TO SHOW EVERYTHING JUST FOR HIM. As he leafed through the crisp, crackling pages, he felt his vision blurring as he realized that the cover wasn't lying.

He told himself that he shouldn't be looking, that he should put it back, close the cupboard up, and go and play with his Top Trumps until his parents got back. He could even try and tell himself that he had imagined the whole thing. Instead, he kept going, his breath escaping in feverish gasps as he stared at the photographic display, turning page after page as he felt a strange, tingling sensation between his legs, accompanied by a heady, warm flush. This was the sort of thing that his dad looked at to pass the time, young women posing with their backs arched and their legs spread wide open for anyone to see, the vacant look in their eyes promising far more in the way of excitement than his timid shrew of a mother ever seemed to. Or perhaps that wasn't the case at all. Maybe his mum was every bit as complicit, her real nature hidden away behind a mask of mouse-like behavior. Jack Mason had talked about THE SEX THING before to anyone who dared to listen to him. Now it all started to make sense; the late-night closing of the bedroom door, the rhythm of creaking bedsprings, accompanied by grunts, moans, and other just-as-disturbing sounds.

Something snapped inside him, almost making a noise like the sharp twang of an elastic band, it was so clear and sudden. He shoved the magazine back, the cover dislodging from the spine as he thrust it back into the middle of the pile, not really caring whether he had returned it correctly. Shoving the cupboard door closed, he rushed from the room with a hand clasped over his mouth to keep himself from being sick on the plush carpet. He made it to the toilet just in time to lose his breakfast of porridge and raspberry jam down the u-bend. A sense of innocence disappeared with it, along with any interest in Christmas or anything to do with it. He didn't know what was worse, the dizzying lightness in his head and stomach, or the unexpected throbbing stiffness in the front of his trousers.

* * *

"O'er the fields we go, laughing all the way…"

They were still singing the same song even though it felt as though they had been standing there for several hours while he was lost in his memories of so long ago. They were a determined bunch, he had to hand it to them, although there was just the slightest edge of possible resignation creeping into some of their voices, the gleam in their eyes, even the vicar's, turning a little more glazed with the cold now tinged with desperation. He recognized most of the faces even though he had little to do with any of them. He had always preferred to keep himself to himself, maintaining a distance from the problems of other people. He glanced across them again, peering through the clouds of frozen breath that hung in the cold air like a fog caught up in the porch light. Things had reached that awkward stage now where he had been standing for just a bit too long to simply close the door on them, despite the growling in his stomach that reminded him of the time only too well.

He looked at each of their faces in turn, trying to assign names to them as best as he could. Of course, there was the omnipresent vicar and his wife standing at the back, gloved hands clasped together. Next to them was the Copperthwaite woman, Agnes or Agatha, or whatever her first name was, he couldn't recall for certain. Wisps of silver hair poked out from beneath her oversized wool hat as though they were trying to escape. Rory, her husband, ran the local corner shop, and there had been all sorts of stories about him involving drink and other women, among other things. Despite all the gossip, she seemed to be bearing up pretty well. In front of her were the Tavistocks, Mary and Joseph; even Max almost laughed at that one. Especially when some of the tales he'd heard about them ruled out any possibility of a virgin birth. In her mid-twenties, Mary was pretty without being strikingly beautiful, and quite a few other men seemed to be inclined to agree, something of which her husband seemed far more proud than was probably healthy in any relationship, or so Max had heard. It was surprising sometimes, the sort of things that you could find out just by listening rather than talking. He had even heard that rumor about that old Miranda woman, the one who liked it to be known just how much good she did for the parish. It was funny how no one ever had got to the bottom of just where that husband of hers had disappeared to. It seemed that pretty much everyone in the village had something that they would prefer to keep to themselves, some dirty little secret or other. Despite everything, though, here they were, a group of them standing together in a show of seasonal unity.

Front and center of the small group stood Sarah-Jane and Sam, the Sutton children, their mother, Tanya, standing behind them. She had a slender hand resting on a shoulder of each child; Max wasn't sure if it was in a gesture of motherly protection or as a means of keeping herself upright. For all the cheer in their voices, each of them, especially Tanya, had a faraway look on their face. Glassy eyes tinged with sadness, at odds with the rosy glow of their cheeks and noses. Husband and dad, Mike Sutton, had been neither seen or heard from in several weeks, the talk around the village being that he had probably done a runner with one of the young hussies that he met on his frequent "business trips." Max could understand the children being upset. At nine and eleven years old, they were at the age where losing someone so close starts to become a very real, painful thing. He was surprised about Tanya, though, having picked up on many of the whispers about her husband's frequent trips away, his visits to the doctor for antibiotics, and just how many times she had bruised herself by walking into a cupboard door or tripping on the stairs. He couldn't get his head around what could lead her to believe that she had anyone fooled. He would have thought that she would be glad to see the back of the man; there was obviously no accounting for other people's thoughts and feelings as far as relationships were concerned.

The two kids held a brightly colored red bucket between them, each gripping the plastic handle with a single cold hand, spots of white showed above the knuckles. Inside was a scattering of loose change and several notes, mainly fivers. Max couldn't help but think that the vicar had probably put a few of those in there himself just to make the collection look a little more respectable, probably going so far as to harangue a few of their fellow carollers into chipping in, too. Almost on cue, Sarah-Jane turned and glanced at her younger brother just long enough for him to take her hint. The two of them shook the bucket in unison, the change rattling around the bottom with a brittle, hollow sound. He looked at their bright, clear eyes peering out from just below the rims of their woolen hats, noses and cheeks tinged pink with the cold. Then he looked at their mother, staring straight ahead at him, yet looking for all the world as though her attention was focused upon something a hundred miles away. Their mouths moved in time with the other singers, a group of people standing together in a show of what they would probably call Christian solidarity, at a time when a neighbor needed it most. Max suddenly felt guilty for everything. Guilty for wishing they would go away, for being so reluctant to answer the door in the first place, *everything*.

He gave out a self-conscious grunt as he stuffed his hand into his trouser pocket, feeling for whatever he could find. He pulled out a crumpled five-pound note, his fingers trembling a little as he unfolded it, although he didn't really know why. Leaning forward a little, he dropped the paper into the bucket, where it fluttered down to rest over a bed of copper and silver coins.

"There you go," he muttered, his voice hoarse thanks to the cold evening air.

"Thank you," both children chimed in unison as the song came to an end. As Max looked up, the vicar and his wife both smiled at him in gratitude, their grins looking just a little too fixed in the cold air. With a collective nod and an air of "mission accomplished," the group turned and walked back up the small garden path, turning to try their luck at the Wilson house next door. *Good luck with that*, Max thought. *They always go away for Christmas; they won't be back for another two weeks.* Stepping back, he closed the front door and locked it behind them, shutting out the cold and everything else with it.

Back in the kitchen, the pot on the stove was still simmering away, the lid continuing to lift and rattle with the occasional burst of escaping steam. At least it hadn't boiled dry. Perhaps they hadn't kept him there for quite as long as it had felt. He closed his eyes and took a deep breath to clear his head, savoring the rich meat odor of the stew. He looked through the glass window of the oven door at the leg, still roasting nicely. Once cooked, he could probably carve the meat right off the bone and make some sandwiches out of it. He had some crusty bread that he had bought especially for that purpose. He had even found a recipe for sausages that he could probably adapt, that would probably put some of the offal to use. It wouldn't be easy, but he could always give it a go.

Seeing the group out there, standing with what was left of the family, had made him feel a tinge of sympathy; it had almost made him feel a little guilty, in fact. He couldn't imagine it being a pleasant feeling to lose someone, even more so close to Christmas.

He *had* deserved it, though, even if they didn't. Horrible, rotten little man, everyone in the village knew that he had treated his family badly, drinking, gambling, far too quick to use his fists, and cheating on his wife more times than anyone cared to count. They just didn't try to confront it, none of them did. So much for Christmas spirit; at least now he was doing something useful. It was supposed to be the season of indulgence after all.

He still took up an awful lot of space in the freezer, though.

Max smiled as he reached into the cupboard above his head and took out a large, deep soup bowl. Allowing himself to smile just a little, he started to hum a Christmas tune to himself as the braised liver stew simmered away in the pan. He took in a slow, deep breath, savoring the rich odor; it smelled delicious.

Jason's Ugly Christmas Sweater Party

Andrew Robertson

"It is so, so ugly," Brad says to me as I hold my iPhone between my shoulder and ear. As he jokingly complains, I keep chopping the carrots my keto obsessed friends will claim to want before they switch to slices of the well-iced Yule Log and After Eight chocolate wafers. "I don't even know if I can stand to wear this for a whole night. And why does it screech like that when I move? Is it acrylic? It sounds like it's crying!"

"Maybe it's just sad you don't love it," I laugh. He's far too alpha for my reindeer games, but he'll need to get used to them.

"I don't," he chuckles. "The felt Santa face on the front looks like a mean drunk, and the tinsel thread is fraying everywhere."

"Brad, you can't come to my patented Annual Ugly Christmas Sweater Party for the first time and not wear an ugly Christmas sweater!" I holler, sure to keep my tone light even though we've had this conversation before. He's lucky he's so fucking dreamy. Those long, white-tipped lashes around apple-green eyes, dirty blond hair in tight curls that feels like silk, and a dark beard flecked with lighter tones... It's like he fell out of a cologne ad. I have no idea how I landed him, never mind started dating him a month ago. "And anyway, you look great in anything, and it's all for fun. Do it for me."

"Yeah, but all these little bells are making every stray cat in town follow me. I'm a little young to be a crazy cat lady. You should have given me the one you're wearing tonight. It's way nicer. And this thing seems to be even tighter than when I first put it on. The neck is so tight I can hardly breathe!"

"It's just all those bulging muscles," I joke and hear him laugh low and sexy on the other end. I know just the face he is making, looking sideways and shaking his head. Just like the day we met at the bar, him in a pair of well-worn jeans and work boots, me in a suit fresh from the city where I spend my weekdays before coming home to the country. I walked right up and asked him if he did house calls. It was ballsy, but I'd seen him on a gay dating app, so all I had to lose was some pride. Instead of the rejection I half-expected, he looked sideways, shook his head, and grinned before asking why it took me so long to ask. When he looked back up at me, his smile could have powered a substation. "The nicer sweater is mine because I bought them, nerd. My friends will be here in about three hours. When are you coming?"

I hear him laugh at the question.

"A dirty mind, that's what I like," I try to say sexily into the phone.

"I'll be there soon, Jason. Maybe we can have a little party of our own before everyone else gets there..."

I feel a bolt of excitement run through my body at his subtext. He has a voice like honey rolling through bourbon. Speaking of which, I could use a shot as a bracer. My Annual Ugly Christmas Sweater Party is always a rager, and once it starts, the booze tends to disappear quickly, so no time like the present.

Pouring myself a stiff Woodford Reserve, I walk through to the living room to check on the décor, but when I enter, the air is ice cold. The curtains are shivering in the draft of an open window. How would the window be open in this weather?

"Listen, I've got to keep getting ready here, but I like that idea. I'll see you soon, handsome."

I hang up and slide the phone into my jeans as I walk toward the window. Must have been the cleaning lady earlier today. I'll need to speak with her about that. The whole house would have been a sheet of ice if I hadn't been here to catch it, and these older country homes are a bitch to heat at the best of times. I pull back the sheers and see the window is open all the way, giving me a perfect view of the huge, dark field at the side of my house. Actually, all the views are the same except for the front door, which looks out on a long, tree-lined driveway to the only sideroad that runs past here from the highway. Everyone will park on the front lawn before the party and stagger back out tomorrow after spending the night in one of the many guest rooms.

While not exactly the social event of the season, the Annual Ugly Christmas Sweater Party is still a must-attend. Who else invites thirty of their closest drinking buddies to a three-story, palatial farmhouse in the middle of nowhere to go crazy all night long? And that's not to mention the ten-man hot tub out back, the guest house, or the basement outfitted with bad disco lights and a makeshift DJ booth for when the nose candy comes out. A white Christmas for sure.

I grab the bottom rail of the window and pull down, feeling it stick a few times on its descent. The whole house creaks and wails whenever you ask it to do anything. The stairs alone could wake the dead in the same way a church pew can cry to heaven when you're late for a visit with God, but despite its protest, I can't have a group of gay popsicles in the morning. It reneges and comes to a shuddering close, slamming hard in a way that makes me worry for the antique glass flopping in the frame. As it comes to a halt, I feel a sliver stab my finger and pull away, surprised to see blood already blooming from the wound, as well as smeared on the frame. But alcohol does thin the blood.

Time to light the fire! I throw a few large logs in the wide mouth of the fireplace and drop in some kindling. A large match does the rest. The fire spits to life before a reassuring flame licks high toward the flue.

Before I return to the kitchen to keep fussing over the buffet, I decide to put on a record in keeping with the season. The party has always had an old-timey vibe in contrast to the actual events that take place so that everyone can feel a touch of tradition as they wade through libations like slush in the gutter.

Bing Crosby croons "Silver Bells" just like he has every year since I was a kid, and I get back to my kitchen, its crowded countertop, and the stacks of appetizers in the oven. Little cheese puffs continue to brown as I turn my attention to the cheese board. It's funny how your life can change so much in only a few years. Ten years ago, I couldn't even afford cheese. Well, I could, but it came individually wrapped and paper thin, a sickly orange hue. And for the record, it was cheese product.

I remember in law school, when I wanted a break from studying for December exams, rather than going out with friends, I would let myself listen to one side of Bing's classic Christmas album before getting back to the books. Coming from a family that could hardly afford to have me in law school, hitting the clubs was not an option. Just me and Bing, a bit of a recharge, maybe some orange cheese product, and then back to torts and transcripts.

Soon I hear the familiar scratch of the record player's needle on the label before the arm automatically returns to its cradle, and I wander through to the living room to flip it over. As I enter the room, I see the fire now raging nicely, the sound of wood crackling and snapping as it turns to ash. I also notice the curtains moving again, fluttering. An uncomfortable flush slithers over my skin, and the room feels stiff in its silence. Maybe it's fatigue after a long week, but I start to panic.

Despite it making no sense, I look to the bottom of the heavy curtains on either side of the window for evidence of shoes like some kind of farcical black-and-white film. There's no way anyone is behind them, but everyone has those moments where their childhood imagination takes over. As the sheers flail, I can see from the living room doorway that the window is actually open again, just a touch. Just enough to slide a hand through. How could it be open again? I glance down the hallway to make sure the front door is closed. It is.

I run over and throw back the flimsy fabric, expecting to see a hostile face or some kind of grotesque mask on the other side of the glass, a flimsy protection against intruders. But there is nothing. Only the same view of the huge, dark field at the side of my house. And more blood on the window rail. Too much blood. There's no way it all came from the sliver in my finger. It's on the wall, on the glass. I reach out to touch it. The blood comes off on my hand, but I never touched the windowpane. And as I smear it, I realize it's on the outside as well, starting to freeze. I'm certain I can see deep red shadows on the snow outside, too. So much blood.

I jump back and start to panic, then shove my hand into my jeans to retrieve my phone. As I pull it out, the phone slips from my grip and soars into the air, my rushed effort giving it all the momentum it needs to arc through the room and land right in the roaring fire.

Screaming, I rush toward it at the same time as my doorbell rings, and I hear an urgent pounding on the door. My heart skips and then slows when I realize that it's Brad. It has to be. Tall, strong, sensible Brad who is here to stop me from thinking that the Ghost of Christmas Past is jumping the gun and trying to rush in through my living room window to save my soul. Maybe it was a wounded raccoon trying to get inside. Quickly using a poker to pull my now-charred phone from the fire's wrath, I flick it to the side of the hearth and then move toward the door.

There is more pounding, erratic and almost urgent.

"I'm coming," I yell as I run down the long hallway toward the door, desperate for company after that eerie experience.

My hand, still wet from the window, slips, desperate to get purchase, as the other struggles with the lock. There is more knocking, and the uncomfortable flush comes back.

"Hold on," I shout just to break the silence in between impacts.

The door swings open as I start to say, "I think I have a ghost," and I can't believe my eyes.

Brad is slouched in the doorway, one hand holding the frame, the other ready to knock once more, but he is covered in blood. Head to toe. His face is scratched and torn, the sweater I gave him soaked with crimson and half off, one sleeve dangling limply in front of him. One of his pant legs is torn, and his knee is bent at an obscene angle. He looks like he is going to fall over any minute. He reaches for me.

"Brad, what happened!"

Brad says nothing before trying to grab onto me and then falling down so hard between the front door and the stairs I'm certain he is dead. I slam the door, hearing it lock, and drop to my knees beside him.

"Brad, Brad!"

His torn lips move slightly, mouthing some words.

I move closer so I can hear.

"Help me..." he wheezes, the sound of phlegm striking tissue as he struggles to breathe. "...so...mad."

He coughs up a blood clot that then pours from his lips, black and thick, followed by a chunk of fleshy meat. Part of his tongue drops onto the floor as he quivers trying to get up on all fours, barely able to hold himself up. One arm buckles and his head drops back on the hardwood with a chilling crack.

"Who's mad?" I ask. "Who?" As I try to pull him onto my lap, I realize there is no part of him that isn't wounded. I hear him wheeze again, then there are no more breaths. I start to gasp with anxiety, rapid and shallow; I start to freak out. I slide him back to the floor as gently as my shaking hands will allow.

"Hold on, I'm calling for help. Stay with me, Brad."

I keep repeating "Stay with me" as I rush back to the living room to get my phone. As I reach down to retrieve it, I realize one of the logs has toppled out of the fireplace, too close to the phone, and it has melted, the screen destroyed and the plastic backing more a puddle than anything with utility. Tears start to sprout in my eyes as I grab the poker to shove the log back in before it sets the house ablaze, but this is no time to cry. With the fire under control, I jump back to my feet and race back down the hall. Brad will have a phone.

When I get to the front door, Brad is lying flat on his stomach, his head sideways, but something has happened. It's hideous. His beautiful blond hair is gone. His handsome, wind-worn face is gone. His entire skull is on display, a red mess of slowly pulsing veins and cartilage with those apple green eyes staring out in disbelief. His body shivers, the head twitching slightly. And the sweater is gone, too, his bare back shining with blood and gore, covered in long scratch marks. I feel bile surge in my throat, and my bowels loosen.

A gory mess trails from Brad's body to the bottom of the stairs in small blotches, and then up the steps, two at a time. Someone is here. Someone is in the house. They must have opened the window after they attacked Brad to come inside and get me. They stripped him and took his fucking face!

Falling to my knees, I try and turn him over, but he is too heavy for me, so I put my lips next to where his ear should be and whisper urgently, "Did you see them? Who's here? Did they leave?"

The warm burn of tears surrounds my eyes again, and I know there's no way he could answer. He rasps, and I'm terrified it's a death rattle. Who the fuck tore his face off? I push my hand into his pants to get his phone and find it in his back pocket. I pull it out and grab the hand closest to me to press his finger against the home button, hoping to unlock it, but they are clotted with sticky crimson and filthy from what must have been his struggle outside. Nothing happens. I wipe them off on my own stupid, ugly sweater and try again. Still nothing. I grab his other hand only to see that the pads of every finger have been shredded to pieces, each dripping with bits of skin and fresh blood. One sparkles with a piece of glittery thread, and I realize that there's part of a tiny Christmas bell from the sweater I loaned him embedded in his palm.

I stab the home button to bring up the emergency call option and tap the icon. In seconds, a woman answers.

"Nine-one-one, what's your emergency?"

"My boyfriend has been attacked by someone outside my house. They've ripped off his face..." My voice starts to break, and I choke trying to suppress a scream. I hear the operator gasp on the other end of the line. This is a sleepy part of the country. The biggest problem is the odd meth head or DUI.

"I'm sorry, sir, but did you say they've taken off his face?"

"Everything! His whole head is bleeding, and they broke his leg. I think they are in my house. I mean, they are. There's blood all over!"

"Sir, I need you to get to a safe place and wait there until the police arrive. Is there anyone nearby, a neighbor who can help? Where are you?"

I recite my address to her.

"Oh my God." She realizes that I am in the middle of nowhere. Precisely where I wanted to be until this exact minute. "I'm getting the call out now, but you need to leave. Can you get to your car? Can the injured party walk?"

And then I hear the intruder.

There is the sound of running footsteps upstairs, light but undeniable. They are in my house. Someone has just tried to murder my boyfriend, and they are in my house.

My voice drops to a whisper. "He's here, I can hear him upstairs."

"Sir, I need you to get out of the house. It will take the police at least twenty minutes to get there. You need to get somewhere safe."

As she repeats the order, I slowly raise my head so I can see up the stairs in front of me. At the top of the dark landing, an arm reaches out just enough to catch the light, and something dangles from the hand. The intruder shakes it out, and I see Brad's face without eyes gazing down at me. A Halloween mask from hell.

"Who's ugly now?" the voice taunts, deep and cold, slowly swinging Brad's face back and forth like a horrible pendulum. The voice doesn't sound entirely human with its merciless mockery.

Choking back a million angry, useless words, I put my hand on Brad's back and feel him breathing, just barely. He has to be in shock. And I have to get his face back. Who could have the skill to deglove an entire human head like that in the minute it took me to run to the living room and back? They must be armed, some kind of crazed doctor. Maybe Brad has a violent ex he never told me about. I need to find a weapon and get out, but there's no way I can lift Brad. Panic starts to make my thoughts spiral, and I can hear the operator still talking to me from the phone. I'm certain I am about to shit my pants.

"I will...I will try..." I whisper to her. "Please hurry." I slide Brad's phone into my own pocket and make for the kitchen. If I can grab a knife and then maybe get to my car out back, bring it to the front, somehow get Brad into the passenger seat, we could escape. As I pass the stairs and peer up past the balcony, I can feel the intruder's eyes burning onto my skin from the darkness.

"Why don't you love me?" the intruder yells before letting out a cackle that turns my spine to ice. It's like a dream where you realize you can't run fast enough to get away or scream or call for help. I feel tiny and helpless as I rush through the kitchen door, certain I will turn around and see a stranger waiting for me, too close, too terrifying. Smoke is starting to billow from the oven as the pastries burn, and there is fresh blood on the counter. My knife block is gone. Stepping toward the back door, I see the handle is also red and slick.

"I've called the police!" I scream into the smoke. "They are on their way. You have to leave!"

My voice sounds shrill and ridiculous. I grab the gore-covered door handle and swing it open, the cold air and snow rushing in. There's a fire outside. It's my car. Orange tongues flicker up the doors and windows against the dark beyond, and I come to the chilling realization that there has to be more than one person involved. I slam the door and lock it even though I know that won't matter anymore.

I start to feel like I am choking, my sweater tightening around my neck, and as I reach up to stretch the fabric, I'm certain it resists. I grab the waistband in sheer terror and pull it up and over my head, feeling the material doing everything it can to prevent me. *This is impossible*, I think to myself, *my sweater isn't alive.* But as I pull it from my body, I'm certain I hear it release a tiny shriek and the sleeves try to crawl back up my arms.

I open the oven and throw it in, watching the fabric quickly start to melt on top of the pastries, now in flames. It screams. The fucking sweater screams and tries to get out. I slap at the sweater, burning my right hand as I close the oven with my left and lean my body against it, the raging inferno inside scalding my legs through the oven door, but there is no doubt in my mind that the sweater is trying to get out during its death throes. This is insanity. I must be going insane.

I see a pair of long scissors on the counter and grab them. It's time to make my stand. Whatever is happening, I need to protect Brad until the police arrive. I need to confront whoever is in my house.

The fury in the oven stops, and armed with my scissors, I quietly make my way down the hall to the bottom of the stairs.

"You can't kill us all," the voice shouts down at me. The top landing is pitch dark, and when I flick the switch at the bottom landing, the lights gutter and spit then fail. And then I hear the wet steps. Wet steps on the second floor, coming down the passage, getting closer. And I see a form coming into the light.

Something short, oddly shaped, oblong in the withering moonlight filtering in through a skylight.

My jaw drops and my mind begins to reel.

Standing at the top of the stairs is the ugly Christmas sweater Brad had been wearing, but it's inverted, standing on the sleeves like legs. Wrong. Awful. Fearful. The tiny bells have all unfurled like tiny brass daggers and the waistband curls slightly down so that it can grasp Brad's torn face as if it was a mask. The effect is horrifying.

"Do you think I'm pretty now?"

The Coal Shed

Christopher Stanley

Lily hobbles down the slope toward the almost-forgotten village of Lee Sodbury. It's a place she's never visited before, a place she's only glimpsed in her dreams. She's walked more than sixty miles to get here, past moss-covered ruins and sacred wells, following the old, straight tracks north from the coast. When there were no landmarks to follow, the wind was her guide, gently pushing her along rivers, roads, and railway lines. Her ankles squeak as she walks, and the hardened leather straps of her sandals have scraped deep, bloody grooves in the skin of her feet. When she can bear the pain no more, she removes her sandals and throws them toward the road. They fly in a high, lingering arc before colliding with the radiator grill of a speeding refrigerator lorry, where they remain pinned until the lorry is out of sight.

"Flesh is a prison," says Lily. "It's a cage like any other, with bars and a lock." Speaking aloud is the only way to silence the voices in her head. "A person with the right skills can pick this lock and release the human spirit with little more than a hairpin and a well-aimed blow." She crosses the road without looking, and a tombstone-gray minivan speeds past, close enough to shine her nose. The driver swerves the minivan and clips the curb, the front driver's side wheel popping like a paper bag. The minivan bounces up off the road and crashes into a tree.

The road is silent. Crows gather overhead, keeping watch while Lily continues down the slope toward the crashed vehicle. The minivan's windscreen is a mosaic of broken glass, and the whole front end has been squished like a squeezebox. The driver's face is pressed into a freshly swollen airbag like he's feeding at his mother's tit.

"The human spirit is a prisoner of the flesh just as surely as free will is a prisoner of the conscience," says Lily as she approaches the wreck. "Liberating the spirit so a person may be closer to God is an act of kindness."

The voices in her head never argue with her.

The driver of the minivan cracks open his door, groaning with the effort. The airbag is a spent balloon hanging limply against the steering wheel. Lily's ancient fingers slip around the edge of the door and ease it open. The driver, red-faced and bleeding from a cut above his brow, manages to unclip his seat belt. He falls toward her, and she catches him by the shoulders.

"Crazy fuckin' bitch," he says when he sees her.

In the backseat of the minivan, there are three booster seats in a row. *A boy and two girls*, thinks Lily, or some other combination. It doesn't matter. She wonders if his children look up to him. Perhaps they're at home right now, playing by the front door, ready to throw their arms around him when he walks in.

"Murder is the devil's word," she says. "But it's not the devil's work."

She runs her fingers through the driver's hair and then

curls her hand into a fist. While Mariah Carey sings "All I Want for Christmas is You," on the radio, she pulls his head down sharply and slams the minivan door against his face. She does this again and again until his nose bursts, until his flesh is puffy and torn like bruised fruit, until she hears his skull crack. The driver's flailing arms fall still, and then she lets go, his limp body hanging half in and half out of the minivan.

* * *

Newspapers call Lily "The Christmas Killer." She's seen it in the headlines of discarded tabloids. And yes, she's killed people. Even if it was for a higher purpose, she's still a sinner. The Lord made her this way when he reached down with his crooked fingers and stole her twins from her while they were still babies. For years, she haunted their nursery, cuddling their toys and burying her face into their clothes. On good days, she called out to their spirits and waited for replies that never came. On bad days, of which there were many, she screamed at the Lord until she was too hoarse to continue. And then her house burned down, leaving her no option but to walk the streets in search of salvation. She's been a mother and a mourner, and now she's a murderer, as cold and lost as any human soul is capable of being.

Christmas in Lee Sodbury is a modest occasion. Ancient strings of lights featuring dancing snowmen and stars of Bethlehem connect the two halves of the High Street. The village Christmas tree is no taller than a bus shelter. The windows of the Post Office contain tinsel and a few feet of spray-on snow. None of the decorations are convincing.

Barefoot against the concrete, Lily hobbles on, gliding unnoticed past cottages and farmhouses, residents and ghosts, toward the far side of the village. She passes telegraph poles and lampposts bearing black-and-white missing person posters. A young woman called Shelly disappeared two weeks ago. Lily likes the curl of the woman's hair and the innocence in her eyes.

She recognizes the guesthouse from her dreams, stark against the dying winter sky. The sign outside says "Vacancies." Inside, the reception area is cool and dingy and smells of nothing at all. On a coffee table between two armchairs, there's a three-foot Christmas tree and a wooden statue of Santa Claus. The tree is undecorated, and Santa looks thoroughly miserable. The owner of the guesthouse—an older woman with a permanent scowl—appears in the hatchway wearing a floral dress that makes Lily think of wallpaper.

"Welcome to The Stables," says the guesthouse owner. "I'm Miz Fairfax." She unfolds a diary with no entries in it and runs her finger along the paper as if searching through an invisible list. "Were you after a room, Missus...?"

"Lily."

Ms. Fairfax frowns. With a red-lipstick smile, she says, "I'm afraid we're full."

"But the sign outside..."

"Signs can be misleading."

Lily hesitates, wondering if the guesthouse owner knows more than she's letting on. "I have a reservation," she says.

Ms. Fairfax's forehead creases as she searches among the imagined entries on the blank page of her diary. And sure enough, there is Lily's name—just Lily, no surname or contact details—written in her own hand.

"Oh," she says. "Oh, yes, there it is. I must have... How silly of me."

"Would you show me to my room?" asks Lily.

"Let me show you to your room." Ms. Fairfax disappears

from the hatchway and emerges from a side door, much shorter than Lily expected. "It's been so busy here recently," she says, "I'm finding it hard to keep track."

There were no other entries in the diary, thinks Lily. *No cars in the carpark. Ms. Fairfax is crazy.*

"Do you have any luggage?"

"Only what I keep in here," says Lily, patting her chest.

Ms. Fairfax smiles uncertainly as she shows Lily up to the second floor. The voices in Lily's head tell her not to trust the guesthouse owner. Lily is here for a reason. Something is going to happen, and Ms. Fairfax has the distracted look of someone who wants to be elsewhere. Lily contemplates pushing the guesthouse owner down the stairs so she can have a proper look around, but she's afraid to act without a sign.

As they pass room number six, Lily feels something inside her, a cold hand squeezing her heart. She hears someone whisper her name and pauses, momentarily, reaching out and feeling—

"This is your room," says Ms. Fairfax from further up the corridor. She points toward a door bearing a bronze number nine. "In here."

Lily pulls her hand away, trying to ignore the voices calling for attention in her muddled mind, and complies with guesthouse owner's taut instruction.

"Let me know if you need anything," says Ms. Fairfax, handing Lily the room key. And then she retreats, disappearing back down the stairs with no mention of breakfast arrangements or wake-up calls. She doesn't even ask how long Lily wants to stay.

❈ ❈ ❈

Lily feels nothing as she enters her room. She'd assumed

that everything would become clear once she arrived. Maybe there's been a misunderstanding. Or maybe the guesthouse owner was right—signs can be misleading. With a sigh of exhaustion, she collapses on the bed, closes her eyes, and dreams she's falling.

When she wakes up, a cool breeze is making the black fabric lampshade sway above her head, causing dust to rain down on her face like a microscopic meteor storm. Her departing dreams leave her with the sensation of being suffocated, and she coughs and splutters, barely able to breathe. In the bathroom, half-blinded by tears, she gropes around the sink until she locates a plastic cup among the complimentary soaps and shampoos. The taps hiss as she fills it up, water splashing onto her clothes and feet. She gulps until the cup is empty. Then she collapses onto the floor next to the bath and waits for her heart to stop racing.

There's a knock at the door. Lily tries to call out, but her throat is too sore. As she leaves the bathroom, she catches sight of her reflection in the mirror above the sink. Her graying hair is painted flat against her skull. Her skin is dry and wind-scorched. Her jacket is stained red around the cuffs.

"Hello," calls Ms. Fairfax. "Lily?"

"What is it?" croaks Lily, standing at the door.

"May I come in?"

"What day is it?"

"It's Friday. Christmas Eve. May I come in, please?"

Lily presses her forehead against the door, trying to feel her way into the guesthouse owner's head. It isn't hard. "That won't be necessary," she says.

"No, it won't," agrees Ms. Fairfax.

"What did you want?"

"You missed breakfast. I was checking if you were okay."

"I need your shoes," says Lily. "Leave them when you go."

"Very good," says Ms. Fairfax.

Lily listens as the guesthouse owner waddles away and then opens the door to retrieve the abandoned slippers. It's Friday already. How has she slept for so long? The sun is falling fast, and she still doesn't understand why she's been brought here. The slippers are a size too big, but they're better than nothing at all.

An out-of-season tortoiseshell flutters against her bedroom window, its wings knocking against the glass. How curious to see a butterfly looking so fresh in winter. Not wishing to leave the pretty insect out in the cold, Lily cracks open the top window and it flies in, circling the lampshade. Lily's pulse quickens. Maybe this is a sign. Seconds later, a tiger moth joins the tortoiseshell, and together they dance around the musty fabric, two riders on an invisible carousel. Lily watches the insects as they circle the lampshade six times, the moth gaining on but never quite catching the butterfly. After the sixth lap, the tortoiseshell attempts to land. To Lily's delight, the tiger moth attacks it, its powerful wings beating against the tortoiseshell until the butterfly's head is separated from its abdomen. The tortoiseshell's torso flutters down toward the bed and remains there, its wings outstretched on the duvet, still twitching.

Lily watches the victorious moth fly away to land on the bedroom door.

She laughs and claps her hands.

This unprecedented act of aggression is, without doubt, the sign she has been hoping for. She exits her bedroom, following the moth into the darkness of the corridor beyond. It flies along the corridor before coming to rest on the door of room number six.

Lily cups the moth in her hand, holding it while she slides a couple of antique hairpins from her hair. They belonged to her mother a lifetime ago, decorated at one end with Chinese knots and sharpened to a fine point at the other. Carefully, she works them into the lock, teasing them into the mechanism. Her fingers aren't as steady as they used to be and it takes her a few attempts, but soon the lock concedes so happily it's like it wanted to be picked. As the door opens, she releases the tiger moth, and its crushed body falls gracelessly to the carpet at her feet.

In all her excitement, she squeezed a little too hard.

❈ ❈ ❈

With the light on, room number six looks identical to her own. The same bedding and furniture. The same salmon-pink curtains drawn across the windows. The same dust swirling in search of a home. Her eyes hurry from one corner to the next, searching for clues. She curses her clumsy hand for extinguishing the moth, which may have had more to show her. It's clear no one is staying in the room, so Ms. Fairfax must have had another reason for wishing to keep her out. Lily checks the drawers and wardrobe for false backs and unusual packages. With a painful grunt, she drops to her knees and searches under the bed, but all she finds is more dust. It's only when she sits up again that she sees what she's been looking for. The moth. The previously dead moth is sitting on the curtains, stretching its wings.

Of course.

Lily switches off the light and hobbles across the room, her fingers trembling in anticipation. This is it. This is what she's traveled all this way for. The even-numbered rooms are on the opposite side of the corridor to the odd-numbered rooms, so they look out over the courtyard and the woods beyond. The moth keeps its distance as she peels apart the curtains.

Outside, night has already thrown its cloak of darkness over the horizon. Too soon, thinks Lily, remembering that there was still a thread of daylight on her side of the guest-house. The woods are little more than shadows, but there's a light in the courtyard, squeezing through a crack in the door of what looks like an old coal shed. The light flickers un-evenly, a ballet of candlelight, but there are shadows in the coal shed, too. Lily watches, glimpsing strange movements and indistinguishable shapes inside. And then something crosses the courtyard. In the uneven light, she sees two fig-ures approach and knock on the coal shed door. She hears the door scrape open.

The light from inside the coal shed falls upon the new arrivals. One is tall and broad, and the other is shorter, with a pronounced belly. Both are dressed in floor-length cloaks with hoods concealing their faces. The taller one removes its hood to reveal the pale, ridged flesh of its bald head. Two rows of small horns—like pointed teeth—reach from its fore-head to the back of its neck.

And then Lily sees the guesthouse owner, Ms. Fairfax. She's holding the coal shed door open, her head tilted low in submission. As the new arrivals step inside, Ms. Fairfax looks up, staring at Lily with the coal-black eyes of the possessed.

Lily shivers in surprise and the bedroom lights up around her. She blinks as her eyes struggle to adjust to the brightness.

"I want my slippers back," says a familiar voice behind her.

Lily spins around but not quickly enough. Something hard and blunt connects with her temple, and the voices in her head are stunned into silence. Before Lily succumbs to darkness, she glimpses the wooden statue of Santa Claus from the reception area flying through the air.

* * *

As they cross the courtyard, the night wind gropes with fingers of ice. The air is seasoned with the uneasy aromas of cinnamon, offal, and dung. Lily shivers violently, her head still throbbing from where she was hit. Her hands are bound in chains. As they approach the coal shed, she can hear the low, nearly monotonous drone of words chanted in some foreign tongue, so rhythmical it seems like the coal shed is snoring. A dozen or so crows hang lifelessly along the fascia of the felt roof, and there are white chalk markings on the door.

"In," says Ms. Fairfax.

Lily ducks her head and enters. Inside, the cinnamon-scented candles are no match for the stench of decay. There's no coal she can see, but the walls are dusted black, and she can taste it in the air. In the far corner, three goats bleat anxiously. A fourth hangs upside down, its life draining into a metal urn through a cut in its throat. The two robed figures stand next to a cloth-covered altar, the shorter one leaning against the edge, its hood still pulled down over its face. The taller figure is a demon, with a sharply pointed chin, swollen forehead, and twin rows of horns curling back across its disfigured skull. On the other side of the shed, hunched over in the shadows, there are two ghouls, a man and a woman, their torsos decorated in deliberate scars. Wide-eyed and broken-toothed, they have an ugly energy about them. The only other person in the coal shed is a priest in dark robes with a wispy moustache. "Another visitor," he says, laughing nervously, his voice high and thin. "I didn't know we were expecting anyone."

"She was spying on us," says Ms. Fairfax.

"No matter," says the priest, although he seems agitated.

Control, thinks Lily. *He's terrified that if he isn't in control, he's doomed.*

To Lily, he says, "I'm so pleased you've joined us. I trust you've brought an offering?"

Lily doesn't know what to say. "The flesh is a prison," she mutters, hoping it will appease the priest.

"What?"

She raises her hands to show that they're empty.

In the middle of the room, the demon removes its companion's hood. Lily sees a young woman, little more than a girl, with high cheekbones and curly red hair. The girl from the posters on the telegraph poles. She's only been missing for a fortnight, but she looks heavily pregnant, nearly to term. And she can't keep her eyes open. Her head rolls forward and back as if she's on the brink of sleep. *She's been drugged,* thinks Lily. *Or poisoned.* She watches as the demon slips the cloak from the woman's shoulders, letting it fall to the floor around her ankles. The woman's skin is pale like the moonlight and stretched tight over her swollen breasts and distended belly. The demon helps her to lie down on the altar, easing her gently onto her back. She closes her eyes and doesn't open them again, quietly shivering in sleep. The demon straps her to the altar with a length of leather above her belly, fastened with a buckle underneath.

"When Jesus was born," says the Priest, turning to face Lily, "there were kings and shepherds. They traveled miles to witness his birth. They didn't have a Post Office on the street corner, or Amazon or eBay, and yet they still managed to bring him gifts." He kicks an empty coal scuttle across the floor. "And here we are, two thousand years later, when the great Master has deemed it appropriate to send us his only child, and what I want to know is: where are our wise men? Where are our shepherds? And where, in the name of all that is unholy, are our gifts?"

Lily doesn't like the priest's tone. "The flesh is a cage like any other," she whispers. "With bars and a lock."

"You have blood in your veins," says the priest. "We'll take that."

Lily looks down toward her bare feet. Is this what she's here for? Is this her purpose? To feed the offspring of the Master?

"No," says the demon, its voice halfway to a lion's roar.

"But goat blood will only sate the baby's hunger," says the priest. "Human blood will help it grow."

"Gifts are unimportant," says the demon. "And the woman is impure. She has madness in her veins. I can smell it."

"You're not thinking straight."

"The mother's blood will suffice."

"I thought Mitchell was supposed to be bringing us a carload of foster kids."

"Mitchell never collected the children," says Ms. Fairfax. "We don't know where he is."

Lily remembers the crashed minivan with the booster seats in the back. "A person with the right skills should be able to pick the lock," she whispers, "and release the human spirit with little more than a hairpin and a well-aimed blow."

The young woman wakes up screaming. Her eyes are wide, and she's clawing at the leather strap, trying to wriggle free. She looks at Lily, her head shaking, and says, "I d-d-don't belong here."

"But you do belong here," whispers the demon, stroking her hair. "You were chosen." It collects the urn of blood from beneath the dead goat and paints swirls and crosses on the young woman's face with its fingers.

"P-p-please don't," she says. "I'm s-so cold."

"Of course you are," says the demon.

As it paints symbols on her shoulders and chest, the

young woman starts to groan. Her belly is swollen and throbbing like some immense boil, and whatever is inside is pressing upwards, as if trying to force its way out. The more the demon paints, the more violently her belly moves. Eventually, the woman lets out a long, high shriek, her teeth clenched, her eyes squeezed shut. "I can't do this," she moans. "I can't do it. Please make it stop!"

The priest steps forward, slipping something from within his robes: a fine dagger with a jewel-encrusted hilt and symbols on its blade. The sun and the moon; the beginning and the end. *It's a thing of beauty*, thinks Lily. *A hairpin will free a human soul, but a blade like that could send a demon back to hell.* She longs to touch it, to feel its weight, to hold it in her hands.

The priest lifts the young woman's arm away from the altar. Speaking quietly, as if reciting a private prayer, he slips the tip of the blade into her wrist and draws it along her vein until blood bubbles and spills across her skin. Then he drapes the young woman's arm over the edge of the altar so her blood trickles down her fingertips and collects in a trough on the floor.

"It won't be long now," says Ms. Fairfax.

Lily has tears in her eyes. Her thoughts are muddled but her feelings are true. She doesn't want the young woman to suffer.

The priest points the bloody tip of his dagger toward the painted dome of the young woman's belly. The baby presses upwards, reaching for the blade. Slowly, the priest lifts the dagger away, and the baby presses harder and harder until the young woman's body can stretch no further. She screams weakly as her skin splits and her belly is ripped open.

The coal shed is filled with the sound of crying.

✳ ✳ ✳

Lily feels numb as the baby is cut from its mother. She never dreamed she would be part of the inner circle that ushered in the end of days. The baby is a girl. She has no hair on her head, so it's possible to see her little horns, curled like those of a goat. As the priest lifts her from her mother's body, she kicks her legs and whips her tail. The priest bites his index finger to draw blood and lets the baby suckle. "There, there," he whispers, and the baby gurgles in agreement.

Lily doesn't know what to think. The baby will need feeding, and the goats' blood will only go so far. If it would please her Lord to die for this creature, she would happily do so. But everything is ambiguity. There are no signs, just dark coercions.

"It's done," says Ms. Fairfax.

"This is a great day indeed," says the demon.

The ghouls move in, stroking their hands over the dead woman's shoulders and hips, pinching and peeling her flesh, their fingers slipping into her mouth and ruptured belly, drool spilling from their lips. There'll be nothing left but bones by the time they've finished.

Lily watches everything, present but not present, remembering the cry of her own babies when they were pulled from her, so young and sweet and—

Something tickles her hair. She shakes her head, but it tickles again. She flicks her head more violently, and the tiger moth flutters briefly in the candlelight before returning to pester her once more. She raises her manacled hands to brush it away, and her fingers connect with something long and hard.

A hairpin.

* * *

The following morning, Lily leaves the guesthouse in sunlight without settling her bill. There's no record of her staying on the premises, and nobody saw her arrive or leave. The coal shed is in flames, its occupants reduced to ash, dark smoke rising into the sky before being dispersed by the breeze. On her feet, Lily wears Ms. Fairfax's slippers. In front of her, a goat trots wearily on a makeshift leash, sniffing for tufts of wild grass. In her arms, swaddled in clean sheets from room number six, the new-born baby girl twitches in her sleep. Like all babies, she's perfect. In her heart, Lily knows there's no one else capable of raising such a special child. The voices in her head agree.

A priest of the good Lord would drown the baby or lock her in a dungeon and throw away the key. A priest of the Master would coerce her into a life of depravity. This is why the Lord sent Lily—Lilith—the stealer of babies. Because no baby is born evil. Because every infant deserves a chance. And some of them need a mother who will dock their tails and curdle blood into their milk. They need a mother who will file the horns on their foreheads so that one day they may walk alongside their mortal brothers and sisters as one of them.

In the distance, Lily hears church bells ringing. It's Christmas day. She squeezes the baby girl tightly to her chest and kisses her forehead. Some babies need a little more love than others, and Lily has a lifetime of love to give.

ABOUT THE AUTHORS

Evan Baughfman works in a very scary place: a middle school! He writes all genres, but horror is where he is most comfortable. Much of his writing success has been as a playwright. He's had many different plays produced across the globe. Heuer Publishing has recently published Evan's script, "A Taste of Amontillado" (an adaptation of Edgar Allan Poe's "The Cask of Amontillado"). Additionally, Evan has penned a collection of 13 short scary stories titled *Twisted Tales from Edgar Allan Poe Middle School*. From that collection, opening story "Loud Mouths" was dramatized as a radio play by Chicago's Small Fish Radio Theatre and Thespinarium as part of their horror podcast, "The Creatures Inside." Furthermore, Evan has adapted a number of his *Twisted Tales* into short film screenplays, of which "The Emaciated Man", "The Tell-Tale Art," and "A Perfect Circle" have all won awards in various film festival competitions. More about Evan's writing can be found at www.evanbaughfman.com.

David Bernard is a native New Englander who hightailed it to South Florida as soon as he was informed that grown-ups can live anywhere they want, and that in spite of opinions to the contrary, he was considered to be an adult. He does still keep an ice scraper by the door, because you never know. His previous works include short stories in anthologies such as *Snowbound with Zombies*, Post Mortem Press; *Legacy of the Reanimator*, Chaosium; and *The Shadow over Deathlehem*, Grinning Skull Press.

S.E. Casey grew up near a lighthouse. He always dreamed of smashing the lighthouse and building something truly grotesque with the rubble. This is the writing method for his broken down and rebuilt stories published in many horror magazines and anthologies that can be found at secaseyauthor.wordpress.com.

B.L. Daniels is a writer of horror and weird fiction. His short stories have been featured in Corner Bar Magazine, Helix Magazine, and various anthologies. He lives in New England with his wife, kids, and a couple of devious cats. Follow him on Twitter @bldauthor

Neil Davies was born in 1959 and has found everything else to be an uphill struggle. He currently lives in the North West of England with his wife, two grown-up children and a cat. He divides his spare time between writing, painting and music. For more information please visit his official website—http://www.nwdavies.co.uk

Alan Derosby, a Maine native, has spent the past several years focusing on his passion: writing. He has made it to the second round of the Amazon Breakthrough Novel awards with his young historical fiction novel Purgatory. Since that time, he has placed his focus on creating original and spooky short stories, having "The Ghost at Old Pier's Pub" published online. When not writing, Alan is teaching history at Messalonskee High School in Oakland, Maine or spending time with his family.

Mark L. Eshbaugh is an Author, Artist, and Musician. He has written a number of non-fiction books about photographic subjects, and contributed to several textbooks about art. To date his creative writing has appeared in anthologies, graphic novels, on film, and in song. He lives in Massachusetts with his wife and son.

Dan Foley grew up in Northern New Jersey. He has lived on the east coast, the west coast and points in between, including two nuclear submarines. He has lived in Manchester, CT. since 1985. His genres of choice are horror and paranormal suspense.

He is the author of the novels *Death's Companion, Reunion, Abandoned,* and *Wolf's Tale*, the novellas, *Intruder* and *Gypsy,* and a collection of short stories *The Whispers of Crows*. All are available through Amazon and B&N. He has also published in various anthologies and magazines in the U.S. Canada, England and Australia. Find him at www.deathscompanion.com, or on Facebook at www.facebook.com/dan.foley.31

Despite what you might think, **Lee Glenwright** loves Christmas and can't imagine why anyone would be disturbed by the thought of a total stranger climbing down their chimney in the dead of night. His writing has been featured in several anthologies and magazines, including 'Mrs Rochester's Attic' (Mantle Lane Press), *Millhaven's Tales of Terror*, Millhaven Press; *Twilight Madhouse Vol. 4*, Schreyer Ink; and 'Lovecraftiana' (Rogue Planet Press). He lives in Sunderland UK, with his family and a menagerie of pets.

R.A. Goli is an Australian writer of horror, fantasy, and speculative short stories. In addition to writing, her interests include reading, gaming, the occasional walk, and annoying her dog, two cats, and husband.

Check out her numerous publications including her fantasy novella, *The Eighth Dwarf,* and her collection of short stories, *Unfettered* at http:// ragoliauthor. wordpress.com/ or stalk her on facebook https://www. facebook.com/RAGoliAuthor/.

Born in South-Africa and raised in a small farming community, **Wiebo Grobler** only had his imagination to keep him occupied until he discovered the magic of books. Soon he started to create his own worlds and stories in his head. These stories developed voices, which clamored to be heard. So, he writes.

Shortlisted for his Flash Fiction and Poetry for the Fish Publishing Prize, he's had stories published in *Molotov Lit, National Flash Fiction Day, Reflex Fiction*, and more. You can follow him for updates on twitter at : @Wiebog; Website: Wiebog.com

Todd Keisling is the author of *A Life Transparent, The Liminal Man*, and the critically-acclaimed novella, *The Final Reconciliation*. His most recent releases are *The Smile Factory* and the horror collection, *Ugly Little Things: Collected Horrors*, available now from Crystal Lake Publishing. He lives somewhere in the wilds of Pennsylvania with his family where he is at work on his next novel. Share his dread: Twitter, @todd_keisling; Instagram, @toddkeisling; website: www.toddkeisling.com

In print, **Vicky MacDonald Harris's** poems reside in the *NaPoChapBook* collection published by Big Game Books, and *The Lincoln Underground*. Most recently, her poem, "Disaster Capitalism" was published in *The Flat Water Stirs: An Anthology of Emerging Nebraska Poets*. Online her poems can be found at *Tiny Poems, Two Cities Review, Poets and Artists, Hobble Creek Review, the24project*, and in *Women Poets Wearing Sweatpants Tumblr*.

Another origin of Santa story of hers was published in *Return to Deathlehem: An Anthology of Holiday Horrors for Charity*. Despite recently moving back to Canada, she is glad to have returned to Deathlehem!

Terry Miller lives in Harlan, Kentucky and attends Southeast Kentucky Community and Technical College in pursuit of his degree as a PTA. His work has appeared in Sanitarium and Devolution Z. His own dark verse anthology, "Fleshlings", is available in paperback on Amazon.

Kurt Newton's dark fiction and poetry have appeared in numerous publications including *The Shadow over Deathlehem, Weird Tales, Dark Discoveries, Weirdbook, Shock Totem, Black Infinity*, and *Hinnom Magazine*. He lives in Connecticut.

Andrew Robertson is an award-winning queer writer and journalist. He has published articles in *Xtra!, fab magazine, ICON, Gasoline, Samaritan Magazine, neksis*, and *Shameless*. His fiction has appeared in literary magazines and quarterlies such as *Stitched Smile Publications Magazine Vol 1, Deadman's Tome, Sirens Call, Undertow, katalogue, Feeling Better Yet?*, and in anthologies including *Alice Unbound: Beyond Wonderland, A Tribute Anthology to Deadworld, Gone with the Dead, Group Hex* Vol. 1 and Vol. 2, *Cuarenta y Nueve*, and the upcoming anthology *First Hand Accounts*. He is also the editor of *Dark Rainbow: Queer Erotic Horror*, a bestselling anthology from Riverdale Avenue Books. A lifelong fan of horror, he is the founder and co-host of The Great Lakes Horror Company Podcast, official podcast to Library of the Damned, and a member of the Horror Writer's Association. Find him on twitter at @AndrewAwesome76.

Debra Robinson is an Appalachian author of short and long fiction. She enjoys writing horror, paranormal, post-apocalyptic, and science fiction. She is happiest when scaring someone, or making them think—preferably both.

Her eight books and many short stories, fiction and nonfiction, are released through several publishers, including: *Red Death: a Post Apocalyptic Thriller*, series with Severed Press, *The Evil in the Tower*, and an upcoming two book series *The Door Beyond the Grave*, with Digital Horror Fiction, *A Haunted Life* and *The Dead are Watching*, both nonfiction with Llewellyn Worldwide, and a regional haunting book in the *Haunted America Series* with History Press.

Most recently, her short stories *The Skeench*, and *Chaos and Void* were released in *Killing It Softly 2*, and *Test Patterns: Creature Features*. Soon to be released, *Beauty Suffers* will be in the upcoming *Don't Cry to Mama* anthology.

She lives happily with a husband and a Havanese , in a one hundred and one year old haunted house.
Amazon Author Page: http://www.amazon.com/Debra-Robinson/e/B00BMHA032/ref=ntt_dp_epwbk_0
Goodreads: https: //www.goodreads.com/author/show/6981130.Debra_Robinson
Facebook: https://www.facebook.com/debrarobinsonauthor?ref=hl
Twitter: https://twitter.com/reb_robinson
Linkedin: www.linkedin.com/pub/debra-robinson/11/71a/336/

Christopher Stanley lives on a hill in England with three sons who share a birthday but aren't triplets. His stories have been published by *The Arcanist*, *The Molotov Cocktail*, and *The Infernal Clock*, and are forthcoming in *Unnerving Magazine* and *Econoclash Review*. Follow him on Twitter @allthosestrings.

DJ Tyrer is the person behind *Atlantean Publishing* and has been widely published in anthologies and magazines around the world, such as *Chilling Horror Short Stories* (Flame Tree), *All The Petty Myths* (18th Wall), *Steampunk Cthulhu* (Chaosium), *What Dwells Below* (Sirens Call), *The Mad Visions of al-Hazred* (Alban Lake), and *EOM: Equal Opportunity Madness* (Otter Libris), and issues of *Sirens Call, Hinnom Magazine, Ravenwood Quarterly*, and *Weirdbook*, and in addition, has a novella available in paperback and on the Kindle, *The*

Yellow House (Dunhams Manor). DJ Tyrer's website is at http://djtyrer. blogspot.co.uk/. The Atlantean Publishing website is at http:// atlantean publishing.blogspot.co.uk/

Karen Thrower was born and raised in Tulsa, Oklahoma and received her B.A. in Deaf Education from the University of Tulsa in 2005. She has various stories in anthologies and magazines, both online and print. You can check out her works on her Amazon Author Page: amazon.com/ author/karenthrower.

Steven Van Patten is a celebrated writer and Brooklyn native. He has penned five novels; The *Brookwater's Curse* trilogy is about an 1860s Georgia plantation slave who becomes a vampire. *Killer Genius: She Kills Because She Cares*, features a hyper intelligent black woman who becomes a serial killer. The sequel, *Killer Genius 2: Attack of The Gym Rats* dropped in late 2018.

SVP's short horror fiction is popping up everywhere, including *Hell's Kitties, Hell's Hearts,* The *Shadow over Deathlehem,* and *New York State of Fright.* There's even a children's book, *Rudy's Night Out,* which is loosely based on the childhood of one of the characters from the *Brookwater's Curse* series. He can be found on Facebook by name and under @svpthinks on Twitter and Instagram.

When he's not creating scary stories, he can be found stage managing television shows. This includes various MTV, VH-1 and FUSE shows over the last twenty years as well as Comedy Central vehicles, *The President Show* and *The Nightly Show w/ Larry Wilmore* and syndicated broadcasts like *HARRY.* His more recent work includes Netflix's *The Break w/ Michelle Wolf,* BET's *The Rundown w/ Robin Thede,* Discovery's *Borders LIVE* and filling in regularly at ABC's *The View.*

His affiliations include The Director's Guild of America, The New York Chapter of The Horror Writer's Association and the Delta Chapter of the professional artists fraternity, Gamma Xi Phi.

Patrick Winters is a graduate of Illinois College in Jacksonville, IL, where he earned a degree in English Literature and Creative Writing. He has been published in the likes of *Sanitarium Magazine, Deadman's Tome, Trysts of Fate,* and other such titles. A full list of his previous publications may be found at his author's site, if you are so inclined to know: http://wintersauthor. azurewebsites.net/Publications/List

 Grinning Skull Press Presents

The Place where it all started

O Little Town of Deathlehem

Twas the fright before Christmas,
And all through the town,
Not a soul stirred,
No one dared make a sound…

Welcome to Deathlehem, where…
…Krampus, not Santa, brings the holiday cheer…
…the lights on the tree, so festive and bright, skitter and crawl and possess
a lethal bite…
…malicious little elves, not a jolly one, know if you've been naughty—or
nice…
and
…family gatherings often turn deadly.
So enter…if you dare.

A collection of 23 holiday horrors benefiting the Elizabeth Glaser Pediatric
AIDS Foundation.

Return to Deathlehem

Slay bells ring,
Kids are screaming,
In the lane, snow is blood stained.
There's nowhere to hide,
Krampus has arrived,
There'll be feasting in a winter slaughter land...

Welcome back to Deathlehem,
...where the office Secret Santa proves more dangerous than a game of
Russian roulette...
...where trips to Grandma's house are fraught with danger...
...where a traditional Nutcracker poses a threat to a pair of would-be
thieves...
...where ghosts of Christmases past haunt and take vengeance against the
living...
...and many more!

Twenty-three more tales of holiday horror benefiting the Elizabeth Glaser
Pediatric AIDS Foundation

Deathlehem Revisited

You make this a Christmas to dismember,
Killing feelings in the middle of December,
Strangers meet, one unwillingly surrenders,
Oh, what a Christmas to dismember...

Welcome back to Deathlehem...again!...
where a mutated Christmas has a taste for human flesh...
...where a trio of trespassers are terrorized at an abandoned holiday-
themed tourist attraction...
...where elves thrive on the torment delivered to others...
...where holiday shopping drives people to commit extreme acts of
violence...
...and many more!

Twenty-three more tales of holiday horror to benefit The Elizabeth Glaser
Pediatric AIDS FoundationPediatric AIDS Foundation

The Shadow over Deathlehem

O little town of Deathlehem,
Within you death doth lie!
Beneath thy deep and rutted streets
Tormented souls do cry.
Yet in your dark streets shineth
A cold and ghostly light.
The fears and tears of all the years
Are met in thee tonight.

Well, here we are again, folks — Deathlehem ...
... where Krampus isn't the only creature to fear
when the holiday draws near...
... where holiday treats aren't safe to eat ...
... where not even the apocalypse will keep
people from celebrating the holiday ...
... where even Chanukah isn't safe to celebrate ...

Twenty-five more tales of holiday horror to benefit
The Elizabeth Glaser Pediatric AIDS Foundation

And don't miss our latest releases...

THE FEAR IS GROWING

From the moment he saw the ancient castle rising out of the picturesque Scottish countryside, filmmaker Dan Martin knew he'd found the ideal location for his vampire horror movie. And nothing could make him leave. Not the eerie legends of soul-stealing beasts of the night…nor a bizarre series of freak accidents. Not even his pregnant wife's tragic miscarriage.

THE TERROR IS BORN

Except that now there is another fetus growing in Vicki's womb. But little Darian is not going to be a normal baby. The Martins' adopted ten-year-old son Marty will soon find that out. In fact, Marty will soon know exactly what his new brother really is.

Shrouded in Mystery

The locals call it *Isla de los Perdidos.*
Island of the Lost.
According to the legends, those who venture onto the shores of this cursed
island never return.

Abandoned

Valarie DeNola and her sister Julie have chosen to ignore the legends and
the warnings. They have been selected to lead a team of explorers to the
island to discover the mystery surrounding it. But once ashore, they become
cut off from the outside world, and what they discover is something they
could never have prepared for.

Inhabited by Death

Now they must fight against an unknown presence that is picking them off
one by one. No one can be trusted, and when even nature rises up against
them, all seems lost. Their one hope is the extraction team they know is
coming.

But will any of them survive to see it arrive?

Welcome to Tornado Alley, where the tales are as dangerous and as twisted as the storms that ravage the great plains of Kansas.

Here, you'll meet an arachnophobe whose plans for a romantic weekend become a nightmare far worse than anything she could ever have imagined.

Holidays are all about food and family, but this year there's a darkness hovering over Don Carmelo's Thanksgiving feast.

A hen-pecked husband finally decides to heed his wife's advice to man up and become a man, but will she like the changes in her husband?

They say you should never judge a man until you've walked a mile in his shoes. Harv Perkins is about to find out what it's like to not only walk in another man's shoes, but to wear his skin as well.

Ding, dong, the witch is dead, that's what the residents of Beckham County are proclaiming. But down in the morgue, something is stirring.

All these and more! Eleven tales to thrill and chill you!

www.ingramcontent.com/pod-product-compliance
Lightning Source LLC
Chambersburg PA
CBHW071256250626
47159CB00004B/1206